Meet ~~cute~~ Not

THE DEMPSEY SISTERS

D. E. Haggerty

A Christmas for Chrissie
A Valentine for Valerie
A Love for Lexi
About Face
At Arm's Length
Hands Off
Knee Deep
Molly's Misadventures

Chapter 1

"HOLY HIPPIE COW!"

My mouth gapes open as I survey the bar. Did a hippie puke in here? Wait. No. Puke makes it sound bad, and it isn't bad. It's freaking cool.

The walls are covered in peace signs, daisies, and musical posters from folk singers. None of the chairs in the place match. And, to top it off, there are colored lights on the walls and ceiling giving the place a purplish haze. I can't imagine how out of this world it would be to end up drunk here with those lights, but I'm willing to give it a try.

Aspen hip checks me. "Awesome, isn't it?"

"Totally."

Cassandra snorts next to me. "Weird is more like it."

I refuse to get annoyed. I will not bicker with my sister today, but, man, she gets on my last nerve. Since we moved to Colorado a year ago, all she does is complain. I want to tell her to go back to Saint Louis if she's not happy, but I don't since I'd miss her grumpy butt. I must be a glutton for punishment.

Gabrielle clears her throat. "Should we sit down?"

I frown at how my baby sister practically whispers the question. Don't get me wrong. She's always been shy, but she turned into a meek, scared woman over a year ago and I don't know why. I'm kind of afraid to learn what happened since I'm pretty sure it's going to be heartbreaking.

"Oh, hey, Forest," Aspen greets, and I turn to meet the man.

My eyes bug out of my head when I realize he isn't wearing any pants. No underwear either. Nope, he's completely bottomless. He is wearing a top and shoes, though, which confuses me.

Cassandra elbows me. "Don't stare."

"I'm trying not to, but it's hard. Really hard."

"It's not hard," Forest says as he glances down at himself, and I realize what I said.

I slap a hand over my mouth as I'm finally able to drag my eyes away from the man's private parts. "Sorry."

Cassandra giggles. "She's the queen of saying awkward shit."

"It's not nice to call someone awkward," Aspen scolds.

Cassandra shrugs. She doesn't apologize for her behavior – ever.

"And you, Forest," Aspen waves toward his nether regions, "put on some pants."

"Do I have to?" He pouts. He sticks out his bottom lip and everything.

I giggle at the sight of the gray-haired elderly man wearing no pants pouting like a two-year-old.

"Do it or I'll tell Lilac."

Mentioning my brother's girlfriend does it. He pulls in his lip and marches off.

"Lilac isn't coming tonight," Gabrielle points out.

Aspen shrugs. "What he doesn't know won't hurt him." She motions us toward a booth. "Come on. Let's get our drink on."

"Whoo-hoo!" Cassandra throws her arms in the air and shouts. The woman should never be encouraged. She doesn't understand what the word moderation means.

I start to follow them, but I'm stopped when an arm circles my waist, and someone leans close to whisper in my ear.

"Hey, babe. I can't wait to find out if the carpet matches the drapes."

I groan. Typical. It's always the same when you have red hair. Men think it's hilarious to make jokes about whether the color is natural or not. Why in the world would I fake having a curly mop of ginger colored hair?

I grab the man's hand and twist his wrist until he's forced to let me go. When I turn around to confront him, he blanches.

"Shit. Sorry. I thought you were someone else."

I wish I could say I lash out at him for being a jerk, but I don't. Why not? Because I'm staring at an honest-to-goodness fashion model. Well, not an actual fashion model since we're in the small town of Winter Falls, Colorado, but he could totally be a model if he wanted to be.

He's tall. Since I'm five-seven and have to tilt my head way back to look at him, I'm guessing he's over six-foot. And, judging by the way his t-shirt strains to contain his muscles, he's hiding a spectacular body underneath his clothes.

His body may be hot, but his face is absolutely gorgeous. He has a short beard trimmed to perfection, which hits all my sexy man buttons since I'm a beautician and have seen way too many unruly beards in my life. You don't want to know some of the stuff I've found in a man's beard. Gross. To complete the picture, he has bright green eyes and a slightly lopsided smile.

His beard and hair are auburn. I never thought I'd find someone with red hair attractive, but this man breaks all my rules. Hell, he fed me some atrocious pick-up line two seconds ago and it did nothing to stop me from drooling over him.

"Elizabeth! Aren't you coming?" Cassandra shouts, and the spell is broken.

"See ya around, Green Eyes." I wave and rush off before I decide to break my rule about one-night stands.

"I can't believe we lived in White Bridge for a year and never discovered Winter Falls," Cassandra says as I sit down.

We recently 'discovered' the small town when our brother, Beckett, fell in love with Lilac who grew up here. Lilac is actually Aspen's sister. She has four sisters in total. I feel sorry for her. I have three, one of whom, Olivia, doesn't deign to be considered part of our family, and it's more than enough. I don't know what I'd do with another sibling to handle.

"I'm jealous you live here," Cassandra tells Gabrielle.

For once, I agree with Cassandra. Winter Falls is the bomb. I'd love to live here. The town is full of quirky people. I refer to exhibit number one – a pantless man walking into a bar. I don't think most people would notice my tendency to spout sexual innuendos at the most inopportune of times here.

Gabrielle tucks her chin into her chest and allows her blonde hair to form a curtain in front of her face. Sigh. She never used to hide from us. I need to get over my fear of learning what happened to her.

"Where's Aspen?" I ask instead.

I search the area and spot her sitting on her fiancé's lap. She and Lyric are staring at each other like they're alone, but they're not. Lyric's brother, Phoenix, a goat farmer we met at a pagan festival a while back – told you this town is cool – is there along with Green Eyes.

Of course, Green Eyes isn't alone. He's surrounded by women. Judging by the grin on his face, he's loving it. Ah, he's a player. I should have known. Anyone as sexy and handsome as he is isn't going to be attracted to me, aka Ms. Awkward.

Phoenix glances over and his gaze catches on Gabrielle. Hmm… Intriguing. Is the goat farmer interested in my baby sister? I know she has a major crush on him. She can't hide from me. It's cute she thinks she can.

Aspen jumps to her feet and grabs Phoenix's hand before she drags him across the room toward us. Interesting. Is Aspen playing matchmaker? I'm all for it. I scoot out of the booth where I was sitting next to Gabrielle to make room for Phoenix.

Aspen shoves him into the booth next to my shy sister, and I cover my face to hide my smile. This is going to be fun.

"Hi, Phoenix," Gabrielle murmurs, and Phoenix's eyes flare. It appears someone's crush isn't unrequited. Awesome.

"I'm Cassandra. Gabrielle's big sister." Cassandra narrows her eyes on Phoenix. "And gatekeeper."

Before I can correct her, Gabrielle huffs as her cheeks darken. "You are no one's gatekeeper," she mumbles in a soft voice.

"Yeah," I agree. "You can't guard the gate when you're always sneaking out of it." I wave to Phoenix. "I'm Elizabeth by the way."

"I'm River," Green Eyes says and winks at me. "I'm the favorite son."

I should have guessed he's related to Lyric and Phoenix since they all have the same tall, rugged appearance.

Lyric shoves him. "You wish."

"We should get some margaritas."

No sooner are the words out of Aspen's mouth than the bartender is setting a pitcher of strawberry margaritas down on the table.

"It's been a bit boring around here. Have at it."

Aspen giggles. "I guess he forgot about how you and your brothers enjoy skinny dipping in the falls."

Cassandra whips out her phone. "When does this happen? I need to make a note in my calendar."

I knock the phone out of her hands. "You are not going to play peeping Tom."

"Don't worry. I won't be playing. It'll be real." Her eyes sweep over the men, and she licks her lips.

"No one sees my fiancé naked except me," Aspen declares.

"No worries. He has two scrumptious brothers I can feast my eyes on."

She's not wrong. Phoenix isn't as gorgeous as Green Eyes…er… River, but he's awful easy on the eyes, nonetheless.

"What else do you do for fun around here in this Podunk town?"

At Cassandra's question, the music screeches to a halt, and quiet descends on the bar. "I believe Ms. Cassandra of the big city of Saint Louis has thrown down," Forest announces from the small stage.

"Holy crappolo, do you have listening devices planted all over the bar?" Cassandra claps and squeals. "Awesome. How does this throw down work?"

She doesn't wait for an answer before jumping to her feet and lifting her arms in the air. "I accept your challenge."

River stands. "I'm in." He smirks.

Cassandra rushes off, and River chases her. I frown as I watch them leave.

Typical. Cassandra always steals the men I'm interested in. She's been doing it since the second my boobs appeared when I was thirteen. Why would River be any different?

Chapter 2

Temptation – wanting something you think you can't have because you're a dumb ass River

RIVER

"Thanks for filling in, brother." Lyric slaps my back.

"No problem. The ladies love a man in uniform." I wink before hitching the suspenders of my fire kit over my shoulders.

He grunts. "When are you going to stop fooling around and find a nice girl to settle down with?"

I feign barfing. "Why would I settle for one woman when I can have all the women I want?"

"Because the love of one woman will make all those nights with other women feel like wasted time."

I roll my eyes. Since Lyric's high school girlfriend, Aspen, came back to Winter Falls and they reconnected, my oldest brother's been shoving love down my throat. I know better than to drink the Kool-Aid. Love is bullshit. When a woman says she loves you, the best course of action is to run far, far away.

"No thanks."

"What about Cassandra? You two ran off together the other night." He waggles his eyebrows.

I punch his shoulder. "Nothing happened. Cassandra is too close to being a local."

I learned my lesson early on in life – don't get involved with a local when you're not in the market for more than a woman to warm your bed for one night.

"You and your no local girls rule. Rules are made to be broken."

"Said by the Chief of Police."

"You know what I mean. Why not make an exception for Cassandra? She's crazy, which is right up your alley."

"What are you? A member of the gossip gals now?"

The gossip gals are five elderly women who are determined to match all the single people in Winter Falls. They can keep their claws away from me.

"River Atlas Alston," Sage snaps. Speaking of the gossip gals, Sage is their self-proclaimed leader.

I paste a smile on my face. "How ya doing, darling?"

She narrows her eyes on me. "I'm not one of your floozies."

I dial up the charm. "No, you're not, but you are a darling."

She giggles. "You're trouble, River Atlas."

I wink. "But tons of fun."

Lyric huffs behind me. "Aren't you supposed to be working, Sage?"

Sage is the police dispatcher, although she spends more of her time gossiping than actually working at the police station.

She holds up a walkie-talkie. "I'm available."

He rolls his eyes heavenward. If he's searching for solutions on how to handle the leader of the gossip gal gang up there, he's shit out of luck. She's uncontrollable. He should know this by now.

"Bane of my existence," he mumbles.

"Target has been spotted," the walkie-talkie squawks.

"Duty calls." Sage rushes off before Lyric can berate her for handling personal business with the town's equipment.

Now it's my turn to slap him on the back. "You need to give up. They're never going to change. You're the one who wanted to live in Winter Falls for the rest of your life."

"I better go see what she's up to," he mutters before following her.

I don't need to figure out what she's up to. I already know her and her gossip gals have their sights set on matching my brother Phoenix next. As long as they leave me alone, they can match up whoever they want.

And good luck matching my brother. A woman got her claws in him, and he hasn't finished licking his wounds yet. I can tell he's interested in Gabrielle, but I'd bet my house against him acting on it.

I step into my boots before making my way outside to the festival. Today's festival is Lammas. Lammas Day, otherwise known as Loaf Mass Day, is to celebrate the beginning of the harvest season. Winter Falls loves its pagan festivals.

As do I. The festivals bring in the tourists. And since today is August first and about eighty-five degrees out, the women tourists are sporting shorts and tank tops. It's my lucky day.

I stroll down Main Street past all the shops with booths set out in front of their stores selling their wares until I spot the Dempsey sisters – Cassandra, Gabrielle, and Elizabeth. Despite what Lyric said, it's not crazy Cassandra who appeals to me. No, it's Elizabeth.

She's not my usual type. She doesn't wear a ton of make-up or style her hair to perfection. I don't think her wild curls can be tamed. She also doesn't dress to show off her body. But, damn, I wish she did. She's got curves in all the right places, and I've always been a sucker for a curvy woman.

She twists to the side and her face with its ivory skin covered by freckles appears. I've never thought freckles were sexy before but, on her, they are. I can't help but wonder if the freckles continue over the rest of her body.

My legs travel closer to her without my brain's permission.

"Holy batman! Is that a loaf of bread? I've never seen anything this big in my life." Elizabeth's blue eyes sparkle as she indicates the giant loaf of bread in the town square.

Part of the Lammas custom is to display a large loaf of bread. Visitors are encouraged to take a portion of the bread home as a celebration of the first bread made from the new crop.

"Oh, darling," I croon, "I can show you something big."

She rolls her eyes. "What are you wearing? Is it 'dress up in the outfit of the person you want to be when you grow up'-day?"

Usually, a spunky woman is a huge turn off for me. I don't need a challenge. But I smirk in response to her snark.

"I'm a volunteer fireman. I put out fires of all kinds," I say and wink to make myself absolutely clear.

Cassandra wiggles her eyebrows. "You can put out my fire anytime you want."

My body has zero response to her innuendo. What the hell? Normally, outspoken, easy girls are my weakness. Instead, I'm gazing at Elizabeth to gauge her response. When her sister flirts with me, her shoulders fall, and I want to reach out and comfort her.

What am I thinking? I am not the man who comforts a woman. I'm the man who sneaks out of the hotel room while she's sleeping to avoid the awkward morning after.

Baa.

The sound of a goat bleating brings me out of my reverie. My brother, the goat farmer, has arrived. Phoenix always brings a goat to town with him.

"Hey, Gabrielle," he greets her while ignoring the rest of us. He better watch out before the gossip gals have him hitched to her.

"Hey," she whispers back. She's a shy thing. After Phoenix's last girlfriend, who was brash and bitchy, I can understand why he gravitates to shy.

"Is this Pan?" she asks.

"She wouldn't let me leave the farm without her."

"She's such a good girl."

"Depends on how you define good girl," he mutters.

I roll my eyes. "My brother, the dorky farmer."

He shoves me. "Nothing wrong with farming. Or did you forget you grew up on a farm, too?"

Phoenix is the youngest of us three Alston boys, but he inherited the farm from Mom and Dad when it became obvious neither Lyric nor I were interested. My parents are still around, but they want to spend their golden years having fun instead of farming from dawn to dusk.

I lean back as I pull on the suspenders of my uniform. "And now here I am all grown up." I wink at Elizabeth who blushes in response.

I'm not a full-time firefighter, but I volunteer when the town needs me. My real job is giving green tours to tourists. Since Winter Falls' claim to fame is being the first carbon neutral town in the world, the town's policies and procedures can be helpful for other locations seeking to lower their carbon emissions.

Green energy may sound boring but, trust me, the tour is fun. I make sure it is. Especially when women are part of the group.

Maa, Pan bleats and jerks on her leash before darting off. Phoenix holds on as she barges into a group of tourists.

I notice the group is comprised of women and smirk. "Duty calls, ladies."

And not a moment too soon. A minute more in Elizabeth's presence and the temptation to reach forward and touch her would have been too much.

I grin as I stroll toward the women. It's obvious from the way they ogle my body, I wouldn't need to make much of an effort to get one of them in my bed. Unfortunately, my cock doesn't appear interested. No, he wants to return to Elizabeth and get better acquainted with her.

Not happening, buddy. She's not a one-night stand kind of woman and those are the only women we're interested in getting to know.

I wink at the women before making my way past them. I need to get my head straight before I do something incredibly stupid such as break my rules about women. Did I say stupid? I meant completely idiotic.

Chapter 3

Gooey middle – the stuff a player hides from the world, so no one realizes there's more to him than his playboy ways

I STARE AFTER MY baby sister as Phoenix leads her out of *Clove's Coffee Corner*. I can hardly believe what's happening. Gabrielle and Phoenix are now fake dating because her ex-boyfriend is phoning every business in Winter Falls searching for her. How did I not know about what her ex Patrick did to her?

River squeezes my shoulder. "You okay?"

I blow out a puff of air causing my curls to fly up from my forehead. "I don't know. My sister was emotionally abused, and I didn't realize what was happening. Thus far, I'm in the lead for worst sister of the decade."

He uses his hold on my shoulder to draw me near before he wraps me in his arms. His outdoorsy scent engulfs me, and I melt into him.

"It's not your fault. Gabrielle probably misled you on purpose." I grunt. "I don't mean to say your sister's a bad person but—"

"I get it," I cut him off before he has to backpedal too far.

"I'm certain you're an awesome sister." He kisses my hair before stepping back and releasing me.

Too bad. I was enjoying feeling his hard muscles wrapped around me. *Shake it off, Elizabeth.* Player, remember? And we don't do one-night stands.

Can't we make an exemption? My body asks. Nope. No exemptions. Not even for players who give the best hugs when you're in desperate need of one.

"Come on," he says and takes my hand.

"Where are we going?" I ask as he drags me out of the café.

"You look like you could use a pick me up."

"Then why are we leaving the café where they have coffee?"

He leans close to whisper. "Because the gossip gals are in there." He shivers.

I glance behind me and notice Sage watching us. She's the police dispatcher for Winter Falls, but she spends the majority of her time gossiping. Thus, the moniker 'gossip gal gang'. The rest of the gang – Feather, Petal, Cayenne, and Clove – join Sage, and she points to us. I quickly glance away.

In addition to having a love for hot pink tops and gossip, those women think they're the best matchmakers in the world. The second Gabrielle moved to Winter Falls, they showed up at her place with a list of local men she should choose from.

"Are you afraid of them?" I ask River.

He rolls his eyes. "No, but I don't want them getting any ideas about matchmaking me."

I should have known. The player doesn't want to be matched. Duh. Since I have no interest in discussing his womanizing ways, I change the subject.

"Where are we going?"

He motions to a place past the courthouse. I read the sign. *Bake Me Happy.* I quicken my pace.

He chuckles. "In a hurry?"

"I wonder if they have anything strawberry flavored."

"Strawberry? Not chocolate?"

"Chocolate's okay, but strawberry's divine," I say as I open the door.

I inhale a deep breath when I enter the bakery. The scent of sugar, chocolate, and vanilla hits me and I sigh. River was right. I need a pick me up after the shit show at the café.

"What can I get you, darling?" the man behind the counter asks.

"Do you have anything strawberry flavored?"

"We have strawberry muffins, strawberry shortcake, strawberry blondies, and strawberry oatmeal bars."

Heaven. I've found heaven.

"Will you marry me?"

He bursts into laughter. "Sorry, darling, you're not my type. Wrong equipment." His gaze finds River. "Now, him," he purrs as he licks his lips, "I wouldn't mind taking for a ride."

"In your dreams," River responds with a wink.

"I'm Bryan," he says and holds out his hand.

"Elizabeth."

"Tourist or new arrival?"

I shrug. "Neither."

"Her sister is Gabrielle Dempsey," River answers.

"The latest gossip gal project is your sister?" Bryan asks and I nod. "I wish those women would find me a match." He puffs out his chest. "I am a catch after all."

I giggle. "Maybe you can ask them."

"Nope. They have to choose you."

"Choose?" River snorts. "He means target."

Bryan leans close to whisper-shout to me, "Mr. Alston is afraid of them."

"I know," I whisper back.

"I like you, Elizabeth Dempsey," he announces. "You can have a treat on the house."

"A treat on the house? What's the catch? Do I take one bite of your goodies and become addicted?"

He coughs. "One bite of my goodies?"

I blow out a puff of air. "I didn't mean your goodies as in your… you know…"

River bursts into laughter behind me. I elbow him but he ducks out of the way at the last second and I meet air. With nothing to stop my momentum, I fly backwards. Fortunately, River catches me before I can do a swan dive into a table.

"Whoa, there, klutzy girl."

"I'm not klutzy," I claim despite not being steady on my feet from my latest clumsy move.

Bryan claps. "This is going to be fun."

I frown at him. Watching the biggest klutz in Colorado make a fool of herself is fun? Gee, thanks.

"You're not a klutz," he declares. If he doesn't think I'm a klutz, what's he talking about? He hands me a plate filled with strawberry goodness and I forget all about asking him to explain himself.

I lift the plate to my nose and inhale. I moan as the smell of baked strawberry goodness hits me.

"Are you sure you don't want to marry me?"

He chuckles as he shoos me away. "Go find a table and I'll bring you a coffee."

River and I settle at a table near the window. He reaches for my plate, and I slap his hand away.

"Ow. Aren't you going to share?"

I drag the plate closer to me. "No. Get your own."

"I thought we were friends."

"Friends?" I wrinkle my nose. "Since when are we friends?"

"We're going to be seeing an awful lot of each other now that your sister and my brother are together. We might as well be friends."

"Wow. Thanks. With an offer like that, how could I refuse?"

His lopsided smile appears and his green eyes sparkle. "I'm glad you see things my way."

I narrow my eyes on him. "I was being sarcastic. Besides, Gabrielle and Phoenix are merely pretending to be in a relationship."

He snorts. "You and I both know there's more to them than pretend."

"True."

Gabrielle's been crushing on Phoenix since she first met him, and Phoenix is clearly attracted to my sister as well, but he's fighting it. Maybe them pretending to date will help push him along. I hope so. My baby sister deserves a good man after her ex-asshat.

Bryan arrives and sets two coffees on our table as well as another plate of goodies. When I eye the plate, River snatches it.

"No, you have your own plate. I don't share."

I raise my eyebrows. "And yet you expected me to share? Hypocrite."

"I prefer the term charlatan."

I giggle. "You're trouble."

He waggles his eyebrows. "But fun."

I roll my eyes. "I bet."

"Ah, you understand me. This is the beginning of a beautiful friendship."

"Fine. I'll be your friend as long as you keep your filthy paws off of my strawberry goodies."

"Don't you worry. My paws will go nowhere near your goodies." He winks.

I force a smile as I know he's joking. What I really want to do is tell him he can put his paws on me any time he wants. *Stop it, Elizabeth.* You are not allowed to dream about River and his hands on you. He's a player. Besides, he's obviously not interested.

"Now shush," I scold. "I need quiet to properly enjoy these baked marvels."

He mimes zipping his lips shut and we fall into silence as we eat. I pat my stomach when I finish the plate. I probably shouldn't have eaten it all, but I never can say no when strawberry's involved.

"I'm stuffed."

"Feeling better?"

I jolt at his question. I'd forgotten all about Gabrielle and her troubles.

"Yeah. Thanks."

He winks. "Anytime, friend. Anytime."

Dang it. My body was already attracted to him and now it turns out he's also sweet and kind and considerate. I'm in big trouble.

Chapter 4

Friendzone – a place where players go to hide

"This is exciting," Cassandra declares before starting to sing and dance down the street toward the town square in Winter Falls.

We're on our way to Aspen and Lyric's wedding. It's being held outdoors to accommodate the attendance of the entire town. Although Cassandra and I aren't inhabitants of Winter Falls, Aspen insisted we attend as we're now her 'sisters'.

I didn't correct her to explain how our brother being involved with her sister doesn't make us family. Nope. She said sisters and my heart latched onto her immediately. In my opinion, family is the most important thing in the world. Even more important – dare I say it? – than ice cream.

"Calm down, Ms. What Is Pitch. It's a wedding, not a carnival," Gabrielle insists.

I smile at my baby sister teasing Cassandra. She's slowly returning to her old self since she began fake dating Phoenix. Fake? Snort. There's nothing fake about the way those two look at each other.

Cassandra whirls around to shake her finger at Gabrielle. "You don't get it. It's a pagan wedding. I've never been to one before."

"How do you know it's a pagan wedding?"

"And here I thought she was excited because weddings are the sacred hunting ground for single men," I grumble.

Unlike me, Cassandra is the queen of love and leave 'em. Sometimes I wish I could adopt her casual attitude toward relationships, but it's not me. I put the cling in clinger.

"Single men such as me?" River jumps out in front of me before twirling his hand and doing a bow.

My heart thumps in my chest. And not because he scared me. But I ignore it. River and I are friends. Nothing more.

"Who are you supposed to be?" I motion to his white billowing blouse. "Robin Hood?" I indicate his khaki pants. "You're missing the tights."

He wiggles his eyebrows. "I save the tights for the special ladies."

I giggle as I shove him. "Poor Maid Marian. She won't know what she's getting into with you, will she?"

"Do you know in some of the early tales of Robin Hood, Maid Marian is supposedly a virgin?" He feigns gagging.

"I was wrong. You're not Robin Hood. You're Casanova."

He perks up. "Casanova. Classic. Handsome. Adventurer. I accept." He holds his elbow out to me. "Does the lady wish to accompany Casanova to the nuptials?"

Duh. Of course, I do. I want to accompany him wherever he's willing to take me. *Calm down, Hussy Girl.* He's talking about a wedding, not his bedroom.

I thread my arm through his. "Let's go, Casanova."

River begins skipping, and I laugh as I join him. We skip down the street until we reach the town center where a crowd is gathering near the gazebo.

We join Aspen's sisters – Ashlyn, Ellery, and Juniper. My brother, Beckett, beckons me to where he and Lilac are standing on the other side, but I'm not moving anywhere away from River. Stage Five clinging has officially begun.

Ashlyn throws her arms around me. "It's good to see you, sis!"

Her husband, Rowan, growls. She rolls her eyes before smiling up at him. "I'm being careful, big guy. Geesh. You'd think I'm the first woman in the world to have a baby."

He captures her arm and draws her near. "You're the first woman to have *my* baby," he says before kissing her hair. Her eyes fall closed, and she melts into him.

I should probably look away as their tender moment is private, but I can't. I want what they have. What my parents had. I was only ten when they died in a car accident, but I remember how Dad would come home from work and immediately search the house for Mom as if he couldn't stand to be parted from her for the hours he worked.

Yes, I'm a hopeless romantic. I've made my peace with it. I glance at River underneath my lashes. Maybe not.

"You ready for this?" Ellery asks as she bounces her baby girl.

I open my arms and she places Willow in them. I cradle the baby close before leaning down to blow bubbles on her exposed tummy. She giggles and I sigh. I want this. Maybe more than I want some great love.

Cole grunts. "Give me back my baby."

Ellery elbows her fiancé. "Let her be. She's held Willow for a grand total of five seconds.'"

"Don't care. Elizabeth's ready to kidnap her."

I am, but I giggle and hand over the baby.

Juniper hip checks me. "It's nothing personal. Cole believes everyone is out to steal his baby."

Her fiancé chuckles. "Lucky for him Willow's a human. If she were a capybara, you'd totally steal the vicious thing."

She rolls her eyes at Maverick as if he isn't the biggest romantic comedy movie star in the world. I guess, to her, he isn't. Me, on the other hand? I'm staring at him with my mouth gaping open. At least, I haven't asked him for his autograph. Yet.

"Capybaras are cute," Juniper argues. "They're not vicious."

River leans close to whisper in my ear. "You might want to wipe the drool from your mouth."

I slam my gaping mouth shut. "I'm not drooling. What's a capybara?" I ask to change the subject.

"It's an adorable giant rodent. They're very affectionate." Maverick snorts at Juniper's reply. There's a story there.

"Are beavers rodents? Beavers are my favorite animals."

River barks out a laugh. "I didn't know you love beavers."

"What's wrong with—" I cut myself off when I realize what I said. My face warms and I shove him. "Stop it. You know I didn't mean … Whatever. Grow up."

River's reply is cut off when Aspen's mom summons us, "Let us gather in our sacred circle."

Everyone shuffles to stand in a circle around the gazebo where Lyric awaits his bride. I scan the area for Aspen's arrival. I laugh when she appears sprinting toward the gazebo.

I'm sure her dress is beautiful but all I notice is the happiness radiating from her. Her smile stretches from ear to ear and her eyes sparkle as she throws herself at Lyric.

I sigh and River elbows me. "Don't go fainting on me."

"Don't be a hater. It's beautiful how they love each other."

"Gak. Love." He wraps his hands around his neck and feigns choking.

I slap his hands. "Knock it off. Love is wonderful."

"Love is a fantasy. It was invented by Hallmark and Disney."

I purse my lips. I know River's a player, but I didn't realize he's a cynic, too. "You don't believe in love?"

He doesn't hesitate to answer. "Nope."

My brow wrinkles, and I motion to the gazebo where Aspen and Lyric are standing. "But the proof is standing in front of you."

He snorts. "Sell me your story in twenty years when they're miserable."

"Aren't your parents still married?" I've yet to meet them, but I know they live in town and are still together.

"Don't try and use your logic on me. Love doesn't exist."

I open my mouth to use more of my 'logic' on him, but he places a finger over my lips and indicates the gazebo. Oh right. During the recital of the vows is not the time or place to have a discussion about love with the groom's brother. It's probably also not the time to notice how soft River's finger is or how yummy it smells. I wonder how it tastes.

I tug his finger away before I lose whatever sanity I have left where River is concerned and suck his finger into my mouth. I concentrate on the ceremony in front of me instead.

"Aspen Cloud West soon to be Aspen Cloud Alston," Lyric begins, and Aspen rolls her eyes. "I've loved you from the moment you stole my chocolate pudding in first grade."

"I didn't steal it. You gave it to me."

"And I loved you throughout high school despite your irrational hate of math and love of fire alarms."

"Math sucks."

"And I loved you when you needed to leave to seek out adventure before you could return to Winter Falls to settle down. I'm honored you've chosen me to settle down with. I will love you until we're old and gray even if you never stop stealing my pudding."

He wraps a ribbon around her hands.

"Lyric Journey Alston, I've loved you from the moment you shoved Love Hill in a pile of mud to protect my honor, although I was six and had no idea what honor was." She waits until the laughter dies down before continuing. "And I loved you for ten years while I lived in Dallas despite believing you were the scum of the earth."

"I'm not."

"I know, which is why I'm tying myself to you for all-time today."

Mrs. West steps forward to help them tie their ribbons together before leading them to a broom. They throw their tied hands in the air and jump the broom.

"We're married!" Aspen shouts.

Phoenix struts to the gazebo and takes center stage.

"What's happening?"

"Family and friends are invited to tell stories about the couple," River explains.

"Are you going next?"

"Nah. Lyric asked me not to speak."

I quirk up an eyebrow. "He did? But you're his brother."

He shrugs. "Who doesn't believe in love."

Huh. He's serious about this not believing in love stuff. Dreams of my showing him how wonderful love can be crash and explode upon impact. Boom! This plain girl is not the woman to change his mind.

"Come on," River grabs my hand, and I realize everyone is leaving as the ceremony has finished.

Oops. I guess my mind drifted off. Don't judge. It's what tends to happen when the man your heart is yearning for tells you he doesn't believe love exists.

"Let's go party. I see quite a few out-of-towners here. You can be my wing woman."

Wing woman? I inhale a deep breath and let it out. *This is not news, Elizabeth.* The man has made it perfectly clear he's not interested in you.

"Earth to Elizabeth. Come on, friend. I want to get to the buffet before all the good stuff's gone."

Friend. Good reminder. River and I are friends. It's all we can ever be since the man put the word *play* in player.

As of this moment, he is officially friendzoned. No more dreaming about how he looks naked, how he tastes, or how it would feel to have his lips devour mine. Nope. No more.

Chapter 5

Wing woman – a lousy excuse to hide how you feel

I SCAN THE LOBBY of the movie theater in White Bridge for River. He's still not here. I check the time on my phone and scowl. Of course, he's not here. I'm fifteen minutes early. I may be a bit eager to see him.

It doesn't matter how many times I remind myself River and I are friends – just friends – I still yearn to spend time with him. Oh, who am I kidding? I yearn for more than to spend time with him. My body has about five gazillion different ideas of things we can do with him. Naked things.

I need a reality check.

I hear a commotion near the entrance. Ah, there's River now. And he's not alone. Naturally. He's surrounded by a group of women who are practically tripping over themselves to get near him. My stomach churns as jealousy hits me.

I did say I needed a reality check.

I want to be the type of woman River would be interested in. But I'm not. I'm plain Elizabeth with the uncontrollable curly hair, pale skin, and freckled face. And I'm not exactly skinny either. But if I have to choose between skinny and strawberry ice cream, strawberry ice cream is winning every dang time.

River spots me and waves. He extricates himself from the women with a show of his lopsided smile before making his way to me.

"Hey, Bessie." He kisses my cheek in greeting.

I shove him. Bessie is the name of a horse or a woman from the eighteenth century. I hate the nickname. "My name is Elizabeth."

"You'll always be Bessie to me."

I glare at him but decide to let it go. I know River. If I make a stink about the nickname, he'll only use it more to tease me. Too bad the only teasing he does with me is verbal. I shut those thoughts down. River teasing my body belongs in the 'never gonna happen' category.

He throws his arm over my shoulder and leads me to the refreshment stand. "What are we watching today?"

I smirk. "A romantic comedy."

He groans. "The things I do for my friends."

He orders popcorn for him and Twizzlers for me. "I can't believe I'm friends with someone who has such bad taste in candy," he says as he hands me the licorice.

I snag the bag and hold it to my chest. "It's strawberry flavored. Need I say more?"

He ruffles my hair. "You and your obsession with strawberry."

I don't correct him, because he's not wrong.

We enter the cinema and climb to the very top row. I prefer the middle row where I don't have to squint to see the screen but, according to River, the cool kids sit in the back. Sometimes I think he forgets he's in his thirties and no longer a kid.

We're barely settled when a woman claims the seat next to River despite the theater being almost empty. I roll my eyes. Here we go.

"Hey, handsome," she says in a breathy voice.

"Hey," River grunts before turning his attention to me. "What's this movie about anyway?"

I open my mouth to answer but the woman speaks again before I get the chance.

"I'm talking to you," she says as she taps River's hand.

He pulls his hand away. "And I'm talking to my friend."

She leans over the armrest to shove her chest into his arm. "Wouldn't you prefer to get out of this place with me instead?"

River stares down at her cleavage, and I decide to give him an out. I am his wing woman after all no matter how much I may hate the distinction.

"You can go if you want. I don't mind. I can watch the movie by myself."

Technically, I'm not lying. Do I mind watching a movie alone? No. Do I mind River taking off with another woman? That's a different story. A story which will remain untold because nothing will ever happen between River and me.

"Don't be silly, Bessie. I'm not leaving you alone to go off with some blonde bimbo."

"Blonde bimbo!" the woman screeches and River shrugs in response. "How dare you? You don't know what you're missing."

She stands and marches off. My stomach gets all warm and fuzzy as I watch her. He chose me over you, I want to shout after her.

"Now." River drapes an arm over my shoulders. "What's this movie about?"

The lights dim. "Shush. Previews."

Thank goodness for previews because he's not going to be happy when he figures out this movie isn't your run of the mill romantic comedy. In fact, it's not a romantic comedy at all. It's romance with a capital R. A genre he vetoed as being too sissy for him to watch.

The movie begins and I lean my head against his shoulder. He kisses my hair and I swallow my sigh. Damn. He's perfect. Except for the whole player thing. And not believing in love. Other than those two minuscule issues, he's the ideal man for me.

As the movie plays, I immerse myself in the film and forget all about River and real life. My bag of Twizzlers lays open but uneaten on my lap as the story grips me.

When the lights switch on as the credits roll, River pinches my chin and turns my head until I'm facing him.

"Fuck, Elizabeth. Don't cry."

"I can't help it," I sob as the tears roll down my cheeks.

He uses his thumbs to wipe my tears away. "You need to stop crying, sweetheart."

"B–b–but it was so s–s–sad." I hiccup.

"It was only a movie."

I slap his shoulder. "Only a movie? How can you say that? It was a beautiful story."

He chuckles. "Got you to stop crying, didn't I?"

I do the mature thing and stick my tongue out at him. "You're a menace."

"But I'm your menace."

I wish he was mine. Mine in every way and not merely a friend. *Stop it, Elizabeth.* Friends. Only. F-R-I-E-N-D-S. Friends.

He stands and gathers our trash before holding out his hand to me. "Come on. I'm starved."

"How can you be hungry?" I ask as he leads me down the stairs to the exit. "You literally just ate a gallon of popcorn."

"Popcorn can't be measured by the gallon. A gallon is a liquid measurement."

I shove him with my free hand. "You know what I meant."

"But how fun is it when your face turns red with agitation?"

I growl. Not fun at all if you're me. I hate my light complexion. The smallest irritation and it becomes bright red to match my hair.

What I wouldn't give to be a blonde. But I learned my lesson. I tried dyeing my hair blonde when I was a freshman in high school. Blonde dye on red hair equals orange hair. I looked like a troll doll on the first day of school. Never again.

We make our way through the crowd of movie-goers in the lobby. Women bite their lips and bat their eyelashes at River, but he ignores them.

"Where do you want to eat?" he asks once we're standing outside on the sidewalk.

I wrinkle my nose. "Are you certain you want to eat with me?" I motion toward the lobby. "There are at least a dozen women who you could go out with instead. All you have to do is snap your fingers."

He pulls on one of my curls. "Nope. Tonight is friend night."

Friend. As if I need a reminder of how plain Elizabeth can't compete with those women.

"There's a bar down the street that serves the best onion rings in town."

I know because a girl cannot live on strawberry snacks and ice cream alone. At least not this girl.

"Lead the way," he says as he wraps an arm around my shoulder.

I snuggle into him as we walk to the bar. If all River and I will ever be is friends, then at least I can enjoy the feel of his arm around me. More, my heart whispers. I want more. Shut up, I tell it. There is no more.

Chapter 6

Target – when the gossip gals have their sights set on you

I STOP MY CAR in front of the River's place and stare up at the house. I'll be damned. This is the house of my dreams. And River – aka the man I want but can never have – lives in it. Life is unfair. Un-freaking-fair.

The house is a one-story ranch. The wooden structure is stained a warm, walnut color. On the right side is the garage and in the middle is a porch with a porch swing. Smack dab in the middle is a bright red door. It's cozy and quaint and the house I've always dreamed of.

It reminds me of the home I grew up in with my family in Saint Louis. My parents inherited a bunch of money when I was a baby, but we stayed in the simple single-story ranch. After they died, Beckett took on the monumental task of raising us four girls at just nineteen years old in that house.

When he sold the house after Gabrielle left for college, I was devastated. I wanted to buy it and raise my family in it. But then he got offered a job in Colorado and my sisters – except Olivia, of course – and I followed him to White Bridge. I might have been the one to rally Cassandra and Gabrielle to follow him since I wasn't allowing the family to be split up. No way.

Family is everything. Too bad Olivia doesn't feel the same way. I've tried and tried with her, but she ignores my phone calls and messages. I finally had to give up. There's only so much heartbreak I can take.

"Hey!" River greets as he opens the car door. "Fancy car."

"Yep." I never know what to say when someone remarks on my wealth. It's not my money. I didn't earn it. Besides, most of it is tied up in investments.

"You're lucky you have an electric car. Gasoline engines are banned in Winter Falls."

Since the town is carbon neutral, they're very picky about what types of vehicles are allowed past the town borders. Most of the locals ride around in golf carts or pedal bikes to wherever they're going. It sounds weird, but it's actually cute as all get out. I want to live here so bad. In fact, plans are in the works to make it happen.

"Did you notice the new Marvel movie is out next weekend?" he asks as I drive us to the bar.

I glance over at him and wink. "I already bought us tickets."

He rubs his hands together. "Yes. Popcorn and candy. Whoo-hoo!"

I giggle. "Do you even want to see the movie?"

"Sure. It gives me something to do while I stuff my face."

I park behind *Electric Vibes.* The hippie place is the only bar in Winter Falls. I peek next door to the empty property in between the bar and *Naked Falls Brewing.* The property – and my ability to secure the lease – are integral for my plan to move to Winter Falls to succeed. But since my plans are top secret, for now, I tear my gaze away.

"What's happening tonight anyway?" I ask as we walk to the entrance of the bar.

"It's couple's trivia night." He throws an arm around my shoulder. "And you, my dear bestie, are my plus one."

"Lucky me." I infuse as much sarcasm into my voice as possible to hide how much it hurts to hear him refer to me as his best friend. I don't want to be his best friend. I want to be his lover. His everything.

Friendzone, remember? I remind myself for the millionth time.

He drops his arm to open the door for me. "I need to chat with my brother. Be back in a sec." He kisses my cheek and struts off.

I should look away. I shouldn't keep my gaze glued to his tight rear end as he walks away. Guess what I do?

"Did you say John Lennon?" Cassandra says and brings me out of a fantasy where I'm biting those luscious globes of River's.

"John Lennon's dead. You do realize there are events which transpired before your birth?" I point out as I join her where she's standing with Gabrielle and Phoenix.

While I've been playing friendzone footsie with River, Gabrielle has done the impossible. Her relationship with Phoenix is no longer fake. They've officially knocked boots and

Phoenix declared he cares for her for all the world to hear. I'm not certain whether I should swoon or be jealous.

I'm also the worst liar in the world. I'm jealous. Don't get me wrong. I'm happy for Gabrielle, but it turns out you can be happy for someone and be consumed by jealousy at the same time. The benefits of being socially awkward.

"Nope," Cassandra insists. "The world didn't exist before I was born."

I throw my arms in the air. "I don't know why I bother."

River arrives and drapes his arm around my shoulders. "Don't know why you bother with what?"

I want to snuggle into his hold, but I can't. Friends don't snuggle.

"Why I bother with the lot of you humans," I grumble as I shove him away.

He pretends to fall, and I reach out to save him but trip on a chair I swear wasn't there a second ago and slam into him. We crash to the floor in a heap and my face ends up in his crotch.

"Why am I the one who always ends up in embarrassing positions?" I mutter.

River's body vibrates with his laughter, and I want to lay on top of him naked while he laughs. Alert! Alert! *Get up, Elizabeth!* But do I get up? Spoiler alert: I don't.

"I could argue my position is more embarrassing."

I lift up to glare at him. "Why? You have women burying their faces in your crotch all the time."

He bursts out laughing. "I usually prefer to remove my pants first."

He stands and helps me to my feet. "Come on. Let's find our table."

Our table is in front of the stage next to a table filled with Lilac's sisters and their partners. I spot Sage and the gossip gals studying me from their location in front of the room.

"What are they up to?" I try to speak without moving my lips as I have a feeling those ladies can read lips.

River drapes his arm over my chair and plays with my hair. "Probably some bet."

"What would they be betting on?"

"Everything and anything. Who will win tonight's pub quiz? When will the next West daughter become pregnant? When will Phoenix and Gabrielle admit they love each other?"

"I thought you didn't believe in love."

He doesn't get a chance to answer as Cassandra pulls out a chair next to mine and plops down in it. "Gross. Please tell me we aren't discussing love." She sticks a finger down her throat and pretends to gag.

"Way to be a grown-up."

She rolls her eyes. "Being a grown-up is boring. Girls just want to have fun."

"There's more to life than fun. Maybe you should think about your career."

"I have a career."

Cassandra doesn't have a career. She works as a bartender. There's nothing wrong with being a bartender, but she graduated near the top of her class in college. She could do more if she'd learn to wake up before noon.

"A career means there are opportunities for progress. Where's the progress in slinging drinks?"

Phoenix and Gabrielle arrive and sit down across from us. Beckett and Lilac are behind them.

"I—"

Cassandra's rebuttal is cut off when Aspen stands from the table next to ours and points at Lilac. "Traitor!"

"How are the Sisters of Mayhem supposed to win when we're missing a sister?" Ashlyn asks.

"Lyric is substituting for me, and you have your partners to help you," Lilac answers.

"All of their brains together aren't as big as yours," Aspen whines.

Lyric frowns at his wife. "Thanks, Sunshine."

"I'm merely telling the truth."

"All bets are now final," Sage hollers from her table near the stage.

"Damn this town and its betting," Phoenix mutters.

River bumps his shoulder. "Not as much fun when you're the target, is it?"

I guess he wasn't kidding when he said people were betting on Gabrielle and Phoenix's relationship.

"I'd be careful if I were you. You might be next." Phoenix nods toward me, and I glance away before he can notice the hope spark in my eyes.

"Nah." River plays with my curls. "Bessie and I are just friends."

There's the f-word again. Stupid word. I'm ready to have it removed from the dictionary.

"Ahem." Lennon – aka the bar owner who resembles the Beatles' guitarist – climbs onto the stage. "Usual rules apply. The first person to raise their hand will be called on for the answer. If the answer is correct, we'll continue to the next question. If the answer is incorrect, the second person to have raised their hand will be asked to answer the question. And so on."

Ashlyn slams a pitcher of beer down on our table.

"What's this for?" Lilac asks.

"Maybe if we get Ms. Smarty Pants drunk, she'll miss some questions."

Lilac leans back in her chair and crosses her arms over her chest. "Maybe you shouldn't divulge your brilliant plan to the enemy."

"Oops!" Ashlyn giggles before returning to her table.

The quiz begins and I try to pay attention. I swear I do, but I'm too overwhelmed by River touching my hair and shoulder constantly. How am I supposed to get the message about 'just friends' if he touches me all the time?

I'm brought out of my reverie when Beckett kneels in front of Lilac. My eyes widen. Is he going to propose? Am I going to get a new sister for real? I lean forward in my chair to make sure I don't miss a thing.

"Lilac Bean West—"

She frowns. "Why am I getting the middle name treatment if you're going to propose? You are going to propose, aren't you?"

Beckett reaches into his pocket and pulls out a jewelry box. "Yes, Lilac no-middle-name West, I'm trying to propose."

"You may proceed."

He smiles. "Lilac, my love, will you marry me?"

"That's it?" Ashlyn asks. "No profound statements about how much you love her and can't live without her? Worst. Proposal. Ever."

Beckett gazes into Lilac's eyes. "My Lilac doesn't want flowery statements or professions of love. She wants to beam me over the head for proposing in front of her family and nearly all of the residents of Winter falls."

"If you are aware of my adversity to you proposing in public, why are you proposing in the middle of a crowded bar?"

Beckett lifts his chin toward her parents. Mr. and Mrs. West are sitting to the side of the stage. Mr. West has an arm around Mrs. West's middle, probably to keep her from jumping into the fray.

"My mother forced you to propose in public?"

Beckett leans close to whisper, "She promised she wouldn't bother us about having children for at least a year if I proposed in front of her."

"My mother is a master blackmailer."

"I prefer the word negotiator," she hollers from her table where she's now actively trying to escape her husband.

"Say yes, Lilac," Sage yells.

"Why? Have you bet on when the proposal would happen?"

Sage whistles and glances away. Yowzah! This betting thing is not a joke.

"If you say yes, you'll be our sister for realz," Cassandra says.

"I don't think being *your* sister is a redeeming quality in a marriage proposal," I grumble because I can never resist the opportunity to needle my older sister.

"May I see the ring?" Lilac asks Beckett and he opens the box before holding it out to her. She picks it up and studies it for a moment.

"I will not take your last name. You will allow me to help pay the bills. And I want two children. Are these terms acceptable to you?"

"Will you use my last name in a social setting?" Lilac nods. "What about three children?"

"Only in the event I have twins, the likelihood of which is one in 250."

Beckett smirks. "I believe we have a deal, Lilac West."

"Yes!" I shout and jump to my feet. "I'm getting a new sister!"

"Sisters!" Ashlyn corrects since the woman apparently can't keep her thoughts to herself.

River wraps his arms around me from behind and kisses my hair. "Congrats, Bessie."

I allow myself to lean into him. What can a bit of leaning hurt between friends? My heart claims a lot, but I ignore it. This is not the moment to worry about how my desire for River will never be reciprocated by him. Nope. I'm not thinking about it. Not even a little bit.

Chapter 7

*Kiss – The first step in taking a relationship out of the friendzone
aka ruining everything*

RIVER

"You ready for this, Bessie?"

Her eyes spark with irritation – she hates when I call her Bessie, which, naturally, means I do it as often as I dare – but she blinks and the irritation disappears. Too bad. Annoying Elizabeth is the highlight of my day.

Instead, she bounces on her toes. "Beyond ready. What's more ready than ready? Ready, ready? Uber ready?"

I chuckle as I grasp her hand and we begin walking toward Main Street. I know friends shouldn't hold hands all the time, but I can't help snatching every opportunity I can to touch her.

I love the feel of her hand in mine. This from a man who disapproves of public displays of affection of any sort. All my rules fly out the window when it comes to Elizabeth.

"This is beyond romantic," she sighs as we walk.

I happen to agree with her, but I don't comment as I don't want to encourage her. Elizabeth Elaine Dempsey needs to stay firmly in the friendzone where she belongs. It doesn't matter how much I want to throw her over my shoulder and drag her back to my house like a caveman. It's not going to happen. I'm not ruining one of the best friendships I have with sex.

And make no doubt about it, sex will ruin our relationship. It's happened a thousand times before. A woman says she's happy to 'stay friends' and 'sex won't change anything'. Lies. It's all lies. Sex changes everything. Feelings get involved. Feelings get hurt. It's a shit show.

We reach Main Street where both of our families are waiting for Phoenix to make his grand gesture to prove his love to Gabrielle. Despite my rejection of love as real, I'm happy for the two of them. They found the real deal. Too bad I can't trust a woman to offer me what Gabrielle gives Phoenix.

I glance over at Elizabeth. I wish she could be the one woman who's different, but I've had those thoughts before. And been burned.

Phoenix walks into the middle of the street and the rest of us gather behind him to take our places. Ashlyn presses play, *The Way You Make Me Feel* from Michael Jackson blares through the quiet street, and we begin to dance our choreographed routine.

Phoenix keeps his eyes glued to Gabrielle and her reaction, but I'm not interested in Gabrielle's reaction. My gaze is fixated on Elizabeth. She's laughing as she dances. The only other time I've seen her this happy was when Beckett proposed to Lilac. Damn. I wish I could be the one to make her happy every day.

I miss a step and slam into Elizabeth. "Pay attention, Mr. Two Left Feet."

She laughs and pushes me away before beginning to dance again. When I stand there like an idiot staring at her, she motions for me to continue.

"Come on. Don't make us look bad."

The gossip gals arrive wearing hot pink sweatshirts with the words *Gossip Gal Dance Team* on them. They're also carrying pink and silver pompoms. They shake the pompoms in time to the music as we finish up the choreographed dance.

The second the music cuts off, Gabrielle rushes to Phoenix and throws herself into his arms.

"That was awesome!" she squeals.

"Grand gesture enough for you?"

"It was perfect! Absolutely perfect. Who knew you could dance? Maybe you should do a private dance for me later." She waggles her eyebrows.

I groan. "Help! My ears are burning. I don't want to know what my brother and sister-in-law get up to in the bedroom."

Elizabeth hip-checks me. "Oh please. You're not an innocent."

I place my hand over my chest. "I'm wounded. How can you think I'm not innocent?"

She snorts. "I have literally witnessed you score a woman in less than five seconds."

"You don't know. Maybe I took her home, tucked her into bed, and left."

Which is exactly what happened the last time I picked up a woman in front of her. I couldn't have sex with her. My cock was completely uninterested in anyone other than Elizabeth.

She bursts out laughing. "Do you even know what it means to tuck a woman into bed?"

I am not discussing this with her. Instead, I grab her hand and tug. "*Naked Falls Brewing* set up a stand outside the brewery this morning. Let's grab some beers."

"Why do they have a stand set up this morning?" she asks as I lead her down Main Street toward the brewery.

I wave toward *Clove's Coffee Corner* and *Nature Coop*, both of which have stands set up in front of their stores.

"Winter Falls will use any excuse to have a party."

"I can't wait to live here."

I screech to a halt. "You're moving to Winter Falls?"

Shit. If she lives here, if I see her every day, I won't be able to continue resisting her. I can barely resist the temptation to gather her into my arms and meld my lips to hers as it is.

"What? Am I not good enough for the town?" she teases but the hurt is plain to see in her eyes. I'm a fucking asshole.

"Of course, you're good enough. Maybe too good. But I thought you enjoyed living in White Bridge?"

I'm grasping at straws here. I know she wants to live in Winter Falls. She hasn't made a secret of the fact. But I thought she'd never move here since Beckett and Cassandra are in White Bridge. She loves her family something fierce. Plus, her job is there. A thirty-minute commute every day is not fun. Not to mention ecologically ill-advised.

"Never mind." She shrugs. "It was merely an idea."

Great. Her dejected tone makes me feel like an even bigger asshole. She tugs on my hand for me to release her but I'm not letting her go. Not when she's hurting.

I drag her down Main Street past the library, *Eden's Garden,* and *Bertie's Recording Studio* until we're at the brewery. I don't stop there. Instead, I pull her into the alleyway between the recording studio and the brewery.

"What are we doing here?" she asks as she surveys the area.

"I need to apologize." I may be an asshole, but I can apologize for my mistakes.

Her nose wrinkles. "What for?"

"I hurt your feelings."

"No, you didn't."

She can deny it all she wants but her hurt was too obvious to miss. Besides, she's my friend. I know when her feelings are injured. I maneuver her until her back is against the wall and I'm looming over her.

"Bessie," I plea.

When she doesn't respond, I frame her face with my hands. "Tell me what I did wrong."

"You didn't do anything wrong," she lies.

"I don't want you mad at me. You're one of my best friends." She flinches. "What's wrong?"

She blows out a sigh. "You don't want me living in Winter Falls."

"It's not that," I claim but glance away to hide how I'm lying.

"I hear a but at the end of your sentence."

I return my gaze to her and smile. "I can never fool you, can I, Bessie?"

"I grew up with three sisters and a brother."

"I do want you to live here," I half-lie.

I'd love to have her nearby. No more driving a half-hour for movie night or to drop by and see her. But dropping by to see her is also the problem. I'm not good at resisting temptation.

"Your wish may be granted."

I wait, but she doesn't add to her statement. "You're not going to tell me more, are you?"

"Nope."

I tuck one of her curls behind her ear. "You certain you don't want to tell me?"

She shoves at my shoulders, but I don't budge. It's cute how she thinks she can move me. I'm five inches taller than her. Not to mention I'm not addicted to strawberry ice cream the way she is.

"Don't try your seduction tricks with me. I'm immune."

Crap. She had to say the word seduction, didn't she? My gaze dips to her lips and her tongue slips out to lick her bottom lip. I should be the one licking her lip. Not her.

My head dips and her breath hitches. Her gaze falls to my lips and I decide, screw it. Just this once I want to feel how soft her lips are and how they taste.

I'm done hesitating. I crash my mouth to hers. She sighs and I immediately take advantage by shoving my tongue into her mouth. Her sweet taste of strawberries overwhelms me, and I groan before I begin to devour her. I cradle her face to allow me to feel her soft skin as I explore every crevice of her mouth.

Her hands on my shoulders pull me near until my hard length hits her belly. I grind into her, and she groans. Hell yeah.

"Well, well, well, what do we have here?"

At Cassandra's question, I tear my mouth from Elizabeth's. I stare down at her. I'm fucked. Plain and simple. One taste and I'm addicted. I was worried this would happen.

"I need to… I should …"

I give up trying to formulate a rational sentence and rush off down the alley in the opposite direction of Elizabeth's sister.

I've ruined everything.

Chapter 8

Secret – something for me to know and you never to find out

I FROWN AS I walk down Main Street in Winter Falls. I should be excited – I'm meeting with the town lawyer to discuss the lease on the building I want to rent – but I'm not. Instead, all I can think about is River. I've lost him. He hasn't phoned or messaged since 'the kiss'.

Which is exactly what I feared would happen if we ever went beyond friends. And yet, I fully participated in the kiss. I couldn't help myself. His lips touched mine and I promptly lost whatever semblance of self-control I had. Poof! Gone!

I reach the building and skid to a halt when I notice Lilac's dad waiting for me. "Can I help you, Mr. West?"

He grins. "You can call me Daniel."

"Okay." I still don't understand what he's doing here.

"I'm the town lawyer."

He chuckles. Probably because I'm doing an imitation of a gaping fish. But who would suspect the laidback, long-haired, sandal-wearing man to be a lawyer? Not me.

"I didn't know."

"Come on. Let's go inside and discuss the contract."

"The contract?"

Don't I still need to jump through several hoops before the townspeople will allow me to rent the place? Apparently, all the businesses on Main Street – except *The Inn on Main* – are owned by the town itself and you need approval from the town council before you can sign a lease agreement.

He opens the door and gestures me inside.

"You're in," he says once the door is closed behind him.

"I'm in? I have approval?" He nods. "Yes!" I throw my arms out to the sides and spin around. Because it's me, I don't see a cable laying on the ground and trip. I fly forward and Daniel catches me in his arms.

"Whoa there, darling," he says as he steadies me.

My face heats and I probably resemble the gingersnap River labels me sometimes. *River.* I rub a hand over my heart. Damn. I miss him.

Stop it, Elizabeth. No mooning over a man you can't have during a business meeting.

"Do you want to hear what I want to do with this place? I'm going to transform it into a day spa no one will ever want to leave. It's going to be a lot of work. I need new floors, new walls, new paint. The list goes on and on." I blow out a breath. "I'll be down on my knees all day and night working, but it will be worth it."

"Down on your knees?"

I whirl around at the amused voice to discover Daniel's wife has joined us. At her obvious amusement, I rewind my words in my mind. I cringe when I realize what I insinuated.

"I didn't mean …"

She waves away my embarrassment. "I'm happy our Lilac found your brother. Now I have three more daughters."

"There's actually four of us, Mrs. West."

"It's Ruby. And I've yet to meet the mysterious Olivia."

Mysterious? Snort. Olivia would love people to think she's mysterious. She's not. There's nothing mysterious about attempting to get into trouble at every step you take. She succeeds way too often to be referred to as anything other than a troublemaker. I wonder how she's doing now since Beckett's not there to bail her out of jail.

It's never her fault when the police arrest her. It's always a 'misunderstanding'. One time is a misunderstanding. Maybe even twice. But more than twice? Misunderstanding flies out the window and is replaced by culpability.

"You'll meet Olivia at the wedding," I claim, although I have no idea if Olivia will bother to show up for our brother's wedding.

My oldest sister doesn't understand what it means to be part of a family. She probably tells everyone she's all alone in the world. My stomach sours. Freaking Olivia. She's not here and yet she's ruining one of the best days of my life.

The door flies open, and Ellery rushes in. "I came as fast as I could."

My brow wrinkles. "As fast as you could? What are you talking about?" I turn to Daniel. "Is the lease not certain?"

I feel sweat gather on my forehead. Shit. Shit. Shit. I told Beckett the deal is solid. It's the reason he agreed to cash in some of my investments to help me pay for the renovations I want to make. Hold on. 'Agreed to' makes it sound as if my brother has control of me. He doesn't. But he does manage my finances.

If he learns the deal isn't final, he'll lecture me until the end of days. I'm not exaggerating. Big brother takes being the protector of the family very seriously. I need to solve this before he learns about the situation.

"Do I need Ellery to sponsor me?"

Ellery's the one who actually gave me the idea of building a day spa in Winter Falls. She mentioned one of the most frequent requests of her guests is if there's a spa in the area and, since I've always wanted to have my own spa, I ran with the idea.

I'm currently working as a hairdresser in a salon in White Bridge, but I'm a trained aesthetician and massage therapist as well. I went to college, too. But I dropped out after sophomore year. Sitting still in lecture halls was not for me.

I want to pamper people. Make them feel beautiful before sending them out into the cruel world, although there's nothing cruel about Winter Falls.

Ellery squeezes my hand. "I've got your back."

"Thank you. Now, how does this sponsorship work?"

"You don't need—"

Daniel's words are cut off when the door slams open and in storms Sage with Feather, Petal, Cayenne, and Clove on her heels. Uh oh. What are the gossip gals doing here?

Sage's gaze meets mine and she smiles. I shrink back. She's hilarious until she has her sights set on you. Then, she's terrifying. *Please. Please. Please. Don't have your sights set on matchmaking me.*

"I'm glad we caught you." She glares at Daniel. "Especially since someone forgot to put this meeting in the city calendar."

"You shouldn't have access to my agenda."

She pats his arm. "Thirty-four years in Winter Falls and you still don't get it."

"There's a back door." Ellery nudges me toward it. "Run for your life."

Is she serious? Her nudge becomes a push. Yep. She's serious. I inch backwards, but Ruby blocks my path. "You're not going anywhere."

"Mom," Ellery whines.

Ruby shrugs. "All of my daughters are paired off. I need something to occupy my time."

"What about your granddaughter Willow? And Ashlyn's pregnant, too."

"And aren't you the high school principal?" I add.

"Now," Sage interrupts, "I have a list of eligible bachelors for you."

Crap. I was afraid of this. Since Gabrielle is now paired off with Phoenix, the gossip gals are in search of another target. Apparently, they think I'm it. They're wrong. I have no interest in being matched. If I can't have River, I don't want anyone.

Hold on. Where did those thoughts come from? I know I can't have River, but I do want a husband and children. I'm not giving up those goals because my heart is latched onto a man I can't have.

"Elizabeth doesn't live in Winter Falls. You can't match people who don't live in town," Ellery says.

What is she saying? She knows I'm planning to move to Winter Falls as soon as this deal is finished. I need to search for a place, but I'm hoping Gabrielle's apartment will become available soon. She might as well move out. She doesn't spend any time there anyway since she's always out at the goat farm with Phoenix.

Ellery winks at me. Okay, she's not being mean. She must be trying to fend the matchmakers off. I can get on board with this plan.

"Yeah. I live in White Bridge, remember?"

Feather laughs. "We weren't born yesterday. We know you're moving into Gabrielle's place this weekend."

I am?

"I already have your candles made," Petal says.

Yikes. Petal doesn't make 'normal' candles. She makes 'sexy' candles of all varieties. Yes, apparently there is more than one type of sexy candle. Who knew? Petal evidently.

"And I have a welcome basket prepared," Clove says.

A basket from the coffee corner owner sounds perfect. I love coffee, although nothing can compare to ice cream. Except coffee flavored ice cream. I'd kill for it.

Sage waves a notebook in the air. "And I have the men you should date all ready."

Curiosity gets the better of me. "Which men?"

"Peace, Freedom, or Cedar."

Ellery rolls her eyes. "Cedar doesn't live in Winter Falls."

"Who's Cedar?" I remember the name being mentioned before, but I don't think I've met anyone named Cedar.

"Rowan's brother," Ellery answers. "He's a recluse."

"I believe he prefers the term wanderer," Ruby corrects.

"Whatever." Ellery waves her hand in dismissal. "He's not here, so you can scratch him off your list."

Sage cocks her eyebrow. "Are you certain he's not in town?"

"Yes. We'd know if Rowan's brother showed up."

"Okay." Sage focusses on me. "Now, who do you choose – Peace or Freedom?"

"Um."

Why didn't she mention River? He's a single man in town, isn't he? He's not secretly married, is he? No, I would know. Besides, he's made it perfectly clear what he thinks of love and commitment. My chest gets tight and breathing becomes difficult.

Since everyone in the room is staring at me, I resist the temptation to lift my hand and rub my chest. These women are entirely too astute. I won't give them any more fuel to use against me.

"Do I have to date anyone? Maybe I'm happy being single?"

Cayenne pats my arm. "You're funny."

"I wasn't being funny."

"Sure, you were."

Sage slams her notebook shut. "We'll give you some time to think about who you choose. I'll send you profiles of both men."

"What about River?" Ruby asks before they can leave.

By body warms at the mere mention of his name. He doesn't believe in love, I remind it. We can teach him. No, no, we can't.

Ruby smirks as she studies me. "Never mind. They're just friends."

"Exactly," Sage says but I have the feeling she's not actually agreeing. There's a twinkle in her eye. I fear it doesn't bode well for me.

Sage leaves with her crew following her. I stare after them with my mouth gaping open.

"Someone tell me I'm dreaming."

"Welcome to Winter Falls."

Chapter 9

Catch – usually played with a ball but a vibrator will do in a pinch

"CAN SOMEONE TELL ME how many times we're going to move one of my sisters into this apartment?" Cassandra whines as she drops a box of my stuff on the floor.

It's moving day! As I had hoped, Gabrielle 'officially' shacked up with Phoenix and her apartment became available. I didn't suspect it would happen this quickly, but those gossip gals know their stuff! They were right on the nose when they said I'd move to Winter Falls this weekend.

Phoenix and Beckett set my sofa on the ground. "What are you complaining about? You carried a total of one box up the stairs and we're nearly finished," Beckett says, and Phoenix grunts in agreement.

"Besides, there are no other sisters," I remind her.

"There's Olivia," Gabrielle points out.

Gabrielle is holding onto the fantasy of Olivia becoming an active member of this family. She should know better. People don't change. No matter how much I wish it otherwise. If they did, I could be the one to change River and convince him love does exist.

How can he not believe in love? Love is all around us. Both of his brothers are smitten and happy. Is he blind? And why can't I stop errant thoughts of him from popping into my mind at all times of the day and night?

Cassandra completely ignores Gabrielle's comment about Olivia. "Where do you want this?" She motions to the box she dropped on the floor.

"Huh." I tap my chin. "The word bedroom is written on it in big letters, so maybe bedroom?"

"Smartass," she mumbles. She reaches down and picks the box up by the flaps. As she lifts, the bottom falls out, and the entire contents of the box spill out and spread across the room.

My eyes widen as I realize the box contains all the stuff from my bedside table. As in, *all the stuff.* I drop to my knees and grab for my things.

"Well. Well. Well. What do we have here?" Cassandra waves my vibrator in the air.

Crap. I should have packed the toy in my clothes or double-boxed it or something.

"None of your business. Give it here."

I reach for it, but she jumps on the couch and holds it above her head. I'm surprised she doesn't stick out her tongue and sing, *na na na boo boo.*

"Grow up, will you?"

"Boring."

I rush to tackle her, but she springs from the sofa and dashes to the chair. "You can't catch me. I'm the gingerbread man."

I stalk toward her, and she smirks as she lifts her arm with the vibrator in the air. Before I have a chance to launch myself at her, Gabrielle pulls on my sleeve.

"Here," she says and hands me a lit candle.

Now, it's my turn to smirk. Cassandra's afraid of fire. I lift my arm and wave the candle toward her, and she squeals. What she doesn't do is give me my vibrator. I shuffle closer until she's on the edge of the chair.

"Why are you playing catch with a vibrator?" Lilac asks as she enters the apartment.

"Someone is being a child," I answer, but before I can explain I feel my skin heating. Oh no. The candle is dripping wax all over the place. "What in the world? Is this not a no-drip candle?"

Lilac blows out the candle before grasping my forearm and dragging me to the kitchen sink. She drops the candle in it and turns on the tap to pour cold water over my hand.

"I don't think the burn is serious," she says as she studies the affected area. It's a little red but the pain is completely gone now. "Where did you get the candle?"

"From the gift basket someone left in front of the door," Gabrielle answers.

"I believe this is one of Petal's sex candles."

"Sex candle?" My eyes are probably the size of saucers as I stare at Lilac. "I thought when Petal said she made sex candles, she meant candles to set the mood or massage candles."

"She has those, too. But I believe this is one of her drip candles for wax play."

"She makes those?"

"She not only makes them, she uses them."

"Wait. What? Petal tests out drip candles for wax play herself?"

"Not herself. With her husband, Orion."

I hold up my hands. "Enough. I don't need to know anymore."

"Sex is perfectly natural," Lilac says.

Beckett draws her to him. "It's also an activity my sisters don't partake in."

Cassandra guffaws. "How does it feel to live in the Land of Denial?"

Beckett's cheeks darken. "I don't know what you're talking about."

"Ha! And you didn't catch me with Jared in my bedroom while he was going—"

"I have wiped the event from my memory," he interrupts.

"You do realize you can't actually wipe an event from your memory?" Lilac has a problem with euphemisms. They can be misinterpreted and therefore shouldn't be used, according to her.

"Hold on. Wasn't Jared Elizabeth's boyfriend?" Gabrielle's gaze ping pongs between Cassandra and me.

Yes, yes, he was. I was totally and completely enamored of him in my junior year of high school. Until Cassandra came home from college for the weekend and crooked her finger his way. It's always the same. Men don't want to stay with me. River wouldn't be any different.

But Winter Falls is going to be different for me. Not only because it's a small town where everyone knows everyone, but because there are no secrets here. No way can Cassandra steal a man away from me here. The news would spread around town before she could put her panties back on.

"He wasn't a very good boyfriend if he was, since he didn't hesitate to switch sisters."

Cassandra doesn't appear the least bit remorseful. In her opinion, she did nothing wrong. My nostrils flare and my jaw clenches. I'll teach her what wrong means. I crack my knuckles as I set off in her direction.

Beckett steps between us. "No fighting."

"Why not? I can take her." Cassandra raises her fists.

"You go on believing that," I taunt.

"This is ancient history," Beckett reminds us.

"I wouldn't say thirteen years is ancient," I mumble.

"I agree. Ancient history refers to events that occurred up to the fall of the Western Roman Empire in 476."

Leave it to Lilac to know the date of the fall of the Western Roman Empire off the top of her head.

Cassandra grunts and drops her hands. She thinks the trivia Lilac sprouts is annoying. I think it's amusing. As does Beckett if the smile he's giving his fiancée is any indication.

Speaking of fiancés. "When do you think Phoenix will pop the question?" I turn to ask Gabrielle, but she's nowhere to be found.

"Gabrielle and Phoenix snuck off to your bedroom a while ago," Lilac informs me.

"You better not be having sex on my bed!" I shout in their direction.

Cassandra bounces on her toes. "Let's go catch them in the act." She bounds toward the bedroom.

I chase after her. "Leave them alone."

"Do you want them having sex in your bed?"

Yuck! No! But they deserve their privacy.

Before we make it down the hallway, Phoenix strolls out of the bedroom holding Gabrielle's hand.

"We weren't having sex," he declares but guessing by Gabrielle's blush they were up to something sexy in there. Good for them. Gabrielle deserves to be happy after what her asshat ex-boyfriend put her through.

"We put your… um… things away."

Thank you, I mouth to her since I know she's talking about my vibrator. But my sister's shy and I won't be taunting her with her shyness and allow her to withdraw into herself again.

"We're going to get going since the big stuff is done," Phoenix announces.

"Thanks for helping," I tell him as I open the front door. He lifts his chin and leads Gabrielle into the hallway.

"We're off, too." Beckett kisses my hair before leaving with Lilac. "You coming?" he asks Cassandra who follows them.

As soon as I'm alone, I make my way to the bedroom to unpack my clothes. The doorbell rings before I manage to open the first box.

"What are you doing here?" I ask when I open the door to River.

"What am I doing here? I'm your friend and you're moving. I'm here to help."

"Friend? We're still friends?"

"Why wouldn't we be?"

"Because your kiss was hot enough to melt the frozen tundra!" Cassandra shouts from behind me.

Holy cow! She scared me. What's she doing here? Did she sneak back inside my apartment when I was in the bedroom? I wouldn't put it past her. The woman doesn't know what boundaries are.

"I thought you got a ride with Beckett."

"I've got my own car here."

I motion to the door. "Maybe it's time for you to use it."

"And miss this? No way. Do you have popcorn?"

I snatch her arm and drag her out of the apartment. "Out!"

She sighs. "This whole ritual was more fun when Gabrielle was the target. She never kicked me out of her place."

I wait until she's tromping down the stairs before returning my attention to River. "Do you want to come in?"

Chapter 10

Choices – a bunch of sucky options that hold no appeal

I swing the door wide open and motion for River to enter. He scans the area as he swaggers inside. And make no doubt about it, he swaggers wherever he goes. I realize I'm focused on his ass and force my gaze higher.

"Do you want something to drink?"

When he spins around to answer me, he's frowning. "There's nothing left for me to do. All the heavy lifting is done."

"My brother and your brother helped out," I explain.

His frown deepens. "Why didn't you ask me for help?"

I shut the door. I don't want anyone to hear my answer. "Because I haven't heard from you since the flash mob when we …"

I trail off. He doesn't need me to tell him what we did. He was an active participant.

"About the …"

I wait but he doesn't continue.

"About the what?"

He shrugs. "I should probably apologize for sticking my tongue down your throat."

Wow. Way to make me feel the moment was special. Dick-head. How dare he— Oh wait. He's doing this on purpose. He wants me to know the moment wasn't special. At least, not to him. To me, on the other hand? Best. Kiss. Ever. Hands down.

The little girl inside of me – the one who believes in fairy tales despite growing up with Cassandra the boyfriend stealer – hopes River will want me for more than friendship. That the kiss meant more to him than he's willing to admit.

When I study his face, however, I realize I have to dash that little girl's hopes. River is obviously not interested in more than friendship with me. To be fair, he made it perfectly clear he'd never want more than friendship. He never lied. He never pretended to believe in love.

It's me who thought he was putting on a show to keep himself from getting hurt. It's me who invented a whole back story about him having his heart broken so badly he was afraid to get hurt again. None of which appears to be true.

This is the moment. I have to choose. Accept River as a friend or let him go. Can I do it? Can I be friends with him while my heart longs for more? I blow out a breath. Time to toughen up my heart because I can't let him go.

If friendship is all he has to offer, friendship is what we'll have.

"There's no need to apologize," I force those words out of my mouth as if they aren't choking me. "I was kind of an active participant."

He chuckles. "Yes, you were."

I feign indifference. "Hey! I wanted to check out the supposed best kisser in Colorado's skills. Who can blame me?"

"Best kisser in Colorado?" He cocks a brow. "Not the entire United States?"

The entire world, I think but know better than to say.

I shove his shoulder. "Don't get cocky."

"It's not cocky if it's true."

I wrap my hands around my neck and pretend to choke. "Hard to breathe in here," I cough out. "With your ego stealing all the air."

He slaps my hands away and winds an arm around my neck before grinding his knuckles over my head. I shove him.

"Do you have the first clue about how hard it is to keep my mop of hair untangled, you ogre?"

He tugs on a curl. "Your hair isn't a mop. It's cute."

Cute. Not beautiful. Another reality check.

"Whatever. Do you want to watch a movie?"

He nods toward the boxes piled up in the kitchen. "Do you want some help unpacking first?"

"Um." I consider. Are there any embarrassing items in those boxes? I don't need a repeat of the vibrator-incident. Especially not in front of him.

He smirks. "Or are you worried there's another vibrator in one of those boxes?"

I gasp. The incident happened less than an hour ago. How can he possibly know about it already?

"How do you know? Who told you?"

He shrugs. "It's all over the Facebook group."

"What? What Facebook group?"

"It's for the residents of Winter Falls."

"I'm a resident of Winter Falls." My eyes widen when I realize what this means. "I should be in this group." If I am, I can erase a post about my vibrator.

I survey the apartment. Where's my phone?

"Before you tear the place apart, maybe you should search your pockets."

Oops. I forgot I put my phone in my back pocket a while ago so I wouldn't lose it. I yank it out and open the Facebook app. I hit notifications and discover an invite to the Winter Falls Facebook group. I immediately accept and start scrolling.

My mouth drops open as I read. "There are fifty comments about the incident."

"I especially enjoyed the comment from Clove with a recommendation of her ten favorite vibrators. And also, Feather's comment about how her candles would never have burnt your hand."

My face warms until it's hot enough to heat all the houses in Winter Falls for the entire winter. Geesh. "How do I delete it?"

"You can't. No one can delete posts except the admins."

I groan. "Let me guess. The gossip gals are the admins."

"And Ruby West."

Ruby isn't any better than those gossip gals. How dare she mention River to them? What a shit stirrer. I throw my phone onto the sofa.

"I don't think I want to be a member of the Facebook group anymore."

"Don't worry. Forest will get caught without his pants on somewhere embarrassing soon enough and steal the spotlight from you."

Spotlight? As if I'm a star? Hardly.

He rubs his hands together. "Now, don't you want to discover what else is in your welcome package?"

I rub a hand over my forehead where I feel a headache coming on. "I don't know. The drip candles were bad enough."

He ignores my trepidation and hauls the basket onto the coffee table. He tosses the card at me. "Read it."

"Welcome to Winter Falls. We hope these items come in useful in the near future. Wink. Wink. Nudge. Nudge."

I groan. What's in the basket? Whatever it is, I don't want to discover it with River. Especially since I've spent every night since the 'kiss' remembering how his tongue felt dueling with mine while lying in bed. And, okay, maybe I used my vibrator while imagining where the kiss could have gone.

"I'm tired. It's been a long day. I think I'll go to bed early."

He barks out a laugh. "It's barely five o'clock in the afternoon. You're not tired. You're scared to find out what's in the welcome basket."

"Can you blame me?" I mutter before reaching for the basket. "Fine. Let's do this."

I remove a set of three long black taper candles. "We already know what these are."

"Are you going to use them?"

"Um. No. I think burning my hand is enough candle play for me."

"Sweet. Can I have them?" he asks but tucks them in his back pocket before I can respond.

"They're all yours." I try to keep my voice light despite the pit of jealousy roaring to life in my stomach. I will not be jealous of whoever he's using those candles on. I will not!

"A box of condoms. Need these?" I wave them in front of his face.

"Normal size." He chuckles. "Nope. I need extra-large."

I roll my eyes. "Said by every man who doesn't know how to measure six inches."

"Six inches?" He waggles his eyebrows. "I can count to ten."

I ignore the tingle those words create. Friend, remember? F. R. I. E. N. D. Friend. As if spelling the word is going to help.

"Wait. This is actually handy. An eye mask."

River snatches the mask from my hands. "This isn't an eye mask to help you sleep. It's a blindfold."

"What's the difference?"

He rummages around in the basket. "I believe it belongs with these." He dangles some black straps from his fingers.

"What are those?"

"It's a bondage kit."

"A what?"

"Bondage," he repeats with a waggle of his eyebrows. "When you tie your partner up and have your wicked way with her while she's unable to move."

His words cause every nerve in my body to spark to life. I've never had a boyfriend tie me up before but the idea of River tying my arms up and blindfolding me while I'm naked and he licks every inch of my body makes tingles explode in my core. I rub my thighs together to alleviate some of the pressure.

"What is this? The kinky welcome gift set?" I try to joke but my voice comes out breathy. I clear my throat and try again. "Do they give this to all new residents of Winter Falls? Wait. Is there a sex club in town I should know about?"

"No, but wouldn't a sex club be fun?"

The tingles in my body evaporate as I imagine River at a sex club being pleasured by a woman. A woman who isn't me.

"This is not what a welcome basket should contain. There should be maps of the local area, some snacks and drinks, maybe some local gift cards and a delivery menu."

"There are no delivery services in Winter Falls. Bad for the environment, but you can get take-out at the brewery or the diner. You need to bring your own containers for the food, though."

I rummage through the bottom of the basket. Edible underwear? No, thanks. Finger vibrator? Interesting, but who would I use it with? Wait. There are some papers at the bottom.

"Aha!" I shout as I wave the papers around. "Maybe there's a map and some take-out menus after all."

I skim the papers and gulp. Not a map.

"What is it?" River doesn't wait for a reply as he reads over my shoulder. "Profiles of Peace and Freedom." He barks out a laugh. "I guess the gossip gals have chosen their next target."

"Why me?" I whine.

"Because you're the woman who wants a white picket fence."

He's not entirely wrong but, "I actually don't think much of fences."

"Let's clean up your sex box and dig out your DVD player to play a movie." I guess it's not a suggestion as he stands and walks over to the box marked 'television' and begins rooting through it.

Welp. If River hadn't made it obvious enough already, I'd get the message now. He doesn't want a wife. Message received.

Chapter 11

Broken – when your 'equipment' doesn't work in its usual manner

RIVER

I bound up the stairs to the courthouse. It's going to be a great day. The sun is shining. I'm back on track with Bessie on the 'friends' path. And I've got a group of tourists signed up for a full-day green tour.

"Good luck." Lyric slaps me on the back as he exits the police station located inside the courthouse.

What's he up to? He never wishes me luck before a tour. Whatever. I'm not letting his negativity bring me down.

"Thanks, bro."

He chuckles in response.

"He's here!" a woman shouts.

I gaze over at her to discover she's standing amongst a group of women dressed as if they're ready for a night on the town. Since there isn't much nightlife in Winter Falls, I'm confused as to what they're doing here.

"How can I help you, ladies?"

"Isn't he as dreamy as Lara said he would be?" one of the women mock whispers to another.

I smirk despite not knowing who Lara is. Probably some tourist I met. Tourism is the life blood of Winter Falls.

"Do you need directions?" I ask them.

"Directions? Don't be silly. We're here for the tour."

Well, shit. This isn't my first all-women tour. But usually, they stick to the two-hour tour I give of town. A full-day tour includes a lot of walking, some of which is through mud and high grass. I study their high heels.

"And you signed up for the all day tour?"

"Yep. You've got us to yourself all day long." She winks.

"This tour includes hiking. Did you ladies bring spare pairs of shoes?"

She giggles and kicks up her leg to show off her sparkly heels. "We'll be fine, won't we girls?" They all sigh in response.

Great. What do I do? They can't be tromping through the mud around the dam at the falls or the tall grass around the wind farm. But there's no way I can keep them busy with a tour in town. I'll think of something.

I clear my throat. "Is everyone here?" They nod. "To start off with, I'm River Alston. I'm the owner of *Turn It Green Tours*. I grew up in Winter Falls, which as you probably already know was the first carbon neutral town in the world."

One of the women's hands shoots into the air. "Are all the men in Winter Falls as hot as you are?"

I chuckle and wink. "Of course not, doll. I'm one of a kind."

"I bet you are," she mutters.

I wait for the zing of excitement I normally feel when a woman hits on me to occur, but nothing happens. My cock is apparently still asleep this morning. Hopefully, he'll wake up later because this tour is prime hunting ground.

"Today, I'll be showing you around the town and surrounding areas to demonstrate how Winter Falls manages to maintain its carbon neutral status."

"You can show me around anywhere you want," one of the women whispers.

Once again, the sexually provocative words don't cause a zing of excitement to bolt through me. I must be tired. I haven't been sleeping well lately. It's hard to rest when you've ruined your relationship with your best friend.

"We'll start with how the town handles the no car policy. Follow me, ladies."

"I'll follow you wherever you want to go."

This time I'm not surprised when my body doesn't respond to the insinuation. I'm tired is all, I remind myself. Tonight, I'll get some sleep, and tomorrow all my parts will be ready to stand at attention.

I lead the women out of city hall toward the bike and golf cart rental outside. It's one of many rental areas in town. Rental is a misnomer as the bikes and golf carts are free to use. Both tourists and residents alike are welcome to borrow the vehicles provided they stay within the city limits of Winter Falls.

A rule I might have found difficult to follow in the past. But when a sexy lady asks you how far a golf cart can go without being recharged, who am I to say no? It's all in the name of science after all.

"This is Winter Falls' answer to avoiding carbon emission from gasoline engines." I motion toward the line of bicycles and golf carts.

"Is this why we were forced to park our cars at the bed and breakfast down the road and told to leave them there?"

Forced? I grit my teeth. Don't they understand what carbon neutral means?

A gust of wind barrels down Main Street and hits us. Considering it's November and the smell of snow is in the air, the wind feels like ice smashing into me.

"Holy crap. It's freaking cold out here." The women huddle together.

I stare at their legs bared by their short skirts and their high heels and grunt. These women are in no way prepared for a tour through nature in November. Time for Plan B.

"How does everyone feel about touring the ecological shops in town?"

They cheer and I bite back a groan. I have no desire to spend the day chaperoning a bunch of women on a shopping bender, but it's apparently my job for the day.

"First stop, Eden's Garden." I motion across the town square to the flower shop.

"Hey, River," Eden greets when I herd my group into the shop.

"Hi! I have a group of tourists who are interested in learning all about your store."

She glances at the group of women and raises her eyebrows at me. I shrug. What can I say? She recognizes what's going on with these women. She knows me inside and out since we grew up together. She's a year younger than me, but in a town the size of Winter Falls, all the kids know each other and hang around together.

"Wait. Your name is Eden? As in the garden of Eden? And you have a flower shop?" The woman giggles.

Eden rolls her eyes. She's used to tourists making fun of her name. In Winter Falls, Eden is a perfectly normal name. In fact, her mom was named Eden, too. But tourists aren't as used to the hippie names in town.

Despite coming to town to enjoy our pagan festivals, most tourists don't bother to try and understand the values behind the founding of Winter Falls. Values I usually try to impart on them during one of my tours. But I can recognize a lost cause when I see one and this group got scratched on to the lost cause category as soon as I noticed their matching four-inch heels.

"This is a flower shop, but we don't have cut flowers."

"You don't have cut flowers? How can you be a flower shop without cut flowers?"

As Eden launches into her spiel about how cut flowers are destroying the earth, I find a spot against the wall to lean against and pull out my phone. I message Miller and Elder from Naked Falls Brewing and ask if they can fit my group in for a last minute tour and tasting. Lucky for me, Elder immediately responds with a message to give them thirty minutes to set up.

A woman from the tour sidles up next to me. "Hi, River," she greets in a breathy voice and it's all I can do to not roll my eyes.

What the hell? *Knock it off, River.* She's obviously coming on to you. You love this. Normally, I wouldn't hesitate to take her hand and lead her out of this place straight across the street to her room at the *Inn on Main.*

Instead, I'm sighing and wishing I could crawl back to bed and start this day over. What is wrong with me?

"Hi, um…"

"Candy. The name's Candy."

Of course, it is. The Candies of this world are my playground, except my body is not responding to her rubbing up against me while batting her eyelashes. I must be even more tired than I thought.

My attention is drawn away from Candy when Eden huffs. Uh oh. The woman is usually calm as can be, but once her temper is engaged? Watch out.

I should know. I accidentally planted a bunch of poison ivy in her locker at school once and she went ballistic on me. It wasn't my fault. I can't help it if she switched lockers with Phoenix without telling anyone. In hindsight, I probably shouldn't have signed the note I left for my brother.

Mrs. West, who was a teacher back then and is the principal now, did not find the prank amusing. What she did find amusing was me spending a weekend cleaning the bleachers in the gym. The things I found under there. I learned awful quick how important it is to dispose of a used condom in a proper manner.

"Do you not understand what waste is? You do know—"

I rush to the front of the group. "Thank you, Eden, for taking time out of your busy day to explain your business to the group."

She narrows her eyes on me as I clap. I grin as the other women join me in clapping for her.

"Now, ladies. I've arranged something special for you."

"I hope it involves a bed," someone whispers and I groan. Did this entire group of women swallow horny pills this morning?

"We're going next door to the *Naked Falls Brewing* company where we'll be getting a tour of their ecological brewing process before having a tasting."

"Yeah!" they cheer and rush out of the door.

Eden laughs behind me. Her anger forgotten as quickly as it arose. "Have fun, Lothario."

I'm not a Lothario. Not when my body isn't interested in any of the women throwing themselves at me this morning. What on earth is wrong with me? Maybe I need to go see Dr. Blue for a check-up.

Chapter 12

Broken record – when you repeat the same lie over and over again

"Awesome! You made it," Cassandra says as I walk into Beckett and Lilac's house on Friday night.

"Why wouldn't I make it?"

Lilac declared Friday nights as family dinner night. According to her, we need a ritual to bond us together. I didn't mention how growing up together after our parents died already bonded us. If someone wants our family to spend more time together, I'm all for it.

Cassandra waggles her eyebrows. "It's Friday night. I thought you might have a date."

"A date? With who?"

She slaps her forehead. "How could I forget? The man you fancy doesn't 'date'."

"River and I are just friends."

Because he doesn't want more no matter how much I do. I should probably create an Unrequited Love Anonymous group. First step, admit you have a problem. I, Elizabeth Elaine Dempsey, want to do wicked things to my best friend and have him do wicked things to me.

Second step …. Hmm. Maybe I should research how a twelve-step program works before I form my group.

"It didn't look like 'just friends' when you were playing tonsil tennis with him."

"Tonsil tennis? Way to be a grown-up. Are you certain you're older than me?"

"Call it what you want. I saw you and River k-i-s-s-i-n-g," she sings.

Someone gasps behind me, and I whirl around to discover Gabrielle staring at me with her mouth gaping open. "Y-y-you kissed River?"

I blow out a breath causing my bangs to fly into the air. "Yes?"

"Not yes. Yeeees. It was hot. You should have seen it. I thought he was going to strip her naked right there in the alley." Cassandra fans her face.

"I don't want to hear this shit," Phoenix mumbles before kissing Gabrielle's forehead and strolling further into the house.

I wish I could follow him. Wait. Why can't I? I start after him, but Cassandra grabs my arm and drags me back. "Where do you think you're going?"

"To help Lilac with dinner." There. I'm not making excuses. Helping out is totally legitimate.

Cassandra giggles. "Beckett's with her." I blanch. "Don't you remember the time you interrupted them when Beckett had his pants—"

Gabrielle slams her hands over her ears. "Na na na."

I want to do the same thing, but I know better. If I make any sort of indication of how freaked out I was to see my brother being pleasured by his girlfriend – yack! – Cassandra will draw out this conversation. No thanks.

"Oral sex is perfectly natural," Lilac says as she joins us.

"What are you doing here?" Cassandra asks her.

"I live here. Or did you forget? Are you having other short-term memory issues? Did you hit your head recently? Should I schedule an MRI for you?"

Cassandra huffs before stomping off. She has no patience for Lilac's brand of weird.

"Thanks," I tell my future sister-in-law.

Her nose wrinkles in confusion. "Thanks for what?"

"For being you."

"Who else would I be? I can't crawl into the skin of another person."

I pat her hand before heading to the living room with Gabrielle following me. As soon as we enter the room, Phoenix's attention focuses on my baby sister. She grins at him and his face lights up with happiness.

My stomach churns. Knock it off. I refuse to be jealous of my sister. She deserves to be happy after the way her ex-boyfriend tried to ruin her life. Besides, she's my sister and I love her. I want her to be happy.

Of course, I also want what they have. A love to stand the test of time. Lilac strolls into the room and Beckett immediately goes to her and slings an arm around her shoulders. The tenderness on his face nearly has me fleeing the room to hide my envy.

"Blech!" Cassandra feigns retching. "Love is all around us. Only Elizabeth and I have remained unscathed. Although, my little sister would love to find love. Too bad she's searching for love in all the wrong places."

I roll my eyes and pretend I don't know what she's talking about. "I'm not searching for love."

"Sure, you aren't." She snorts. "And you're also not in love with River."

Do I have more than friendly feelings for River? Yes, I do. But am I in love with him? No, I am not. Although it wouldn't take much for me to tumble down the rabbit hole to love. I know better, though. I'm watching where I walk and avoiding all holes and uneven surfaces.

"Anyway, what are we having for dinner?" I say in an obvious attempt to change the topic.

"Sausage and onions."

"Yum. I love sausage."

Cassandra bursts out laughing. "Yeah, we kind of figured that out when we found your vibrator."

I feel my face heat. Can't Cassandra be a normal sister? The kind who doesn't mention every embarrassing moment you've ever experienced in front of your family.

"I don't know why this is funny. It's perfectly normal for a female to have a vibrator."

Cassandra sticks her tongue out at Lilac. "Way to read the room."

"Read the room? The room isn't a book."

Beckett grasps her hand. "Come on. Let's check on the food and I can explain what read the room means while you tell me all about vibrators."

Gabrielle's face loses its color, and she clutches her stomach. "Can everyone please stop discussing their sex lives?"

Phoenix frowns at her. "Are you feeling okay?"

"Why wouldn't she be feeling okay? It's not as if she's pregnant." Gabrielle flinches, and I immediately regret my careless words. "Are you two trying?"

She glances away as she shrugs. "Maybe?"

And here I thought my jealousy had reached its peak, but nope, there's more jealousy in me. A fountain of the stuff as it turns out. I want children more than I want a husband to have them with, although a husband would be way more fun than a laboratory.

"No way." Cassandra shakes her finger at Gabrielle. "You're not going to be the first of us sisters to have children. You're the youngest. You should wait."

Phoenix growls but before he has a chance to respond to Cassandra, Gabrielle pats his hand, and he calms down. Wow. If I ever doubted their love – which I haven't – I wouldn't anymore. The way they're in perfect synch with each other's moods is beautiful to watch, despite my jealousy and envy.

"Don't worry, Cassandra. I'm not pregnant," Gabrielle declares.

"Good. My sister will not be having children out of wedlock." Beckett glares at Phoenix. "Nod if you understand."

Judging by the way Phoenix rolls his eyes, he isn't intimidated by my big brother.

Beckett points at me. "The same goes for you, too."

I whip out a salute. "Yes, big brother. Whatever you say, big brother."

"What did I do to deserve four wise-ass sisters?" he grumbles.

Cassandra beams up at him. "You must be the luckiest man in the world."

He winds an arm around her neck and messes with her hair. "Lucky? You guys gave me gray hair and ulcers."

"Stress doesn't actually cause stomach ulcers, although stress can limit the ability of the human body to deal with an infection of the stomach lining."

Cassandra groans. "Ms. Encyclopedia strikes again."

"It's Mrs. Encyclopedia-Dempsey," Beckett corrects.

Lilac frowns at him. "I told you I wouldn't take your name upon marriage. I have fifty witnesses to the agreement."

"It was a joke."

"Oh. Was it supposed to be amusing? I didn't find it amusing." She's not being bitchy. She's genuinely confused.

Beckett sighs before announcing, "Dinner's ready."

Cassandra and I rush to the dining area. "I'm starved. I could stuff two sausages in my mouth right now."

"Two?" She laughs. "Do you often have two sausages in your mouth at one time? Tell me more, dear sister."

I shove her. "Grow up."

She shoves me back and I go flying across the room straight into Beckett who's holding the tray of sausages. My legs give out and I slide to the floor at the same time he loses control over the tray and the contents spill over straight into my lap.

"You got your wish. Plenty of sausages for you to choose from."

I glare at Cassandra. She's going to regret saying those words to me. She's not the only one who knows how to pull off a revenge prank.

Chapter 13

RIVER

I stroll into the library and scan the crowd for Elizabeth. I haven't seen her in a few days and I'm jonesing for my Bessie fix. My platonic Bessie fix I remind myself.

It's movie night. Once a month, Juniper puts together a movie night since Winter Falls doesn't have a movie theater. The movie is always a surprise, which is shocking in and of itself. There are no surprises in Winter Falls. I'm convinced my big brother is helping her because there's no way she could pull off a surprise of this size otherwise. Although, she is now shacked up with a Hollywood star.

"She's not here yet," Sage says.

I pretend I don't know who she's talking about. "Who's not here?"

"Your boo."

I cough to hide my laughter. "My boo?"

"Isn't Elizabeth your boo?"

I can't contain my laughter anymore. It sneaks out in a series of chuckles. "Um, yeah. She's my best friend and my boo."

"Isn't boo a girlfriend?"

"Not necessarily."

She studies me for a second. When I don't begin fidgeting, she raises her voice to shout at Petal who's on the other side of the room with her husband, Orion. "Is a boo always a sexual partner?"

Elizabeth enters the room with her eyes the size of saucers. "Why are we yelling about sexual partners across the library?" she mutters her question to me.

I shrug. "Because this is Winter Falls."

Movie night is the one night of the month the gossip gals are allowed to speak in the library according to the agreement the librarian, Gratitude, made with the Gossip Gals. They can have their 'movie night shenanigans', but they better behave any other time they're in the library.

I wish I was there the night they managed to hack out a deal with the librarian. Rumor has it wine and matches were involved.

"Hello, Elizabeth," Sage greets and Elizabeth steps closer to me. "Did you have a chance to read those profiles in your welcome basket?"

"Um…"

"Is there any information missing? We can find out anything you want to know."

Elizabeth eyes the exit. "Any information? How did you find out the information you already have?"

Sage grins. "Easy. I'm a police officer."

Lyric groans as he joins us. "You're not a police officer, Sage. You're a police dispatcher. And you shouldn't use police resources for your little matchmaking business."

"Lyric Journey Alston, don't you dare speak to me this way. I used to change your diapers."

He drags a hand through his hair. "Bane of my existence."

"And why would I use police resources when I have the best resource known to man?"

This I gotta hear. "What's the best resource known to man?"

Sage winks. "A boy's mama."

My eyes automatically scan the crowd for my parents. I spot them canoodling on a sofa. When my gaze meets Mom's, she waves with a wink. Crap. She'd tell the gossip gals everything they want to know.

Lyric claps a hand on my shoulder. "Not as much fun when you're the target, is it?"

Has no one paid any attention to a word I've said since I returned to Winter Falls after college? "This is a waste of everyone's time. I'm not relationship material."

He chuckles. "I seem to remember another brother of mine saying the same thing."

Phoenix's situation was completely different. He got screwed over by his girlfriend, who was not a nice person to begin with. I don't know why my little brother hooked up with her in the first place. Sure, she was hot, but she was also drama. Not his usual cup of tea.

I didn't get screwed over by *a* woman. I got misled, deceived, and fooled by a bevy of them.

"Settle down, everyone!" Juniper claps her hands. "Find a seat so we can begin."

I shackle Elizabeth's wrist and drag her to a loveseat in the corner of the room. Sage winks at me and gives me a thumbs-up. She's delusional if she thinks Elizabeth and I are more than friends. Except warmth suffuses me from where I'm touching her skin.

If Elizabeth was any other woman, I'd keep walking past the loveseat straight to the rear of the stacks to a dark corner where I'd shove her up against a bookshelf before having my wicked way with her. My pants tighten at the vision of Elizabeth with her lips swollen from my kisses and her hair a mess from my hands running through it.

I need to calm down because there's no way I'm taking my best friend to the rear of the stacks. My cock whimpers, but I ignore it. The same way I've been ignoring it since Elizabeth and I became friends.

We get comfortable on the loveseat. I throw my arm around Elizabeth and drag her close until she rests her head against my shoulder. Maybe this isn't the way best friends usually act, but I don't give a shit. If this is the only way I can have Elizabeth, I'm taking it.

"How was your day?"

Her body vibrates with excitement. "Good. No, great. Sirius began work on the spa today. I need to bring in a plumber and electrician from out of town, but he's getting a lot of the prep work done. Gabrielle's helping with the social media and a colleague of hers is working on the website and logo."

I kiss her hair. "Everything's coming together. I'm happy for you."

She elbows me. "Despite not wanting me to live in Winter Falls."

She's teasing, but I know she's still hurt I was initially against her relocating to my hometown. She doesn't know my hesitation was for completely selfish reasons as in I wasn't sure I could keep my hands off of her if she lived in the same town as me.

And here she is now all cuddled up to me. Maybe I'm not doing a very good job of keeping my hands off of her now, but I can keep her in the friendzone.

"I was shocked is all." Before she can call me on my blatant lie, I mess with her hair. Something I know she hates.

She shoves me away. "Leave the hair alone!"

Juniper stands in front of the room and whistles for everyone's attention. "Is everyone ready to hear what tonight's movie is?"

I use the opportunity to cradle Elizabeth against my chest again, and she settles in.

"Tonight's movie is …."

"Stop keeping us in suspense, Juniper!" Feather shouts.

"I'm not in suspense. I know what the movie is," Sage responds.

Juniper raises her eyebrow at her. "You figured out tonight's movie is *Made of Honor*?"

Ashlyn jumps to her feet. "Pay up, suckers!"

"What is she talking about?" Elizabeth murmurs her question.

I grunt. "She must have guessed tonight's movie."

She giggles. "This town will bet on anything."

"How did you guess the movie, Ashlyn? Or did your sister tell you?" Sage asks.

Ashlyn huffs. "Are you kidding? I didn't need to cheat. It was easy." She motions toward where I'm sitting with Elizabeth. "Best friends to lovers movie."

Elizabeth buries her face in her hands and groans. I rub her back. "Don't worry about it. The gossip gals and Juniper can try to match us all they want. It doesn't mean we don't have free will."

She drops her hands to narrow her eyes on me. "You're not surprised. You knew this would happen."

"It was a distinct possibility, Bessie."

"I've got ten bucks on them making out before the closing credits roll," Ashlyn shouts.

Elizabeth glares at Ashlyn. "I know where you live, Ashlyn West."

"It's Hansley now." Ashlyn waves her left hand. "And I'm pregnant." She rubs her belly. "No pranking me when I'm pregnant."

"Is that a rule?"

"It is now. As declared by me, Empress of Winter Falls."

Rowan sighs. "Dream Girl."

"What? Why am I getting the dramatic sigh? Am I wrong? Am I not an Empress? Am I not your queen?"

He tilts his head back to stare at the ceiling.

"Yeah, Rowan. Is Ashlyn not your queen? Someone's sleeping on the couch tonight," I tease.

"Can we just watch the movie?" Elizabeth asks no one in particular.

"Of course," Juniper answers.

As the movie plays, I realize why Ashlyn won the bet. The movie's about a man and a woman who are best friends. They both have more than friendly feelings for each other, but neither one of them act on those feelings. Not until the woman is getting married and the man realizes he can't handle her marrying another man.

I'm not worried this movie will give the gossip gal ideas. They can get as many ideas as they want. I'm not falling into the relationship trap. Been there. Done that. Have the scars to prove it.

Elizabeth may seem different now but if we change our relationship to something romantic, she'll end up just like all the other women. And I refuse to compare her to other women. She's my Bessie.

Chapter 14

Ambush – can be quite pleasant if Sangria and snacks are involved

"You ready?" Gabrielle asks without preamble when I open my door to her.

"Ready for what?"

"Duh. Book club."

"You were serious about me coming with you? I don't read romance."

"Stop being a romance hater."

I'm not a romance hater. Not reading romance novels is an attempt at self-preservation. I know love and romance is not in my immediate future. Not when the man my heart yearns for has a big ass neon sign flashing *Unavailable* on his forehead.

I wish I had a sledgehammer to destroy that stupid sign, but I'm not the woman who can make a man change his ways. Plain Elizabeth can't compete with all the women at River's disposal.

"Come on." Gabrielle flutters her eyelashes. "Please. For me. I don't want to go alone."

I roll my eyes. "You won't be alone. Lilac and all of her sisters will be there. Not to mention the gossip gals."

She does an exaggerated shiver. "Which is why I need you to protect me."

"Me? Protect you? You and Phoenix are living together. The gossip gals have completed their mission with you."

She tries a different tactic. "Don't you want to get out of your place for a while?" She motions to the dining room table, which is covered with drawings and drafts of business plans. "You need a break."

She's not wrong. Besides, if I stay home, I'll spend half the night staring at the phone waiting for River to ring and tell me whether he's stopping by tonight. I don't want to be that girl.

"Fine." I grab my purse. "But no one better give me a hard time about not reading the book."

When we reach *Fall Into A Good Book,* Aspen's bookstore located on Main Street, the place is already packed.

"I love you and I'm sorry."

At Gabrielle's words, I spin around to confront her, but I'm not quick enough. She shoves me through the entrance before following me in and locking the door behind her.

"Good job, Gabrielle." Sage winks at my baby sister and I lose any hold I still had on my anger.

"What's going on?" I demand of my sister who has the good grace to drop her gaze to the floor.

"It's book club."

"Really? This isn't an ambush?"

"Ooh. Ambush. We need to read a dark romance about a woman getting ambushed," Feather says and rushes off to the bookshelves.

"Here." Aspen shoves a glass of sangria in my hands. "Wine makes everything better."

"And what, pray tell, does this particular wine need to make better?" Despite my snarky words, I take a sip and sigh in pleasure when the fruity taste hits my tongue. It's good.

"I hope there's more food than a bowl of pretzels," Gabrielle mutters and pushes past me.

"Are you abandoning me?" I shout after her.

"Needy much?" she shouts back and my chest puffs out with pride for her. It wasn't too long ago Gabrielle would have fled at my comment but not anymore. I'm so dang proud of her for overcoming what her asshat of an ex did to her.

Bang! Bang! Bang!

I glance over my shoulder to discover Cassandra pounding on the door. "Let me in!"

I debate ignoring her. But I know better. Ignoring my older sister is asking for trouble and I have enough trouble at the moment, thank you very much.

"Took you long enough," she says when I unlock the door for her.

"You're welcome."

"Grab a drink and a seat. We're almost ready to start," Aspen tells Cassandra before leaving us alone.

"Glad to see Gabrielle managed to get your grumpy ass to come out tonight."

Great. My presence at the book club was a concerted effort amongst my sisters. Whenever Gabrielle and Cassandra gang up, bad things happen.

"My ass is not grumpy. In fact, an ass can't be grumpy."

"An ass can too be grumpy when ass is referring to how stupid my sister is being."

"I'm not stupid. You're stupid."

I nearly slap myself in the face for those words. Two minutes in the presence of my sister and I'm no longer a thirty-year-old working on building a business but a teenager acting like a complete idiot. In my defense, Cassandra drives everyone crazy. River isn't the only reason I couldn't wait to escape the apartment I shared with my older sister.

"I'm finding a seat," I say and stomp off before I slap her. Don't worry. I'd never actually do it, but it's better to remove myself from temptation.

Everyone settles in their seats in a circle around Aspen. "Can someone tell me what trope this month's book, *Hot Storm*, by Lynn Raye Harris is?"

"I know!" Feather's hand flies into the air. "It's a friends to lovers romance. Plus, friends with benefits."

"Friends with benefits? You kids and your fancy lingo. What does friends with benefits mean?" Guessing by Sage's wink at me she knows exactly what the term means.

Feather rubs her hands together. "It's when two friends have a sexual relationship before falling madly, deeply in love."

Cayenne fans a hand in front of her face. "And it's sexy as all get out."

"What do you think of the idea of friends with benefits?" Clove asks me.

If I was unsure as to whether I was being set up by attending book club tonight, there's no doubt left. Although, to be honest, I wasn't unsure, to begin with.

"I'm sure a friend with benefits agreement can be mutually satisfactory."

Petal leans in close. "And have you been mutually satisfied lately?"

I groan. Do they seriously expect me to discuss my sex life with them? I don't kiss and tell, although there's nothing to tell about lately. One kiss with River – no matter how hot and explosive – does not a story make.

"Well, um…" I stammer.

Cassandra snorts. "Obviously, no one's giving Elizabeth the business."

"And someone is giving you the business?" I throw the question back at her.

She waggles her brow and bites her bottom lip. "Actually…"

"Who have you been dating?"

"Dating? Barf." She feigns retching. "You mean boning."

Cassandra doesn't believe in dating or relationships or love or anything normal basically. I don't know why. Whenever I bring up the topic, she makes some snide comment about how men don't understand the word faithful. I assume someone cheated on her, but who?

"Are we going to discuss the book?" Gabrielle asks.

Juniper barks out a laugh. "You must be kidding."

"I don't understand what's funny." Gabrielle holds up her kindle. "I read the book, and this is a book club."

Juniper pats her on the shoulder. "This is Winter Falls."

"Why does everyone say those words as if it excuses every-thing?" Gabrielle mumbles. I agree with her.

"Since we've determined this isn't a friends with benefits situation, let's move on to Plan B," Sage announces.

"Wait. Didn't Feather say the book had a friends with ben-efits element?" I'm confused. I feel as if everyone's having a conversation in front of me and I haven't been invited to participate.

"Of course. In the book." Feather nods her agreement.

I'm saved from figuring out what in tarnation is going on when the bell over the door rings as it opens. A police officer saunters in and if I wasn't obsessed with River, I'd probably be interested in him. He's tall and walks with self-confidence. There's something about a man in uniform, isn't there?

There's also the lush, brown hair he's sporting. Good hair is the one thing I can't resist. I'm a hairdresser. I can't help it.

Of course, I will be resisting this man. My heart isn't in-terested in any man other than River. Plus, this is Peace. One of the two men the gossip gals are determined to match me with. I know better than to get involved in a gossip gals matchmaking scheme. Unless the scheme involves River, then I'll throw myself at their mercy.

"I heard there was a disturbance." He smirks as he hitches his thumbs in his utility belt.

Ashlyn's hand shoots into the air. "It was me, officer. I phoned in the disturbance."

"You sure, darling? Rowan has the police department on speed dial."

She slumps back in her chair. "Whatever."

Peace saunters my way. Come on, body. He's hot. Have some kind of reaction. Apparently, my hormones are on the fritz because there's no warm feeling in my tummy or hitch in my breath. Stupid body. Longing for someone it can never have.

He holds out his hand and I take it before allowing him to lead me to the back storage room. As soon as the door closes behind him, his smile drops from his face.

"What's going on? Am I in trouble? Am I wanted for questioning?"

"Why would you be wanted for questioning?"

I throw my arms in the air. "I don't know, but you're a police officer and you're wearing a super serious expression right now. It's freaking me out."

He chuckles. "You're not in trouble."

"Yes, she is!" Sage hollers from outside the room. "And you're the officer who's going to tame her."

My mouth drops open, and I stare at the door as my face heats.

Peace cradles my jaw. "Don't worry about her. I can handle Sage."

"You can?" As far as I can tell, no one can handle the woman.

He winks. "If you go out with me tomorrow night, she'll get off your back."

All the puzzle pieces click into place, and I gasp. "This entire thing was a setup."

I don't get it. Weren't the gossip gals trying to push River and me together at movie night? And what about all the friends to lovers innuendos this evening? Weren't they referring to River and me? Have they given up on pairing me with him already?

I mean, they should. River is a player who has no interest in moving our relationship past friends. But they gave up awful quick. I didn't think the gossip gals knew how to give up.

"Welcome to Winter Falls," Peace says, and I force myself to pay attention to him. "I'll pick you up tomorrow at six. We'll go to the brewery."

Which is how I end up agreeing to go on a date with a sexy police officer with a great head of hair, who puts the butterflies in my stomach into hibernation.

Chapter 15

Slumber – when body parts forget what they're supposed to be good for and fall asleep

"THIS IS STUPID."

There's no response to my declaration since my reflection can't talk back. The doorbell rings, and I sigh before going to answer it.

Peace hands me a potted violet when I open the door to him. He must notice my confusion as he explains, "Cut flowers are bad for the environment."

"Say no more!"

If something's bad for the environment, it doesn't happen in Winter Falls. The town takes being the first carbon neutral town in the world very seriously. Thus far, it's been amazing, but I'm worried about the lack of pizza when my time of the month hits.

"You ready?" Peace asks and his eyes sweep over my outfit with blatant interest.

Come on, butterflies, wake the hell up. They grumble about me disturbing their sleep before rolling over and continuing with their snoring. Are they blind? Did they not get a glimpse of the sexy police officer standing in my doorway?

"Let's do this."

Why do I sound as if I'm preparing to wage battle instead of going out on a date with Winter Falls' number one bachelor? Maybe my hormones are broken, and I should make an appointment with a doctor. This could be some kind of crazy disease middle-aged women suffer from. I am thirty after all.

"You okay with walking?" he asks as we exit my apartment building.

"I don't know. Do you think we can walk the five minutes to the brewery without being accosted by a member of the gossip gals?" I scan the area as if I'm worried about the women jumping out in front of us at any second.

Truth be told, I wouldn't put it past them. Half the time I'm terrified of spotting their hot pink shirts, the other half of the time I can't wait to hear what they'll say next.

"Rumor has it Chip and Dale escaped from Forest and it's all hands on deck."

I gasp. "No way. You didn't set Chip and Dale free, did you?" He winks. "Who are Chip and Dale anyway?"

"Forest's two squirrels, of course."

I giggle. "I love this town."

"Even if the elderly mob in pink are trying to match you with a hot police officer?"

"Even then."

We reach *Naked Falls Brewing* and he opens the door for me. "After you."

He places a hand on my back and leads me to the hostess station. "Hey, Moon. We've got a reservation."

"Yeah, you do." She winks at me. "I'm Moon. You must be Elizabeth."

I wave at her, and she taps her chin as she studies me. My cheeks start to ache with maintaining my smile and I'm beginning to wonder if I have something stuck in my teeth when she finally glances over her shoulder and shouts, "Tonight!"

I lean close to Peace. "What's tonight?" I whisper.

He frowns. "Nothing. Nothing is tonight."

"I know you're speaking English, but I don't understand what's happening."

"Come on." Moon grabs a pair of menus and motions us upstairs. "I've got lover's booth reserved for you."

Lover's booth? Has Moon joined the hot pink t-shirt matchmaking squad?

"Have you been here before?" Peace asks once we're seated and have ordered a couple of IPAs.

"Yep. My business is next door. I've been here for lunch a few times." If being addicted to their fries and eating them on a daily basis is considered a few times.

He cocks a brow. "Your business?"

"What? You didn't get a dossier with all my likes and dislikes plus a detailed background of my career path? In my defense, the D in chemistry wasn't my fault. My lab partner was a bitch who was too busy flirting with the teacher to pay attention in class."

He chuckles. "I won't hold your lack of chemistry prowess against you."

"Phew!" I run an exaggerated hand across my forehead. "And I won't hold the time you pranked Lyric against you."

"Hey now! It wasn't my fault. Freedom was the one who caught the crickets."

"But you didn't stop him from letting them loose in the school, did you?"

He barks out a laugh. "It was hilarious. I thought Mrs. West was going to kill us."

"Lilac's mom was the high school principal back then, too?"

"No. She was still a teacher when I was in high school." He shivers. "Those poor kids. They probably can't get away with anything with her at the helm. The woman is some kind of witch who can read minds."

"She has five daughters. She probably had to learn how to read minds, or they would have all ended up pregnant or in jail by now. Except Lilac. Although sometimes I worry she's building some kind of machine to take over the world."

"And you have three sisters?"

I guess we're continuing with the pretend to get to know each other portion of the evening. I say pretend since those files the gossip gals prepared were extensive. Seriously. On top of report cards for each year Peace went to school, there was a list of former girlfriends including the reason each relationship didn't work out.

"Yep. You've met Cassandra the crazy and Gabrielle the sweet. Olivia didn't come to Colorado with us when we relocated last year. I expect her to turn up any day now."

"What makes you say that?"

I giggle but there's no humor attached to it. "Because there's a limit on the number of times the police will give you a warning before they realize you're not heeding them."

"Olivia's the troublemaker."

Moon plonks our beers down on the table. "Incoming."

"Incoming? What do you…." But she's already gone.

Cayenne bustles over to us. She clings to the edge of the table while she catches her breath. She's wearing a hot pink t-shirt with the words *Gossip Gal Matchmaker* written on it.

"Holy smokes. I won. I can't believe it. I never win."

I raise my eyebrows at Peace, but he shrugs instead of answering my unspoken question.

"What did you win?"

"On a scale from one to ten, how would you rate your date thus far?" is her bizarre response.

"You said they'd leave us alone if we went out on a date," I accuse Peace.

He wrinkles his nose. "I thought they would. To be honest, this is my first time."

"Your first time?"

"Yep. I'm a gossip gal matchmaking virgin."

I bark out a laugh. "Now, there are four words I never thought I'd hear said together."

"Welcome to…"

"Winter Falls!" I finish the sentence for him.

"Can you at least give me some clue?" Cayenne asks and I startle. I'd forgotten she was standing there. "I just discovered a new supplier of all natural yoga pillows. I want to buy a few for *Earth Bliss*."

Earth Bliss is the yoga studio Cayenne operates when she's not off performing her gossip gal duties. I have no idea what her desire for new pillows has to do with our date.

"Sorry, I—"

Peace grasps my hand before he cuts me off. "I'll give us a seven out of ten."

"Seven. Awesome. Have fun!" She waves as she leaves.

I scowl at him. "A seven? This date is a two if it's anything. Don't you know how to score?"

His hand jolts before he releases me. "Score? You don't think I know how to score?"

"Yeah, well…" I slam my mouth shut when I realize what I said. Awkward girl strikes again! "I didn't mean… I'm sure you know how to score just fine."

He laughs. "I do?"

I wave a hand up and down his body. "If you don't know how to score with your physique, it would be a damn shame."

He reaches across the table to squeeze my hand. "Thank you. I'm humbled by your concern about my ability to score."

I groan and drop my head to the table. "Can we stop talking about scoring now, please?"

Moon arrives with our food and more beer.

"We didn't order more beer," I protest.

She indicates a table behind her. "You'll thank me later."

When she moves, I can see who she was indicating. River. And he's not alone. Of course, he's not. The man is never alone. But is he with one of his brothers? Nope. He's on a date with a woman.

Peace tugs the bottle out of my hand and pulls my attention away from River's table. "Sorry. I thought I'd remove your weapon before you can do any damage. Damage equals paperwork. And I hate paperwork."

I give myself a moment to allow my hurt and anger and about a million other emotions rolling around in my stomach to smash through me – now, those stupid butterflies wake up – before I inhale deeply.

"I'd hate for you to have to do paperwork when on a date."

"Now, you're getting it. The gossip gals would kill me if I arrested a date they'd matched me with."

"I wouldn't want you to get on the bad side of those gossip gals."

He does an exaggerated shiver. "Exactly. They scare the ever-loving daylights out of me."

I giggle and motion for him to return my beer to me. He hands me the bottle as he leans in close to whisper, "Besides, he's not worth it."

I nod, despite not agreeing with Peace. River is worth everything. A night in jail? No problem. A bit of paperwork? Piece of cake. A fight with some blonde bimbo who's licking her lips like she's ready to swallow River whole? Let's go.

River glances up from his menu and his gaze catches on me. He winks at me before giving me a thumbs-up.

Did he seriously give me a thumbs-up for my date? What an asshole.

"I think I'm ready to go home."

"Darling, don't let him see how much he's hurting you."

"I'm not hurting," I deny.

"I know interest when I see it."

I lean back in the booth and cross my arms over my chest. "Give me one instance of being interested in a woman who wasn't interested in all Peace the peace officer has to offer."

"Besides you?"

My shoulders slump. "Besides me."

"It's possible I had a bit of a crush on my teacher when I was in high school."

Now, we're getting somewhere. "Tell me it was Mrs. West." I cross my fingers and lift them in the air.

His cheeks darken until the tips of his ears are dark red. "It was."

"What did you do?"

"Mostly, I daydreamed about her husband leaving her and in her devastation, her leaning on me for support."

"And where did you do this daydreaming?"

He wags a finger at me. "Nuh uh. No embarrassing sex tales on a first date. It's in the gossip gals' rulebook."

"Thank you," I say when I manage to calm my laughing.

"Anytime, darling. Anytime."

Welp. It appears I'm now the queen of making friends with hot men. Great. Maybe I can turn this into a hobby. Or write a book. *How Not To Land the Guy of Your Dreams.*

Chapter 16

Jealousy – an emotion best friends should never feel for each other

I sigh as I shuffle up the stairs of *The Inn on Main.* I'm not in the mood to have dinner with Suzie – one of the women who took my green tour today with her friends – but I can't have dinner with the woman I want. Correction. I can't have dinner with my best friend since she's out on a date with Peace.

Ellery frowns at me when I enter her establishment. "Which one are you here to pick up?"

The obvious disappointment in her voice makes me want to cringe, but I'm made of sterner stuff. "Suzie."

She shakes her head at me. "I thought…Never mind." She picks up the phone. "Do you want me to ring her room?"

I stuff my hands in my pockets. "I'm early. I'll wait."

"Yeah, you wouldn't want to appear too eager," she mutters as she returns the phone to its cradle.

"You're sounding awful judgy tonight. What's wrong? Lose a bet?"

More betting happens in Winter Falls than in Las Vegas. It's ridiculous and fun until the gossip gals set their sights on you.

Then, it's not so much fun anymore. Especially when one of the gossip gals follows you around with a pair of binoculars all day. They think they're being sneaky, but they should probably wear a color other than hot pink if they don't want to be seen.

Ellery snorts. "Bet you wouldn't ruin things with Elizabeth by going out on a date with someone else? Do I look stupid to you?"

I grunt. "Ruin things with Elizabeth? When will everyone get it through their thick skulls? Bessie and I are friends. Just friends."

"Which is why she lets you call her Bessie although a blind person could tell she hates the nickname."

A group of women enter the area before I can lie and tell her I'm only teasing Elizabeth by calling her Bessie. In truth, using the nickname she hates is just one more way to push the woman away and keep boundaries between us.

"Hi, River," they greet as one.

Showtime! I smirk. "Hey, ladies. How is everyone doing tonight?"

Behind the group, Ellery rolls her eyes. Fine. I'm laying it on a bit thick today. In my defense, every woman in this group is practically undressing me with their eyes.

Hold up. In my defense? I should be eating this stuff up. What is wrong with me? The women bat their eyelashes and bend over to display their cleavage and my body doesn't respond. Little River has no interest in these women. I frown down at my crotch. *Wake up!*

"Back off. He's mine." A blonde shoves her way through the group to the front. She places a finger on my chest and draws it down to my waistline. "Hi, River."

I snatch her hand before she dives for the jewels. I'm all in for sexy times, but I draw the line at public sex. I don't share my toys. Never have. Never will. Blame middle child syndrome or whatever. I don't care. Sharing and I aren't friends.

"You ready?" I ask the woman. Suzie. The woman's name is Suzie. *Get with the game, River.*

"Yeah," she sighs out with her brown eyes wide as she stares up at me. I don't want to gaze into a pair of brown eyes. I want blue eyes. Blue eyes framed by alabaster skin. Skin covered in adorable freckles I want to trace with my tongue.

Knock it off, River. You don't want your tongue to touch any part of Elizabeth's skin. She's off limits. Off. Limits.

"Don't wait up for me." Suzie waves at her friends as I lead her out of the inn.

I don't miss Ellery's look of blatant disapproval, but I pretend I do because I have more important things to discuss.

"You don't have your own room?" I ask Suzie as we walk across the street to *Naked Falls Brewing.*

"We're sharing." She bites her lip. "I figured we could go back to your place."

I grunt. The chance of that happening is zero. I don't invite women into my home. There's a better chance of us ending up in her hotel room than back at my place. I said I don't share, but I have no problem with two women sharing me.

No excitement courses through my body at the idea of a threesome. No anticipation makes my fingers tingle. Crap. The situation is worse than I thought. I'm thirty-two, nearly thirty-three. Maybe my body isn't interested in sex anymore. Maybe I'm too old.

Except my parents are still as frisky as they always were. As a child, it was embarrassing. As an adult in Winter Falls, it's expected.

"Hey, River," Moon greets when we step inside the brewery. "I've got your table ready."

My table ready? What's she talking about? I didn't make a reservation. I never do.

"Follow me." She motions us toward the stairs.

Suzie latches onto my arm as we ascend to the second floor. "This place is cool. Who would think the Podunk town of Winter Falls would have a brewery?"

I hate it when tourists refer to Winter Falls as a Podunk town. I should be used to it. It happens during nearly every tour I give. I usually let the words roll over me, but tonight I'm agitated by everything.

Why is this date not working? Why is going out with Suzie not helping me forget about Elizabeth? Because you're an asshole, a voice whispers in my head. I ignore it. I always ignore anyone who tells me I'm an asshole. Especially my brothers.

"This is your table."

I start to sit down in the booth, but Moon pushes me until I'm forced to sit on the opposite side.

"What's your damage?"

"Nothing," she sings with a smile before slamming the menus down on the table. "I'll be back."

Suzie watches her go. "Do you know our waitress?"

"It's a small town, darling. I know everyone."

Her nose wrinkles. "Did you sleep with her?"

I don't think she's interested in the time Moon and Ashlyn slept in a tent with me and my brothers because they got lost while trying to spy on us. We ended up rescuing them. Nothing happened except Ashlyn complained about having to pee but being afraid to go in the woods all night. I'm surprised she didn't pee her pants.

"I don't have sex with locals."

"Is this a hard rule?" She wiggles her eyebrows.

Come on, River. Make an effort. She's a nice woman. She doesn't deserve to be treated to grumpy River.

Someone gasps and I glance over to discover Bessie staring at me with her eyes the size of saucers full of hurt. Son of a bitch. I should have known she'd be here with Peace. The whole town knows about their date tonight. I should have gone to the diner.

My stomach churns. I gulp down a glass of water, but it doesn't help. What is wrong with me? Did I eat something bad? Except I know I'm lying to myself. I'm not feeling nauseous. I'm feeling jealous at the sight of Bessie out with another man.

She giggles at Peace and my jealousy grows as anger fills me. How dare she enjoy herself with another man? She should be *my* woman.

"Are you okay?"

I don't respond to Suzie. I'm too busy wondering where the hell the words 'my woman' came from. I don't want a woman. I've organized my entire life in such a way as to ensure I never have a woman.

"Hello! Earth to River." Fingers snap in front of my face.

"Hey, babe. Sorry." I force crazy thoughts of Elizabeth being my woman out of my mind. "I thought I forgot to switch the lights off at home," I lie.

She shrugs. "No big deal. Your house won't start on fire from leaving your lights on."

No big deal? Did she listen to anything I said during the green tour I gave her and her friends today? Switching off appliances you're not using is one of the easiest ways to save energy. So much for getting through to her group.

"True," I grunt instead of giving her a lecture on saving energy. I know a lost cause when I encounter one.

My gaze drifts back to Bessie and Peace. Yep. I know a lost cause when I see one. I didn't forget my lesson. Love is bullshit.

Chapter 17

Mean Girl – a woman who refuses to grow up already and continues to act like the world is high school

SIRIUS POINTS TO THE water hook-ups in the wall. "Is this where you want the sinks?"

I study the drawings for the building of my spa and feel my nose scrunch up. "Yes?"

He chuckles as he swipes the plans from me. "Let me show you how to read these."

"Oh my god. Thank you. I have no clue what any of it means." I'm not a total idiot. I can read the numbers and I understand they're measurements, but all the lines and circles and whatnot? There's a reason I cut hair and don't teach physics.

"It's the least I can do considering I'm married to one of the gossip gals." Except he says the words gossip gals as if he's proud of them.

"Now you tell me. You should give me a discount. A deep discount. The deepest you can go kind of discount."

He coughs and glances away as his cheeks darken. What? What did I say now? I groan when the words hit me – deepest you can go.

"People in Winter Falls are supposed to pretend I'm not the winner of the Miss Awkward award."

"Darling, you're not awkward. You're hilarious." He squeezes my shoulder. "Don't ever change who you are to please another person."

My stomach warms as I imagine my dad saying those same words. I was ten when he died, but I remember how much he encouraged me and my sisters. He didn't bat an eye when I wanted to join the magician's group at school. When I told him I needed a cape and wand, he took me to the store himself.

My eyes itch as I imagine how proud Dad would be of this endeavor. He'd be the one here handling the various contractors while bragging to all of them about how his daughter was the business owner. I sniff. Man, I miss my parents.

"Are you the handyman philosopher? Do I have to pay extra for your philosophical advice?" I sass to hide how nostalgic I'm feeling.

"I'll add it to your bill." He winks. "Explain your vision to me and I'll show you how your vision translates into these drawings."

"Okay. On this side will be the hairstyling. On the opposite side are make-up stations. Behind the hairstyling are the sinks and across from them are where the manicures and pedicures will be done." I walk further into the building. "Down this hall will be two private rooms for massages and wax treatments. And, finally, the storage room slash break room."

"What about your office?"

I point to the rear door. "Here."

"This is your office?" His brow wrinkles. "I thought this was a closet."

"Yeah. Yeah. My office is tiny, but I'll be spending most of my time on the floor anyway. For now, I'll be the only beautician doing hair and make-up."

He spreads the plans out on a makeshift table in front of the windows where the light is best. "Let's review these before you go to my wife's café to buy us coffee."

I can get a hint. I guess it's my turn to buy coffee today.

"*Glitter N Bliss.*" Someone snorts. "How cliché can a name get?"

I spin around to confront the new arrival.

"Do I know you?"

She sticks out her hand. "Love Hill. I'm here for an interview."

Is she for real? She literally insulted the name of my business five seconds ago and now she wants a job?

I indicate the building site behind me. "I'm not interviewing yet."

She smirks. "But you'll want to hire me now. Otherwise, some other spa will snatch me up and you'll lose your chance."

Uh oh. Someone thinks the movie *Mean Girls* is a how-to documentary instead of the entertaining movie it's supposed to be.

I cross my arms over my chest. "What experience do you have?"

She flips her blonde hair over her shoulder, and I bite back my sigh. Her flirtatious tricks won't work on me, let alone impress me. In fact, they have the opposite effect.

"I can do just about anything. Cut hair. Give a manicure. You name it, I can do it."

"And where did you study?"

"Study?"

Study is maybe a big, fancy word for getting a certificate, but I don't care. I worked my butt off to get my cosmetology certificate and license. It was more difficult than college, to be honest.

"You do have your full cosmetology license, don't you? Or are you a nail tech?"

She huffs. "I knew this wouldn't work."

Color me confused. "What wouldn't work?"

"You're afraid to hire me because you're hung up on River and you know I've slept with him."

My mouth drops open. I literally met Ms. Mean Girl Goes Small Town two minutes ago. Why would I know the first thing about her sexual past?

"I have no idea what you're talking about."

"Sure, you don't. It's okay. There's nothing to be ashamed of. Everyone in town has taken River for a ride a time or two. Of course, he always ends up back in my bed."

I ignore the jealousy eating through my stomach egging me on to test how strong her blonde locks are. Will they hold if I swing her around by her hair? Or will they get yanked out?

How long will those hairs need to grow back? Will she use a scarf or a hat to cover up the bald spot?

Sirius wraps a hand around my forearm to stop my forward motion. I didn't even realize I'd moved. "Winter Falls is non-violent."

Love Hill sticks out her right leg and props her hand on her hip. "Oh, did I upset you? It wasn't my intention."

Clap. Clap. Clap.

I gaze past Mean Girl On Steroids to find Ashlyn slow clapping behind her. "Your performance deserves a standing ovation."

"It wasn't a performance," Love Hill snaps.

"I'm sorry. How do you refer to a situation where one party lies her tits off to another person?" Ashlyn taps her chin as she considers. "I remember now. You call the person a lying bitch and escort her out the door." She motions to the open door behind her.

Note to self: Start shutting the door so no one can sneak up on me again. And maybe get a bell for when the door opens. No, not a bell. A thousand bells.

Sirius steps forward and places a hand on Love Hill's back. "Come on, darling. Let's go."

"I don't understand what I did wrong," she whines and bats her eyelashes at him.

Enough with the batting already! Geez. Isn't she worried about her fake eyelashes sticking together?

"And I don't understand where your parents went wrong. I guess the world's a mystery," he mumbles as he escorts her out of the building.

"Please tell me you didn't believe a word she said," Ashlyn says as soon as they're out of hearing range.

I shrug. "It doesn't matter. I know River's a player. What difference does it make if he slept with every single woman in Winter Falls?"

There. My jaw isn't clenched and my hands aren't fisted. Nope. I'm completely unaffected by how the man my body is lusting after is a complete player.

Ashlyn rolls her eyes. "Please don't lie to me. My bullshit detector is finely tuned." She grunts and clutches her stomach.

"Are you okay? Should you be standing?" I grab one of the folding chairs leaning against the wall and open it up for her. "Here. Sit down. You need a rest."

She groans, but she does sit down. "You first."

"Me first? Do you want me to rest?"

"No." She waves a hand in front of her face. Her face is flushed and sweat is forming on her brow. She doesn't appear well.

"Do you want me to phone Rowan?"

"In a minute. First, I need you to listen to me." Her breaths are now heaves.

"Be quick about it, because you're kind of freaking me out."

"River Atlas never slept with Love Hill. He wouldn't dare. Even if he doesn't have a strict 'no locals in my bed'-rule, he wouldn't sleep with the woman who nearly destroyed Lyric and Aspen's relationship. Although, I guess she did destroy them for a decade, but they're back together now, so it's all water under the bridge."

I grasp her hand. "Thank you for telling me. It doesn't matter but thank you."

She squeezes my hand until the bones creak. "You should probably get Rowan now. I've been in labor all day. It's too early, but the baby doesn't care."

"What?" I screech. "You're in labor?"

I rush off to get Rowan, but her hand is latched onto mine. I slam to a halt before slinging my way back to her.

"Speaking of water," she murmurs as a puddle appears beneath the chair.

"Did your water break?" I squeal.

"Duh." She motions to the mess on the ground. "I hope you have a good cleaner."

"You hope I have a good cleaner? Are you crazy? You're having a baby."

She beams up at me. "I know. I can't—" Her words cut off and she screams. She also grasps hold of my forearm and squeezes.

Holy cow. Who knew such a tiny thing could be this strong? Between my hand and forearm, I'll probably need physical therapy for the life of her child to recover.

She grunts. "Why are you still here? Aren't you going to get Rowan for me?"

I lift up our combined hands. "Oh." She releases me before shooing me out the door. Good thing there aren't any cars in this town because I don't bother to check both ways before darting across the street.

Chapter 18

Sex education – a class that would have come in handy when your friend has a baby on the floor of your new business

"Rowan!" I scream as I push the door of *Bake Me Happy* open.

He strolls out of the kitchen with a smile on his face. "Hey, Elizabeth. Are you in need of your daily strawberry fix?"

"I…Not me… Your wife…Labor." Between gulping for breaths of air and the sheer fear surging through my body, I can't manage to form a sentence

The smile drops from his face. "Did you say labor?"

"Her water broke."

"It's go time," he shouts. "You stay here," he orders Bryan.

Bryan whips out a salute. "Aye, aye, Captain. You go become a dad."

"Dad. Whoa. I'm going to be a dad."

But Rowan doesn't move. He stands there imitating a giant statue. Great. I grab his hand and tug. "Come on, Daddy-to-be, let's get you to Mommy-to-be."

He nods. Thank goodness since there's no way I could drag a six-foot-five former NFL quarterback out the door, let alone across the street. He sprints out of the bakery, and I chase after him.

By the time I enter my building, Rowan is kneeling in front of Ashlyn. He's holding her hands and gazing at her as if she's a miracle worker. I guess, to him, she is. Damn. This is the kind of love I want.

I need to stop holding out hope for River. And, make no doubt about it, I have been holding out hope. No more. I'm done being a freaking idiot.

"Ouch!" Ashlyn screams and I remember I have more important things to do than contemplate the bad life choices I've been making recently.

"What can I do?"

"Get the car parked behind the police station."

I don't ask Rowan any further questions. I'll figure it out. I dash outside and sprint down the street toward the police station.

"Car. Car. Car. Parked behind the police station." I mutter to myself, so I won't forget what I'm supposed to be doing until I slam straight into someone.

"Elizabeth." River shakes me. "I've been yelling your name. You didn't respond. What's wrong? Are you hurt? Talk to me, sweetheart."

"Baby. Need to get car. Baby's coming."

"Who's baby?"

"Ashlyn's."

"Where?"

"My building."

He grasps my hand and drags me into the police station. I try to yank away from his hold. "I need to get the car. Ashlyn and Rowan need to get to the hospital."

River lifts his chin toward Lyric who's bounding down the stairs. "The Chief of Police will help them get to the hospital."

"Then, where are we going?"

"To get my kit."

"Your kit?" What's he talking about? He's making no sense.

"I'm a paramedic as well as a volunteer firefighter."

He is? How did I not know this? I screech to a halt. "Geez. Is there anything you can't do? Leap tall buildings? Faster than a bullet? Stronger than a locomotive?"

He chuckles. "I'm not Superman."

Wrong. He's the definition of a superman.

He hitches a large red bag over his shoulder and grabs my hand again. "Come on."

We rush out of the courthouse and down Main Street back to my building where a crowd is already gathering. River shoulders his way through the people until we're inside.

"Status?"

"Status?" Ashlyn screams. "What do you think the status is? I'm having a baby, idiot. What did you think was happening here? We're having an emergency meeting to discuss paint colors?"

River chuckles as he sets his kit down in front of Ashlyn who in the meantime has abandoned a chair in favor of laying on the floor with her back propped up against the wall. "Mind if I have a peek?"

"You want to study my lady parts now? I know you're a player, but this is ridiculous."

Rowan cradles her face with his hands. "He wants to check on the baby, Dream Girl."

"Oh." She nods. "Go ahead. I'm commando. I took off my panties after my water broke."

I quickly snatch a sheet from where the painters left it laying on the floor and hold it up in front of Ashlyn, so the spectators don't get a free peep show.

"What's she doing? We're going to miss the action. How can we figure out who won the bet if we can't see what's happening?"

I raise my eyebrows at Lyric who shoos everyone out of the building until the only people remaining are the parents-to-be, River, Lyric, and me.

"Lyric," River hollers, and his brother rushes over, "get Dr. Blue now."

"Dr. Blue? Not a car?"

"No time. The next West child's arrival is imminent."

Lyric rushes out of the room, and Peace and Freedom assume guard duty at the door. Peace waves at me, and River growls next to me.

"Now is not the time to be flirting."

"Seriously? And here's me thinking Ashlyn having a baby on the floor of my new business while I hold up a sheet to protect her privacy was the perfect moment to find me a husband. Dang. There goes my plan."

River ignores me and returns his attention to the patient. "How long have you been in labor, Ashlyn?"

Her nose wrinkles. "Um, a few hours?"

"How many hours?" he asks as he snaps on a pair of gloves.

"How many hours has it been since ten o'clock last night?"

"What the hell!" Rowan explodes. "You've been in labor since last night? Why didn't you tell me?"

"Because the first baby is supposed to be late and it's not my due date yet and why are you being a big oaf?" By the time she gets to the end of her rant, she's screaming.

"I'm sorry, Ash. I'm just worried about you having our baby in the middle of a dirty floor." His gaze meets mine. "No offense."

"None taken." He's not wrong after all.

"Yeah, well, having a baby anywhere other than a hospital was not part of the birthing plan. If you would have just agreed to the water birth, all would be fine."

"I wasn't going to let you deliver our baby in a plastic bathtub in our living room."

"Let me? You aren't my keeper, Rowan Aries Hansley!"

Lyric arrives to interrupt the couple's squabble. "Dr. Blue isn't in town. He's already at the hospital."

Rowan stands. "Then, we're going to the hospital."

"Sure." River shrugs. "I can deliver the baby in the backseat of the car just as easily as here."

"Backseat?" Rowan gulps and retreats a few steps until his back hits the wall.

"I am not having my baby in the backseat of a car!" Ashlyn screams and I cringe from the high pitch.

She gazes around the area as if searching for a solution. Finally, she slaps my hand. "You check. You won't lie to me. Tell me if I can make it to the hospital in time."

She's got to be kidding. "How would I know? I'm not a doctor."

"You're a woman. You'll know," she claims, and I'm terrified to tell her no. I know better than to deny a woman in labor.

"I've got the sheet," Lyric says as he stands next to me.

I snarl at him. "Thanks."

I gulp as I tiptoe around Ashlyn to where River is kneeling in front of her wide open legs. Gulp. This is really happening.

"Check!" Ashlyn demands as she widens her legs. "Can I make it to the hospital?"

I inhale a deep breath before darting a glance down at her situation. Uh oh. Am I seeing hair? I look back. Fuck. I am.

"I-I-I think you're crowning."

"Already? The baby's coming?" Rowan's skin is more green than white at this point.

"If the hair is any indication, yes."

I have no idea what I'm talking about. I skipped health class in high school more than I attended. If the school district wanted us to learn about sex from a teacher instead of from each other, they probably should have planned the lesson at any time other than Friday afternoon.

"She's coming!" Ashlyn screams, and River elbows me out of the way. He doesn't need to use much force. I'm going already.

"Shouldn't I be boiling water or gathering towels?"

"Grab as many clean towels as possible. A warm blanket for the baby would be great."

Where in the world am I going to get a warm blanket from?

"Here," Peace says and hands me a warm blanket. When I stare at him, he indicates the crowd. "Mrs. West brought it."

"Mom's here? I want my mommy!" Ashlyn yells.

Ruby doesn't need any more encouragement to plow her way through the crowd. Daniel follows after her apologizing to everyone.

"I'm here, baby girl. I'm here," she says and begins bossing everyone around. "Daniel, you hold Ashlyn's free hand. Lyric, you're on the sheet. And, Elizabeth, you're with me."

She kneels next to River and her eyes widen at the sight before her. Her confidence evaporates as she sways, and I grab her and pull her out of River's way.

"One big push and the baby's here," River announces. "As soon as the next contraction hits, all you have to do is push."

"All I have to do is push? Have you tried to push a watermelon through your dick? I think not! So, maybe stop with the—" Ashlyn's rant is cut off when she screams.

"Push. Push. Push," Rowan chants as she bares down.

I want to look away, but I'm in it now. The shoulders emerge and River cradles the head as the baby arrives in the world with a wail.

"Ashlyn. Rowan. You have a baby girl," River announces as he wraps the baby in the blanket.

"How's that for christening your new spa?" Ashlyn asks and I burst out laughing. Leave it to her to make a joke about having a baby on the floor of my building while it's a construction site.

I look over at River expecting him to share my humor but he's staring at Ashlyn holding her baby with longing on his face. Whoa! Does River want the same things I do? A partner and a family? My heart clenches and a zing of excitement courses through my body.

Welp! So much for giving up on holding out hope for River to change.

Chapter 19

Weak moment – an excuse to act like an asshole

RIVER

"I don't know why I have to attend the monthly business meeting," Phoenix whines from next to me.

He hates coming to these meetings. It's too much gossiping for him. Does he not care who got caught running naked through downtown last week? Spoiler alert: It wasn't me. I tend to keep my clothes on when I'm outside in winter. It doesn't matter how fast you run, you can get frostbite on your feet in less than a mile.

"It's December."

December is when we choose the mayor for the next year. All business owners are required to attend. Winter Falls hates rules – or, I should say, we hate rules that don't involve saving the environment – but this is one rule no one dares disobey. Not even my whiny brother.

I, on the other hand, attend all the meetings as the town secretary. But even if I wasn't working, I'd be here. Unlike Phoenix, I love to hear all the gossip. Plus, they serve beer.

"It's December," he mimics.

"You're being more whiny than usual. What's wrong?"

He crosses his arms over his chest and slumps in his chair. "Gabrielle is sitting with Lilac and her sisters."

I chuckle. "You're being a brat because your girlfriend doesn't want to spend every single second of the day with you?"

He play punches me. "I spent the day repairing the fence. I hardly saw her today."

I pretend to crack a whip. "Kuh-POW."

Lyric plops down on the other side of me. He's wearing a shit-eating grin, his shirt is untucked, and his hair is a mess.

"I assume Aspen's doing well," I say and tap my cheek to indicate where a smudge of lipstick is on his.

"Better than well." He smirks as he rubs the lipstick away.

Elizabeth walks in and, despite my best intentions, my gaze is glued on her as she scans the room. She spots her sister and waves but continues walking until she reaches me.

"Hey, River!"

I want to jump out of my chair and pull her into my arms and kiss her silly, but I won't. I know better. I'm not ruining our friendship for a few hours of ecstasy. Not worth it.

These cravings are nothing new, but I didn't have a problem keeping my hands to myself until Ashlyn went and had a baby in Elizabeth's store. Holding her baby flipped a switch in me. And now my body refuses to listen to reason.

I reach down to pull my notebook out of my bag to stop myself from staring at Elizabeth.

"Hey," I grunt.

Lyric elbows me. "Don't be grumpy." He stands. "Here. You can have my seat."

Panic hits me at the idea of sitting next to her for an hour and not being able to touch her the way I want. What is wrong with me? I'm River. The player who doesn't believe in love. I should be able to sit next to my friend without wanting to do wicked things to her.

I jump to my feet. "There's Lilac. I need to discuss the election with her." I rush off before either of my brothers can call me a liar.

I join Lilac where she's standing at the front of the room. She's frowning at a hat filled with pieces of paper.

"Everything ready to go?"

"If by 'ready to go' you mean do I have all the names of the business owners in a hat, then yes everything is ready to go."

"You don't appear happy."

"Because I'm not," she says but doesn't elaborate. If you want information from Lilac, you have to ask her a direct question. She doesn't understand insinuations.

"Why not?"

"The mayor should be chosen based on their leadership capabilities and managerial experience, not picked from a hat."

"Don't be silly," Ashlyn says as she arrives with her baby girl wrapped in a sling on her chest. "I'm the best dang mayor Winter Falls has ever seen, but I didn't have any managerial experience when I became the chosen one."

She also wasn't the chosen one. She volunteered when Ellery's name was picked last year since Ellery was pregnant at the time, although pregnancy didn't stop Ashlyn any.

Lilac ignores Ashlyn's comment and instead remarks, "I didn't expect you to be here today."

Ashlyn's nose wrinkles. "Why not?"

"You gave birth less than a week ago. I assumed you'd be recovering."

Rowan grunts in agreement from his position behind his wife. He's standing with his hands held out as if he expects her to collapse at any moment.

Ashlyn snorts. "And miss my final meeting as mayor? Never."

Mrs. West rushes over. "Let me hold my granddaughter while you conduct the meeting." She attempts to steal the baby, but the little one is practically glued to Ashlyn's body with the baby carrier.

Ashlyn bats her mother's hands away. "No. Patience is sleeping."

"I can't believe you named your daughter Patience."

Ashlyn beams at Lilac. "I know. It's ironic, isn't it?"

Lilac's lips purse. "You not having any patience doesn't mean it's ironic to name your daughter Patience. Irony is—"

Ashlyn shoves her palm in Lilac's face. "Nope. I won't have my little Patience suffer through her first Lilac lecture at the age of six days."

"I don't know why not. She won't understand anyway."

"At least let Rowan hold the baby for the duration of the meeting," Ruby insists.

Ashlyn snorts. "And allow you the chance to steal the baby from the big softie? Not on my watch."

"But I want to hold my granddaughter," Ruby pouts.

Daniel arrives and drags her away. "Give it up, sweetheart. You didn't want anyone holding our daughters when they were less than a week old either."

"But I'm Grandma!"

"Shall we get the meeting started?" Lilac asks.

I return to my seat to discover Elizabeth has gone off to sit with the West sisters.

"Way to be a bonehead, little brother," Lyric grumbles. "What's your damage?"

I pretend I don't hear him as the meeting begins. I can hardly tell him the truth of how I want to do dirty things to my best friend. Dirty things that will ruin our friendship and prove Elizabeth is like all the other women.

"Welcome to the final business meeting of the year," Ashlyn says in a voice slightly louder than a stage whisper.

"What did she say?"

"Can anyone hear her?"

"Do we need to buy a microphone?"

Ashlyn frowns. "Can everyone please not shout in front of the baby?"

"Speaking of the baby, who had River delivering Ashlyn's child in a construction zone?" Sage asks.

Aspen raises her hand. "I had River delivering Ashlyn's baby."

Lilac marches to the front of the room. "Can we discuss the town business before the gambling begins?"

Feather guffaws. "It's cute how you think gambling isn't the town business."

Petal sighs. "She's stubborn. She'll never learn."

"We have two festivals coming up – Yule and Hogmanay. We need to discuss them and choose a mayor. Nowhere on today's agenda is a discussion of who knew what name Ashlyn would give her child."

Clove raises her hand. "I picked the name Patience."

Cayenne wags a finger at her. "You cheated. I know you bought a book of names and highlighted the ones you preferred before you put it in Ashlyn's mailbox."

Clove crosses her arms over her chest. "It's not cheating. It's smart. I can't help it if I thought of the idea before you did."

Elizabeth raises her hand. "Don't I win some sort of prize for the birth happening in my building? There was a lot of cleaning up to do."

"Sorry," Ashlyn says. "I might have mistimed the birth."

Rowan grunts from where he's still standing behind Ashlyn. "Maybe if you had told me you were in labor, we could have made it to the hospital in time."

His wife ignores him. He's probably used to it by now.

Old Man Mercury raps his cane on the floor. "Can we pick the new mayor now?"

No one dares to contradict him. Mercury is one of the original founders of Winter Falls. When he speaks, people listen. Only the gossip gals presume to ignore him.

Ashlyn picks up the hat. "Who wants to do the honors?" She points to Elizabeth. "How about our newest business owner?"

Elizabeth stands next to the hat. "What do I do?"

"Hold on. We need our town secretary to watch the proceedings." Ashlyn winks before crooking her finger at me. There's no use trying to fight her. It's a losing battle normally and now that she's got her Mama Bear thing happening with her daughter strapped to her chest, the battle won't even have a chance to begin.

Elizabeth smiles at me when I stand next to her. I grunt and stare at the hat. I'm not being an asshole to be an asshole. I have to ignore her to stop myself from reaching for her. My hands itch to touch her. I stuff them in my pockets.

Out of the corner of my eye, I notice Elizabeth's smile crumble but she shakes herself and forces the smile back. Damn. She's strong.

"Okay, here we go." She rummages around in the hat before picking a piece of paper. "Do I read it?"

At Ashlyn's nod, she opens it up and reads, "The next mayor of Winter Falls is…Eden."

When Eden doesn't immediately stand up, I search the crowd for her. She's sitting in the back next to Miller, one of the owners of *Naked Falls Brewing.* Neither one of them is paying any attention to the meeting as they're too busy arguing. Huh. Interesting.

Forest claps her on the back and she startles. He motions toward the front of the room, and she scowls. "I'm the new mayor? Crap."

After Eden accepts the gavel from Ashlyn, the meeting adjourns. I ignore my brothers' pleas to join them at *Electric Vibes* for a drink. I don't need a drink. I need to get out of here and get my head screwed on straight.

Elizabeth is my best friend. I can't continue to ignore her because I suddenly can't control my cravings for her when she's around. I need to figure out a way to shove those feelings back in the box they lived in before I delivered Ashlyn's baby because I will never act on them. Never.

Chapter 20

Modus Operandi – a fancy way to say you're stuck in a rut doing things the same way you always have

I SAY A LITTLE prayer River isn't here before I knock on Ashlyn and Rowan's door. I've been snubbing Mr. Idiot Scum since the business meeting last week. How dare he ignore me? What did I do to him? It's not as if he can actually see the cartoon hearts in my eyes when I look at him.

"Come on in." Ruby opens the door wide and waves me inside. "Welcome to Patience's Sip and See Party."

Since Ashlyn didn't want a baby shower when she couldn't drink bubbly, she's having a party for Patience now. I'm surprised she didn't have a baby shower and a sip and see party. The woman does love to be the center of attention – champagne or not.

Speaking of center of attention, Ashlyn's resting in a recliner in the middle of the room with baby Patience sleeping on her chest. Ruby tiptoes up behind her and reaches across Ashlyn and *smack!* Ashlyn hits her hand.

"Stop trying to steal my baby."

"Stop hogging my grandbaby."

Ellery shoves Willow into her mom's arms. "Here, you can hold this granddaughter."

Ruby cradles the baby to her chest before charging out of the room. "I know where you live!" Ellery shouts after her.

Once the door closes on her mom, Ellery grabs Cole. "Let's go. We have at least an hour before she'll bring Willow back."

She giggles as she hurries out the front door with her fiancé.

"Gross." Cassandra feigns gagging. "I didn't know married people still had sex."

"They're not married. I'm the only West daughter who's tied the knot." Aspen waves her wedding ring in Cassandra's face.

"Hello!" Ashlyn hollers. "Rowan and I are married."

"You eloped. It doesn't count."

"I'm fairly certain the lawyer who drew up our prenup disagrees."

Aspen's mouth drops open. "You and Rowan have a prenup?"

"A prenup's smart," Cassandra buts in to say. "Since love is a crock and all."

"Love is not a crock." I motion to all the couples around us. "Are you blind? Love is all around."

"Please tell me you're not going to start singing about love and puppies and rainbows shooting out of your ass."

"I'll have you know I'm an excellent singer."

I'm also a world-class liar because I can't sing. None of the Dempsey sisters can. When we were standing in line for talents, we all missed the sign for 'ability to carry a tune'. Don't think it's possible to get kicked out of a Christmas caroling group? You'd be wrong.

"Besides, rainbows don't shoot out of my ass. They shoot out of my fingers." I pretend to create a rainbow with my hands.

Gabrielle sighs as she enters the living room. "Oh goodie. Bicker sister one and bicker sister two are here."

"I think I enjoyed it better when Gabrielle was afraid of her own shadow."

Phoenix growls, and I shove Cassandra toward him. "She said it. She's the bad sister. She volunteers as tribute."

"I'm not the bad sister. I'm the realistic sister. The one who realizes love is about as realistic as a unicorn charging into this room." She pauses as if to wait for the mythical creature. "Told you so," she singsongs and walks off.

"Where's River?"

I shrug at Gabrielle's question. "How would I know?"

"Aren't the two of you 'best friends'?"

"What's with the air quotes? We are best friends."

Except I haven't seen him in a week, and I've been ignoring his calls and texts. I suck at being a best friend. Amendment. I suck at being best friends with River. Usually, I'm an awesome friend. Boyfriend or girlfriend dump you? I'm there with liquor and snacks and movies. Plus, I'll listen to you bitch about your ex until the cows come home.

But River? How dare he ignore me in front of the entire town? I need some time away from him before I decide to slap the daylights out of him. Violence is wrong. Especially in Winter Falls.

"But you don't know where he is?"

"Is there some rule about knowing the location of your best friend at all times?"

Cassandra returns holding a glass of champagne and a tray of food. "I know where she wishes he was." She thrusts her hips and croons, "Oh River. Yes. Right there. You know how I like it."

I swipe the champagne from her and drain it. "River and I are only friends."

She wiggles her eyebrows. "With benefits."

"No. Just friends." No matter how much I may wish for more, more isn't happening. I refer to exhibit number one – the man ignoring me at a town meeting.

Ruby hands me a box of condoms. What on earth? Where did she come from? And why is she carrying around condoms?

"What are these for?"

"They're prophylactics. They're used to prevent pregnancy and sexually transmitted diseases."

I swallow my snarky reply. Getting on the wrong side of influential town residents is a bad idea. "I am aware of what condoms are used for. What I don't understand is why you gave me a box."

"For when you give into temptation and shag River for all he's worth."

"Do people say shag anymore?" Cassandra's nose wrinkles. "Shag makes me think of shag carpets, which leads me to wonder whether anyone in the seventies knew about pubic hair grooming."

Which reminds me of the first time I met River, and he asked me if the carpets matched the drapes. Player. He's a player. I shouldn't be fixated on him. My heart disagrees. Nope. It's not giving up. Awesome. My heart has a mind of its own now.

"How old do you think I am?" Ruby asks when Cassandra stares at her as if waiting for a response about pubic hair grooming.

"I didn't say you were shagging in the seventies. I figured you'd know all about pubic hair grooming since you appear to be an expert in sex."

Ruby beams. "I am an expert in sex."

Ashlyn groans. "No! My mom is not some sex expert."

"Of course, I am. Don't you remember the time you walked in on me and your dad—"

Ashlyn slams her hands over her ears. "La La La. I can't hear you."

"Works every time," Ruby whispers as she rushes to the chair and steals Patience off of Ashlyn's chest.

"Hey! You tricked me!"

Ashlyn pushes down the footstool of the chair but before she can go anywhere, Rowan's there shoving her back into the chair. "The doctor said you should rest."

She glares at her husband. "I need to pee."

He holds out his arm. "I'll accompany you."

"We can't get frisky. There's no reason to accompany me," Ashlyn grumbles as they pass.

"I love you, Dream Girl."

I sigh at Rowan's declaration. There's no doubt he means those words from the bottom of his soul. I want to find someone who calls me his dream girl and thinks I hung the moon.

Ruby taps the box of condoms I forgot I'm holding. "Your current look is exactly why you need these."

I glare at her before I get a brilliant idea. "Can you open the box for me? I can never get the plastic off."

I hand her the box and she hands me Patience. While she fiddles with the plastic wrapping, I stroll off with the baby.

"Hey! You tricked me."

I wink at her. "I learned from the best."

"Thank you, my dear. I am proud of my capabilities."

There's no wonder why all her daughters are batshit crazy. They learned from their mama.

"And now you're going to learn from your mama, too, aren't you, baby girl?" I coo to Patience. She blinks her blue eyes up at me and – boom! – I fall in love. I want one of these tiny creatures more than anything in the world.

"Where are Ashlyn and Rowan?" River asks as he enters the house.

"They're making out in their bathroom," Ruby answers.

"Ew. No. Mom. Were you spying on us?" Ashlyn asks as she and Rowan return.

Ruby rolls her eyes. "I don't need to spy on you." She points to Rowan's face. "The evidence is in the pink lipstick."

River throws an arm over my shoulder and peers down at the baby. "Hello there, troublemaker."

And because his arm feels entirely too nice around me, I sass back, "She's not a troublemaker. She can't help it her mom didn't let anyone know she was in labor."

He bops the little girl's nose. "But with Ashlyn for a mom, she's on a direct and immediate path to troublemaker. I don't envy Rowan."

"What? You don't want one of these adorable bundles for yourself?"

He shrugs. "Nope."

I want to tell him he'll change his mind when the 'one' comes along, but I want to be the 'one' and I already came along, and he hasn't changed his modus operandi one bit. He's still a player. See exhibit number two – the blonde buxom woman he took out two weeks ago.

"Your loss."

To my surprise, my words come out sounding completely normal despite how my chest is aching. My heart doesn't have such a big mouth now. In fact, it's sulking and begging for a vat of strawberry ice cream. I can get on board with that idea.

Chapter 21

Complication – When you give yourself what you want knowing it's a mistake, but you do it anyway

RIVER

I know I hurt Elizabeth's feelings when I ignored her at the monthly business meeting. What can I say? I was an asshole.

The time has arrived for me to make amends for how I acted. After the party at Ashlyn's yesterday, I realized I can be around Elizabeth and not want to jump her. It helps when she's holding a baby.

She glares at me when she opens the door. "What do you want?"

"Is that any way to greet your best friend, Bessie?"

She rolls her eyes and motions for me to come inside. "You weren't acting like much of a best friend last week."

Damn. I adore this girl. She doesn't hesitate to call me out for my shit. The women in my past never dared to criticize a word I said.

"I'm an asshole."

"You won't hear me disagreeing." She plops down on the sofa. "What do you want?"

"I come offering gifts." I lift the bag from *Bake Me Happy* and her eyes zero in on it. I've got her now. Someone has a bit of a sweet tooth.

She licks her lips and I remind myself it's not okay to fuck your best friend no matter how sexy she is. My cock disagrees. He wants to feel those plush lips surrounding him and test out how hot and wet her mouth is.

"Gimme. Gimme."

I throw the bag at her before hiding behind the recliner to adjust myself. Stupid cock has a mind of its own lately. It wasn't interested in the blonde I took to the brewery. He couldn't be bothered to harden despite the 'I'm a sure thing'-vibe the woman threw out. But Elizabeth? I'm hard around her all the damn time.

Elizabeth moans and my cock jerks. "So good. Strawberry is the best."

"Not chocolate?" I ask as I sit down next to her. Thank goodness for baggy sweats or she'd know all about my fantasy of dribbling chocolate ice cream all over her.

She glares at me. "I'm a strawberry girl."

I tug on one of her curls. "Strawberry hair for a strawberry girl."

She knocks my hand away. "Don't mess with the curly-haired girl's hair."

"Are you going to share your treats with me?" I reach for the bag but she hugs it to her chest. I make a grab for it and end up with a handful of breast. Her nipple hardens and I want to know what color her nipples are. Do they match her hair?

"Um…"

I realize I'm staring at Elizabeth's chest and lift my gaze to discover a blush creeping across her face and down her neck.

"What are you doing?" she gasps out as I caress her breast, but she doesn't move allowing me to continue my ministrations. I glide my thumb over her nipple, and she shivers. "Maybe you should stop."

"Do you want me to?"

I pinch her nipple and she gasps *yes* before arching her chest into my hand.

"Yes. You want me to stop?" I switch my attention to her neglected breast, and she moans.

"Yes. No. Don't stop."

I drop my hand and stand. For the life of me, I can't think of one reason why having sex with Elizabeth isn't the best idea I've ever had. I lift her up and throw her over my shoulder.

"Where are we going?"

"To the bedroom where I can lay you out and feast on you."

She wiggles on my shoulder, and I slap her ass. At her moan, I wish I'd left the bondage kit here for us to play with. I don't get to indulge my enjoyment of tying women up very often. It's hard to find a partner who trusts you enough to let you tie her up when your life is full of meaningless one-night stands.

Meaningless? No, no, no. Those one-night stands weren't meaningless. They were fun. *Meaningless.* I ignore the voice in my head. It's obviously not to be trusted.

I throw Elizabeth on the bed before whipping off my sweatshirt. Her eyes widen and she licks her lips.

"Like what you're seeing?"

She shrugs. "It's okay."

I motion toward her. "Turnaround is fair play. Now you."

Her fingers toy with the hem of her sweater. "Are you certain? I don't want to ruin you for other women."

She's joking, but what she doesn't realize is she's already ruined me for other women.

"I think I can handle it."

"Don't say I didn't warn you."

She removes her sweater to reveal miles and miles of alabaster skin painted with freckles. I plan to spend the night tracing every single one of them with my tongue. She also reveals the red satin bra she's wearing.

"Damn girl. Red is my new favorite color."

She plays with the edge of the bra cups. "I guess I'll leave this on then."

I crawl between her legs and snap her pants open. "If you're leaving the bra on, these have got to come off."

I unzip her jeans to discover she's wearing matching red satin panties with little bows on the side. "You're full of surprises, aren't you?"

I tug her jeans down her legs and she kicks them off. I smooth my hands along her skin and smirk as goosebumps appear in my wake. Her legs begin to close as she tries to rub her thighs together.

I tap her hip. "Nuh uh. I'm in charge of giving you relief today."

"You need to get on with it."

"Impatient? I guess I need to teach you a lesson in orgasm denial."

She throws a pillow at me. "You wouldn't!"

"Don't worry. You'll love every second."

"I—"

Her complaint is cut off when I rub my finger over her panty-covered slit. Her head falls back, and her legs widen for me.

"Good girl," I murmur before diving into her panties to discover her wet for me. No, not wet. Soaking. "What happens when I pull these bows?"

Magic is what happens. Her panties fall open to reveal short, curly red hair. I enjoy the sight of her laid out before me for a few seconds before I fit my shoulders between her thighs and get to work.

I glide my nose up and down her slit until her hands clamp onto my head. Her fingernails dig into my skin and my cock jumps. I do enjoy a bit of pain with my pleasure.

"You ready?"

"I've been ready. Do I need to get out my vibrator to take care of business?"

I glance up at her. Her eyes spark with annoyance as she heaves for breath. I have her right where I want her.

"Maybe later." I can think of about two thousand ways I want to use her vibrator to give her pleasure.

Before she can complain again, I dive in. My tongue circles her clit while my finger toys with her opening. I push my fingertip in just a bit before pulling out again.

"You're a tease," she huffs.

She has no idea. I don't get the chance to indulge my love for teasing very often. But today I will.

I continue to toy with her opening with my finger while my tongue plays with her clit until her thighs are quivering and her nails are piercing my skin. Only then do I latch onto her clit with my mouth and suck while I plunge two fingers into her. She immediately comes.

"Holy cow!" she shouts as her walls pulse around my fingers.

I lick her through her orgasm until her body goes soft. I kiss her thigh before crawling up her body.

"How you doing, firecracker?"

She pats my shoulder. "I'm too satiated to yell at you for the nickname. Remind me to give you hell later."

I chuckle as I smooth her hair away from her sweaty forehead.

"You up for round two?" I thrust my covered cock into her stomach in case there's any confusion about what I mean.

She taps her chin. "I don't know. Can round two beat round one?"

"There's one surefire way to find out."

When I roll to the side to rid myself of my sweats and boxers, Elizabeth props herself up on an elbow to watch. Her gaze zeroes in on my cock and her eyes widen.

"Huh. You weren't kidding about needing extra-large condoms. I guess it's a good thing Ruby gave me that box after all."

Her hand wraps around my cock and I groan as my head falls back and my eyes close. She isn't tentative with her touch. Nope. She squeezes me as hard as she can while she tugs me. Fuck yeah. Exactly how I need it.

I bat her hand away and she grunts. "I was enjoying myself."

I scrounge a condom from her drawer and quickly don it before covering her with my body. "Trust me. This will be even more enjoyable."

"Promises. Promises."

I line my cock up with her opening and push in. Damn. She feels awesome. Hot, wet, tight. She's going to kill me. I freeze before I end up slamming into her. She clamps her hands on my shoulders.

"What are you waiting for?"

"I don't want this to be over before it begins."

"Oh no. Are you one of those three pump wonders?"

I growl. "Three pump wonder. I'll show you a three pump wonder." I slam into her until my balls slap her skin. She pulses around me, and I wonder if she's going to make me into a liar. Three pumps seems about right.

She wraps her legs around my waist and arches her back until we're skin to skin. I should have told her to get rid of her bra. I want to feel those hard nipples against my chest as I plunge into her over and over again.

Promising myself next time, I slowly pull out allowing myself to enjoy every ripple of her walls against my cock. Nothing has felt this good before. Nothing.

She buries her face in my shoulder, but I don't want her to hide from me. "Eyes," I demand, and she immediately obeys my command. Just when I thought she couldn't get any better.

I slam into her again and her eyes widen as she stares into mine. I continue to keep my eyes locked on hers as I thrust into her over and over until I can't tell where I end and she begins. I don't want this moment to ever end.

Her walls tighten. "I'm going to come again."

"Wait."

"I can't wait."

"I want you to come with me."

"I'm …."

"Hold on," I order as I chase my own climax. "Almost there."

"Okay." She bites her lips and pants as she watches me.

The tingling in my lower back hits and I tell her, "Now. Come for me now."

Her eyes roll back in her head, and she moans as she detonates. "Yes," she hisses.

"Fuck yeah," I grunt as my rhythm fails and I climax.

"Round two was definitely better than round one."

At her declaration, I burst out laughing.

Chapter 22

Slip out – not the same as sneak out but pretty darn close

I MOAN AS I roll over. My entire body is sore. Deliciously sore. The type of sore you only get after an exceptional round of sex. I knew sex with River would be good, but I didn't know the definition of good sex until last night.

I reach for River but my hand encounters empty space. I force my eyes open to discover his half of the bed empty. I know he slept here since I woke up to his mouth latched onto my breast sometime in the middle of the night. I passed out after that particularly energetic round of sex.

I search the bed, but there's no note. Duh. What century am I living in? He probably messaged me. I sit up to grab my phone off the nightstand. I scroll through my messages, but there's nothing from River. He's probably busy.

By the time I've showered and am eating breakfast, I'm working on a good mad. I still haven't heard from River. Is he ghosting me? We're supposed to be best friends. You don't ghost a friend. Although, maybe you do after sleeping with them?

There's a knock on the door. Wait. Maybe I'm jumping to conclusions.

I skip to the door and swing it open. "Did you— Crap."

"Not who you were expecting?" Cassandra asks as she pushes her way inside. She doesn't bother waiting for an invite. She won't get one and she knows it.

Gabrielle mutters *sorry* and follows Cassandra inside.

"What are you two doing here?"

Cassandra pours herself a cup of coffee.

"Make yourself at home, why don't you?"

She lifts the cup. "I am."

"I was being sarcastic."

"And I chose to ignore your tone," she says before sipping on her coffee.

I give up on getting answers from Cassandra. Gabrielle's the weak link. "What are you doing here?" I ask her.

"I could use a cup of coffee, too," she says as she rushes to the kitchen.

Gabrielle avoiding answering a question can never be good.

"What is going on?" I sound like a broken record. Ask me if I care. "What are the two of you doing here?"

Gabrielle raises an eyebrow at Cassandra who mouths *no*.

"Oh, screw it! I need to get down to the spa."

Cassandra rubs her hands together. "Now, we're talking. I want to hear all about the screwing."

Crap. I did it again. The return of Ms. Awkward! Can I at least get a cool outfit? Maybe a sweater with a giant A on the front. Oh wait. Not an A. Adultery is bad. The worst.

"I wasn't talking about that type of screwing," I hedge.

They can't possibly know River and I had sex last night, can they? I pat my hair, but I already showered this morning. There's no way I have sex hair. And Cassandra doesn't have x-ray vision. She can't possibly see the beard burn on my thighs.

Cassandra plops down on my sofa. "Maybe you weren't, but I am."

I throw my arms in the air. "I'm not talking about screwing with you!"

Gabrielle pats my arm. "You might as well come clean. Everyone already knows."

I narrow my eyes on her. "Knows what?"

"How you made whoopie with your quote-unquote best friend last night."

I open my mouth to deny it – they can't possibly know what happened in my bedroom – but Cassandra holds up her hand.

"Before you start playing liar, liar pants on fire, the gossip gals saw River sneaking out of your apartment this morning at six."

Six? At least he didn't slink off in the middle of the night like a thief with my heart. Correction. He did steal my heart because I'm the idiot who fell in love with her best friend.

Dang it! This wasn't supposed to happen! I was already more than halfway in love with River before. Him making love to me sealed the deal. And make no doubt about it, we did make love. There's no way he didn't feel the connection between us as he moved inside of me. I saw it in his eyes. He felt it!

Which is why he's lounging around in your living room now and not somewhere else. Ugh! Stupid little voice of reality. I hate her and her 'doses of truth'.

"I want to hear all about the boom boom," Cassandra insists, and I'm brought back to the room where my sisters are waiting for me to reveal all of my secrets. "Did the neighbors phone about a noise complaint? Tell me more. Tell me more."

"I need coffee," I mumble before fleeing to the kitchen. What I need is some kind of magic to get me out of this conversation. Unfortunately, I'm a muggle through and through.

I turn away from the counter and startle to discover Gabrielle standing behind me.

"You scared me. You're sneaky. I should put a bell on you."

"Good idea," she says, and my eyes widen. "No, not for me. For Pan. I should put a bell on her."

"A bell? Whenever I'm around your goat, she's bleating her lungs out."

"She's noisy until she happens upon food she isn't supposed to get into. You know she can open the refrigerator?"

"Which supports my theory that Pan is the devil," Cassandra shouts from the living room. "But we're not here to discuss the devil goat. We're here to get the details on how hot River is without his clothes on."

"Ew." Gabrielle makes a face. "Did you forget I'm dating his brother?"

"I don't kiss and tell. You know this. You tickled me until I peed my pants and I still wouldn't tell you about the time the goalie on the soccer team asked me out."

Cassandra's nose wrinkles as she contemplates me. "Fine. No details. I have one question for you, though. Why did River leave your bed at six this morning? Was it to go for a run? Did he have to work this morning? Did he have a shift at the fire station?"

"I don't know," I admit when she pauses for a breath.

"You don't know?" A smile spreads across her face. "Beckett is going to beat the crap out of him."

"Becket isn't going to beat anyone up." I hope. Big brother does tend to be a bit overprotective.

"I don't know." Gabrielle chews on her lip. "He did try to beat Phoenix up after the first time we … you know."

"Had sex," Cassandra fills in. "Be a big girl and say the word. It's not difficult. S–E–X spells sex."

Gabrielle straightens her back. "I don't need to say the word when I'm actually having it, unlike some people."

"Cassandra's record dry spell continues," I add because I will do just about anything to move this conversation away from my sexual adventures with River.

Cassandra cocks her brow. "Who says I'm in a dry spell?"

I study her but she holds my gaze. She doesn't fidget or nibble on her thumbnail, which is a dead giveaway crazy Cassandra is lying.

"You're not lying. Who is he?"

"That's for me to know and you to never find out," she quips.

My mouth drops open, and I gape at her. "Are you telling me you've gone back for seconds with the same man?"

Cassandra never has sex with the same man twice. Even if he is her sister's ex-boyfriend. She says they 'get too attached' and attachment scares the living daylights out of her. I don't know why. As far as I know, she hasn't had a bad experience with a boyfriend. Technically, she's never had a 'boyfriend'.

"We're not talking about me. We're talking about you and River."

I'm done talking about me and my supposed best friend who snuck out on me. Jerk. Jerk I love to the ends of the earth, but still – jerk.

"At least tell us the name of the mystery man."

"Nope. He can't be a mystery man if you know his name."

"Does this mean he's someone we know?" I tap my chin. "Is it Freedom?"

She gags. "I would never date a police officer."

"You admit you're dating?"

"I didn't say I'm dating anyone. I merely said I would never date a police officer."

Gabrielle's phone beeps to interrupt us. She frowns as she reads the message.

"Do you need to get back to work? I should probably get down to the spa and check on how things are going."

She shakes her phone at me. "You're going to want to change your plans."

I snatch the phone from her and read the message from Phoenix. "Damn it." I hand the phone back to her. "Let's go."

I wish I could ignore the message letting Gabrielle know my brother is on the warpath to teach River a lesson. But I can't. I might not think much of River at the moment, but I still love the idiot.

"How does Beckett know about last night?" I ask as I lace up my boots.

"Probably Lilac. She's a member of the Facebook group."

"The Facebook group?" If my night with River is on the Facebook group, then every single person in Winter Falls knows what happened.

"This is awesome." Cassandra rushes to the door. "Let's go. Let's go. My money's on Beckett."

Gabrielle pats my shoulder. "You get used to living in a fishbowl."

"Whatever." I stand and follow her out of the apartment.

I'm not sure what I was thinking, wanting to live in Winter Falls.

Chapter 23

Blunder – when you open your big fat mouth and say things you don't mean

RIVER

I check the clock on the kitchen wall when my doorbell rings. Eight o'clock in the morning. It's a bit early for visitors. But maybe a visitor will get my mind off the colossal mistake I made last night.

It sure didn't feel like a mistake when I was buried deep in Elizabeth, but when I looked into her eyes and felt the connection with her, terror hit me. Why did I insist she keep her eyes focused on me while she came? What the devil was I thinking?

I woke up this morning and knew I needed to get out of there before all the questions and the planning started. I don't do awkward mornings after.

She's going to be pissed. It'll take more than some strawberry treats from *Bake Me Happy* for her to forgive me this time. If she ever does. Damn. I run a hand over my beard. I don't want to live in a world without Elizabeth as my friend.

The doorbell rings again and I set my coffee cup down on the kitchen counter before walking to the front door.

"Hold your horses, I'm coming."

I frown when I open the door to discover Phoenix on my porch. "Shouldn't you be milking your goats?"

"Sorry, brother." He steps away to reveal Beckett standing behind him.

"What's going on?"

Beckett grips my t-shirt and yanks me out of the house. "I'm here to kick your ass."

I push him away. "Why?"

His hands fist and his nostrils flare. "Because you used my sister."

Freaking Winter Falls. Don't get me wrong. I love living here. I wouldn't want to live anywhere else in the world, but I sure as hell wish the residents of the town would look up the word privacy in the dictionary once in a while.

I literally left Elizabeth's bed less than two hours ago and her brother – who doesn't even live in town – is here to defend his sister's honor. Wait. Beckett doesn't live in Winter Falls. How does he know what happened?

"Why do you think I used your sister?"

A car door slams, and Lilac appears. Mystery solved. "Can the two of you get on with this heathen proceeding? I have a ten o'clock meeting I can't miss."

"I'm the CEO. I'll write you a note."

She frowns at Beckett. "You want to write me a note to excuse me from meeting with one of our biggest clients? Did

River already hit you in your head while I was answering my emails in the car?"

"No," he growls. "River did not hit me. He's not going to hit me. I'm going to take him down."

She sighs. "I'll be in the car where it's warm. Let me know when this male bonding ritual is finished."

"We're not bonding," he yells after her.

She waves and mutters, "whatever", before climbing back into the car.

I chuckle. "Your girlfriend appears supportive."

"She's my fiancée. And it's none of your business." He holds up his fists and shadow boxes. "Let's do this."

I cross my arms over my chest. "Phoenix took you down when you went to 'kick his ass'."

Phoenix moves until he's standing behind Beckett. "Good thing I'm on his side this time."

"What the hell? You're my brother. You're supposed to be on my side."

"This is me being on your side."

He's making no sense. Fine. Whatever.

"Two against one? Seems fair."

It actually sounds like fun. I could use an excuse to get rid of this excess energy coursing through my body. It's not terror. It can't be. Why would I be terrified because I slept with my best friend? Elizabeth will forgive me. Eventually.

"I'm not fighting anyone," Phoenix says and my shoulders slump in disappointment. "I'm going to watch as you lose the best thing to ever happen to you."

"What are you talking about? I'm not losing anything."

He snorts. "Uh-huh. Sure. You're not going to go back to being friends with Elizabeth?"

"We are best friends."

"This is going to be painful to watch."

I snort. "I can kick Beckett's ass in my sleep."

"I wasn't referring to the fight."

"What are you talking about then?"

"You're going to have to figure it out for yourself," he says, and I growl. I'm about done with my brother and his mysterious answers.

"You're my baby brother, remember? You're not some guru because you've found love," I grumble. Another reason love is complete bullshit.

He cocks an eyebrow. "I'm not?"

"I'm done with this asinine conversation."

Beckett grunts. "Good. Time to fight."

I motion to the front yard. "Let's go."

He follows me down the steps of my porch to where a crowd is already gathering.

"I have twenty dollars on River busting Beckett's lip." Petal slaps a bill in Sage's hand.

"You're not supposed to enjoy violence," I remind her. Winter Falls is very serious about 'peaceful' demonstrations. The sit-in they staged when Lyric decided the police force would carry weapons lasted for weeks.

"I didn't say I'm going to enjoy it."

"Sem—" Beckett's fist plows into my jaw before I have the chance to finish my word. I fly backwards at the impact. Once the birds stop flying around my head, I move my jaw around to make sure it's not broken. I'm going to have a killer bruise tomorrow.

Phoenix nods at Beckett with respect. "Someone's been training since the last fight."

"I need to be prepared. I've got four sisters I raised as my own children. I never thought Gabrielle would be the easy one."

Phoenix growls. "Gabrielle isn't easy."

Beckett waves away the comment. "You know what I meant."

I have no interest in listening to them hatch out the Phoenix and Gabrielle story. More love crap. "Are you two done gabbing now? Do you need a break, Beckett?" I taunt.

His nostrils flare. "I don't need a break."

He raises his right fist again, but I'm paying attention this time and block him with my left arm before dancing around him.

"You certain you want to do this?"

This time he comes at me with an uppercut to the jaw. I lean back at the last second and his fist meets air.

"Fucker. Fight me."

"There's no reason to fight. I didn't steal Elizabeth's virtue."

He growls and rushes me. "Don't you dare talk about my sister's virtue." He wraps his arms around me and attempts to punch me in the back. I drop to my knees and spin away before he can inflict any damage.

"You used my sister," he growls as he kicks at me.

"Come on, River. Stop toying with him," Petal yells from the crowd.

"I'm not splitting his lip so you can win a bet."

"I'll make you some of those non-wax drip candles you enjoy using."

I could use some of those candles. Elizabeth would look like a sexy dream with wax dripping off of her breasts.

Bam! Beckett plows his fist into my stomach. I fly back with the force of the punch and land in Phoenix's arms. He pushes me toward Beckett. "Finish this."

"I'll be the one finishing this," Beckett claims. "I'm going to beat you to a bloody pulp for using my sister."

"Will you stop saying I used Elizabeth? I didn't force her to do anything she didn't want to do."

His nostrils flare. "You know she's half in love with you and you don't want a relationship."

Half in love with me? Elizabeth isn't half in love with me. She cares for me because we're friends. She knows I don't believe in love. I've been upfront about my feelings from day one of our friendship.

"It was sex. That's all it was."

I hear a gasp and swear under my breath. Damn it. Elizabeth wasn't supposed to hear me say those words.

"Bessie!" I shout for her but she darts off. Gabrielle attempts to throw lasers from her eyes at me before following her sister.

And here I thought I'd already fucked everything up. Apparently, I can fuck things up even worse.

"What's wrong, River? You miss the inside of my jail cell?" Lyric asks as he saunters toward Beckett and me whirling a pair of cuffs on his finger.

"One time. One time I was inside the jail cell, and it wasn't because you arrested me, you asshat."

He chuckles. "Newbies fall for the 'clean the jail cell walls' every damn time."

He's the one who begged me to help out at the police station and deputized me. Some day I'll learn to say no to my big brother's cries for help.

"You going to arrest me?"

"Nope. I think you've been punished enough." He glances over his shoulder to where Elizabeth is fleeing with Gabrielle and Cassandra chasing after her.

"Whatever. I'm done with this."

"Are you running away? Don't be scared, little boy," Beckett mocks me, but I ignore him. I don't give a crap what he thinks.

A car horn blares before Lilac yells out of the window, "Are you finished? Can we leave now? I have work to do. The next time you decide to perform male bonding with a man involved with your sister, I'm driving my own car."

I climb the stairs to my house and slam the door behind me. I can hear Lyric dispersing the crowd, but I don't care about anyone in Winter Falls except Elizabeth. This is why I tried to keep my hands off of her. I knew it would ruin everything.

Chapter 24

Forgive and forget — about as likely to happen as a goat eating your skirt

"Wow!" My mouth gapes open as I catch my first glimpse of Main Street all decked out for this weekend's celebration. "Winter Falls knows how to do Christmas."

"This isn't Christmas. It's Yule," Cassandra corrects me because she will never miss the opportunity to prove she's smarter than me. As if I care who's smarter. I care when she sticks her tongue down my boyfriend's throat. Whether she's smarter? Meh. No biggie.

I hold up the bag of presents I was ordered to bring with me. Apparently, Winter Falls doesn't believe in shopping for gifts. Thus, all my 'presents' are gently used items I no longer need.

"Close enough. Presents."

"Nope. Not the same thing. Yule is a pagan tradition to celebrate the sun beginning its return to us."

I indicate the mistletoe and ivy. "The decorations appear to be the same, too."

Gabrielle sighs. "It's good to know heartbreak hasn't affected your ability to bicker with Cassandra."

"I'm not heartbroken."

Lies. All lies. I rub my fist over the ache blossoming in my chest at the thought of River. Damn, I miss him. I know – I *know* – I never should have let him into my bed, but I couldn't say no. Not when it seemed as if all my dreams were coming true. I thought River felt the connection between us. But no. It was only sex to him.

Cassandra bursts into laughter. "And I'm celibate."

I latch onto the change of topic for all it's worth. "Are you going to tell us who is assisting you in this bid to avoid celibacy?"

"Nope."

"Hey!" Aspen waves us over before I have the chance to grill Cassandra on her mystery man. I'm not convinced he exists, to be honest. My sister has never been one to keep her sexual shenanigans a secret. She's more likely to hire a skywriter to let the world know how many orgasms she had.

"What's up?" I ask as we join Aspen.

She indicates the bag I'm carrying. "You're not supposed to carry your presents around."

"I'm not? What do I do with them? Winter Falls newbie here."

"You hide them."

"Hide them? Like Easter eggs?"

"We'll have a discussion about where Easter eggs come from later. For now, go hide your presents. The gazebo's a great spot." She shoos us away.

We trek down Main Street until we reach the town square where the gazebo is. I study the best spot to hide my presents and spot wrapped gifts everywhere. In the trees, on the ground, on the benches.

Cassandra picks one up and starts opening it. I slap it out of her hand. "What are you doing? You can't steal the presents."

She points to a sign. *Please choose a surprise.*

"You may proceed."

She snorts. "As if I need your permission." Her nose wrinkles when she unwraps the gift. "A candle. You can have it." She shoves it at me and reaches down to pick out another present.

"This isn't a shopping mall. You can't pick and choose."

"But I hate fire."

I tap my chin. "Hmmm… I wonder why. Tell you what. You spill the beans on why you have this phobia about fire, and I'll let you pick two more presents."

"The very definition of phobia means it's irrational and doesn't have a basis in truth."

"Except you weren't afraid of candles before you left for college. Come on, you can tell me what happened. I won't tell anyone."

"I won't either," Gabrielle chimes in.

"Nothing happened." Cassandra drops the present she's holding. "Let's go make wreaths." She marches off toward a crafting table set up in the street.

Cassandra's going to craft? Whatever happened in college must be embarrassing. My older sister doesn't have a problem sharing her adventures unless she comes out sounding like a fool. And now I'm more curious than I was before.

Eden smiles as we sit at the picnic bench in front of her shop, *Eden's Garden.*

"Hey, Ms. Mayor," I greet.

She groans. "Figures I would get chosen to be mayor the year asshat number one and asshat number two decide to expand their business."

I don't think she's referring to River, although he's definitely asshat number one.

"What are you talking about?" I ask.

"Nothing," she grumbles. "Are you ready to make an evergreen wreath?"

"Why evergreen?" Gabrielle asks.

"Evergreens such as yew, holly, pine, mistletoe, and ivy represent everlasting life, protection, and prosperity. Holly and ivy ward off negative energy, pine has healing magic, and mistletoe brings fertility and abundance."

Cassandra drops the mistletoe she was holding. "Did you say fertility?" She doesn't wait for an answer. "I'm grabbing a beer." She marches off toward the brewery without a backward glance.

"Have you voted on best yule log yet?" Eden asks as we decorate our wreaths.

Gabrielle freezes. "Yule log as in chocolate cake?"

I giggle. My baby sister is obsessed with chocolate. She doesn't know what she's missing. Strawberry is the best.

"It's certainly not an actual log burnt on the hearth anymore," Eden grumbles.

"I'm sensing a story."

"Oh, sorry. Sometimes I forget you Dempsey sisters didn't grow up here."

"Thanks," I say because I can recognize a compliment when I hear one.

"Anyway, when I was young, it was tradition to select a log to burn on the hearth during the Yule celebration. The hearth is usually a fireplace inside a home except this is Winter Falls, and we do enjoy our community celebrations, so a fireplace was built on the town square for the occasion.

But when I was in high school, some prankster thought it would be funny to steal the yule log. Except they used normal gloves instead of fire gloves and ended up burning their hands and dropped the yule log in the middle of the street. Now, we do a yule log cake contest instead."

"I bet I can guess who the pranksters were."

"If you guessed the Alston brothers, you'd be correct."

I am not talking about River and his brothers. "How does this yule log contest work? Does everyone have to use the same recipe?" I ask instead.

"No. The most common cake is a basic yellow cake with chocolate buttercream, but contestants can use whatever ingredients they want – chocolate cake, ganache, expresso icing."

Gabrielle drops her wreath decorations and starts to stand. "I think I need to see a man about a cake."

Eden giggles. "I understand. Go on. I'll finish your wreaths. The booth is set up in front of *Clove's Coffee Corner*."

You don't need to tell Gabrielle twice. She's on a mission now. I follow her. Maybe someone was clever and put strawberry in their yule log cake.

Maa!

A goat butts her in the hip as she hurries across the street. "Hey, Pan," she greets as she tickles its jaw. "Where's your daddy?"

Phoenix groans. "Please don't ever say I'm a goat daddy again. I told you what Billy goats do."

He wraps an arm around her and pulls her near. I glance away before their lips lock and my gaze falls on River.

He's wearing his volunteer fire department outfit as he struts my way. Dang him. He couldn't appear disheveled or drunk? Is it too much to ask for him to become invisible and for me to never see him again? I don't think so.

"Hey, Bessie," he greets, and I roll my eyes so hard I'm afraid they're going to get stuck. I also start to walk away from the asshat. It was only sex. Screw him.

He grasps my arm to stop me, but I shove him away. "Leave me alone."

He lets me go, but he doesn't leave me alone. Of course not. I should be so lucky.

"See? This is why I didn't want to have sex with you!"

I feel my face heat with embarrassment, but I am not letting this go. I'm not some meek woman. I'll show him meek.

"It sure seemed as if you wanted to have sex at the time. Several times if I recall correctly."

Phoenix grunts. "I don't want to hear about my brother having sex."

"Shush. We're getting to the good part," Cassandra quiets him. Damn. Of course, she shows up now when I and my ex-best friend are airing our dirty laundry in public. I wouldn't be surprised if she starts selling tickets.

River runs a hand over his beard. "I meant I didn't want to have sex with you because it ruined our friendship."

Is he really this stupid? Or is he merely a fool? I don't know. What I do know is he's pissing me right the eff off.

"Sex didn't ruin our friendship," I shriek. "You did, you dumbass, when you snuck out of my bed like I'm a two-bit whore."

"Are you saying we could have remained friends after we fucked?"

Fuck? I flinch and trip on my own feet at his crude words. He reaches forward to catch me before I fall but I slap him away. I'd rather fall on my rear end in front of the entire town than let him touch me again. Phoenix clutches my jacket to save me from hitting the ground.

Once I'm steady on my feet again, I hiss at River. "I don't know. But you didn't give me the chance to try."

I'm done with this conversation. I whirl around and march off. My sisters try to catch my attention, but I ignore them. I'm not in the mood to be cheered up by Ms. In Love With Love and Ms. Love Is Bullshit.

Chapter 25

Family gathering – must include at least one crying session and one meltdown

THE DRIVEWAY AT PHOENIX and Gabrielle's farmhouse is crowded with bikes, golf carts, and electric cars when I arrive on Christmas morning. Why are there this many people here? I know it's a celebration, but this is ridiculous. Our family isn't this big. Especially since Olivia decided 'Christmas is too commercial' and she therefore won't be visiting for the holidays.

I knock on the farmhouse door but when no one answers, I push it open and peek inside. My eyes widen at the scene in front of me. No wonder no one answered. It's absolute chaos in here.

Maa! A goat rushes by. Told you. Chaos.

"Is that goat wearing reindeer horns?" I ask no one in particular.

"Phoenix!" Gabrielle shouts. "You better put a diaper on Pan before she pees on the Christmas tree again."

Again?

"You're the one who wanted the damn goat in the house," Phoenix mutters as he trails after the animal.

"I heard you!" Gabrielle yells after him. I join her in the kitchen.

"What's going on? Why is there a circus happening inside your house?"

She wipes the back of her hand over her forehead leaving a smudge of flour in its wake. "Don't be mad."

Great. Now I'm definitely going to get mad.

"Why am I going to be mad?"

She grasps my hands. "I wanted to have Christmas at the farmhouse."

I know this. Beckett and she got into an epic fight about it, which ended when Beckett told her to stop being a baby and she burst into tears, therefore assuring she got her way. Being the baby of the family does have its perks.

"But I couldn't have Christmas with Phoenix without his brothers coming."

My jaw clenches. River is here? I have to spend Christmas with him? The man who thinks I'm not special. The only thing I'm good for is a roll in the hay.

"And his brother Lyric is with Aspen and Beckett is with Lilac and they're sisters. And now all of the Wests are here, too." She throws her hands in the air. "And I decided to make a log cake this morning since they were such a hit at the Yule festival and it's way harder than it looks and now Christmas is ruined."

I study the countertops, which are currently covered in flour and chocolate, and say the one thing guaranteed to get a rise out of her. "I prefer strawberry anyway."

"You will eat my log cake and you will love it. Love it! You hear me," she snarls.

I hold up my hands and retreat a few steps. This is not my baby sister. She's shy and doesn't raise her voice. And she definitely doesn't snarl at people. The nightmare of Christmas must have her in his grips.

Lilac's mom bustles into the kitchen. "There. There. My dear Gabrielle. Shall we set out some snacks for the hungry masses while we finish the cake?"

Gabrielle glares at Ruby. Her nostrils flare and a vein in her forehead pulses. I expect steam to come out of her ears any moment now. I should be recording this.

"Did I ever tell you about the first time I met Daniel's parents?" Ruby asks as she pulls trays of cheese and meat out of the refrigerator. "They're Soviet defectors, you know. Svetlana stood guard outside my bedroom door the entire night we stayed with them to protect my virtue. Never mind Daniel and I were living together by then. In fact, I was probably pregnant with Aspen on the trip."

"Mom," Ashlyn whines. "No stories about having sex. You and dad have never had sex. I was born by immaculate conception."

Ruby smirks. "I guess the time you walked in on me and your father in the bathtub was a mirage."

"You're mean. Babysitting privileges for baby Patience are hereby revoked." Ashlyn stomps off.

Ruby rolls her eyes. "She'll be begging me to babysit in no time." She hands me a tray. "Here. Go mingle."

"At least there aren't any condoms on the tray," I mumble.

"I have extra boxes in my purse if you need them," she hollers after me.

I hurry away before she says anything else to embarrass me and run straight into a tall woman with long, curly brown hair and sparkling brown eyes. Crap. It's Mrs. Alston.

"Oh shit. I'm sorry. I didn't see you there. And now I've said shit on Christmas. Shit. I've said it twice now. Or was it three times. Shit."

She giggles as she snags the tray from my hands. "Ever, serve this food and don't eat it all."

Her husband winks at me as he takes the tray from her and saunters off.

"You must be Elizabeth."

"And you're Radiance." I hold out my hand, but she ignores it to pull me into her arms.

"You're family. Families hug."

Except I'm not family. I'm the ex-best friend of her son and the sister of her soon-to-be daughter-in-law. Assuming Phoenix manages to pop the question sometime in this century. The whole town knows he already bought a ring at *Bohemian Treasures.*

When I try to extricate myself from the hug, she threads her arm through my elbow and leads me to the window seat. She sits down and pats the spot next to her.

"I figure it's time for the two of us to get to know each other."

I shrug. "There's not much about me to tell."

"Except you've captured my River's attention. Not an easy thing to do."

"River and I are only friends." And friends is pushing it at the moment.

"Friends with benefits." She winks.

I groan. I should have stayed home. To hell with Christmas being one of my favorite holidays. To hell with loving to spend the day surrounded by family. To hell with it all. Skipping one year wouldn't kill me.

"No. No. No." I deny. "There are no benefits. There's no screwing or sucking or—"

Radiance giggles and I realize I've caught a case of the awkwards. Again. I slam my hand over my mouth. "I didn't mean. I mean." The words come out garbled since my hand is still over my mouth. I drop it. "I'm sorry." What else is there to say?

"Mom." Lyric rushes over. "I need your help with dad. He snuck off with a tray of cheese."

She sighs as she stands. "A wife's job is never finished."

My shoulders sag in relief as Lyric leads his mom away. Aspen plops down next to me. "You're welcome, sister."

"Just don't come crying to me when your in-laws get into a fight on Christmas day and cause Gabrielle's head to explode."

Aspen frowns as she watches my baby sister scurry around the kitchen. "Twenty bucks says she throws the turkey at someone."

"Twenty bucks says she bursts into tears and convinces Beckett to buy her whatever she wants."

She snorts. "I'm not betting against you. I have a baby sister, too." She nods toward where Ashlyn is sitting on the floor in front of the Christmas tree with her baby.

"What's she doing?" I ask when I notice her picking up presents and putting them down again.

"She's teaching Patience how to figure out what a present is worth by its weight."

"Did she forget Patience isn't yet a month old?"

"Patience is going to know how to break into Mom's house before she's potty trained."

I snort. "Your mom never locks the door. She told me so when she revealed where the condom supplies are kept."

"Too bad Mom's mission to tame Dad isn't as successful as her safe sex mission is."

Aspen motions outside to where her parents are walking across the field. Her dad is covered in mud and her mom is obviously yelling at him. Her dad captures her and throws her in the air before melding his lips to hers.

"Ashlyn!" Aspen shouts. "Look outside! The goats are being adorable."

Ashlyn stands and peers out the window. Her face pales when she spots her parents making out in the field.

"You're cruel," I tell Aspen.

She winks at me. "Being the oldest has its privileges."

Cassandra flops onto the floor in front of us. "What are we going to do about that?" She points to where River is standing with Rowan, Cole, Maverick, and Phoenix.

I pretend I don't know what she's talking about. "Call them Aspen's brothers-in-law?"

She rolls her eyes. "Don't act obtuse. You know what I mean."

Juniper and Ashlyn join us. "What's the plan?" Ashlyn asks.

"Plan? There is no plan."

Ashlyn's nose wrinkles. "You're not plotting the biggest revenge prank in history against River? And here I thought we were sisters."

"Technically, we're not sisters," I remind her.

"You didn't hear it from me, but someone's afraid of skunks." Juniper wiggles her eyebrows. "But don't use a real skunk. The smell is torture to get out."

Cassandra rubs her hands together. "Now, we're talking."

"Phoenix Apollo Alston," Gabrielle shouts and the room quiets. "If you don't get your butt over here this minute, I'm going to feed the turkey to the goats."

Aspen holds out her hand. "You owe me twenty bucks."

I ignore her as I stand and march to the kitchen to sort out whatever meltdown my sister's having now. From the corner of my eye, I notice River watching me and I'd be a liar if I claimed I didn't shake my hips and toss my hair as I crossed in front of him.

Let him stare at what he can't have. He could have had me. He's the one who screwed things up. Asshat. Maybe an epic prank is in order after all.

Chapter 26

Trust – the best gift a woman can give a man

RIVER

"What's going on?" I ask when I open my door to discover Elizabeth crouching on my patio.

"It was an accident."

I cock an eyebrow. "An accident? You have paint in your hair, there are paw prints all over my porch, and all you have to say for yourself is 'it was an accident'?"

She stands and throws her arms in the air. "It was an accident. I wanted to use a skunk but after Juniper told me about her 'skunk experience', I changed my mind and decided to use a kitten. You remember the old cartoon with the skunk who falls in love with the poor French black cat."

She looks at me and I cross my arms over my chest. If she's looking at me to let her off the hook, she doesn't know me very well.

"But the kitten was mean." She shows me her scratched up arms. "And didn't want to play along. I was determined, though. I wrangled her into the corner, caught her, and painted her. Except it was more than a stripe. It was maybe the whole kitten. And then I heard something and—"

I do the one thing guaranteed to stop her babbling. I dig my fingers into her hips and haul her to me before slamming my mouth on hers. She sighs and I thrust my tongue into her mouth. She immediately melts against me.

And I'm done. I'm done fighting this attraction to Elizabeth. I'm done fighting the pull of her. I want her and nothing I've done over the past week has helped to alleviate my desire for her. Fine. I'm jumping in with both feet.

I squeeze her hips. She's in tune with me as she jumps into my arms and wraps her legs around me. I carry her into the house and slam the door shut behind us.

I continue to explore her mouth as I walk to my bedroom. I lay her on the bed and stand to study her. She's wearing the same green dress she wore to the holiday party at Gabrielle and Phoenix's house. It hugs every delicious curve she has. If her intent was to drive me mad all day, it worked.

"What are you waiting for?"

"I can't decide if I want to fuck you in your sexy dress or strip you bare and tie you to my bed." When her body shivers at the second suggestion, my mind's made up. "You want me to tie you up?" I ask to be certain.

Her cheeks darken but she maintains eye contact with me as she nods and gasps, "Yes."

My cock jumps and I fist my hands before I attack her. When I have my body back under control, I kneel at her feet and unzip her boots. I shove the boots off and they fall to the floor with a loud thump.

I run my hands along her legs under her dress and stop to squeeze her thighs.

"I'm going to remove all of your clothes and then I'm going to tie your hands to my bedposts and blindfold you."

"Awesome plan. I give this plan an A plus plus."

Her body is vibrating with excitement, but I ask one more time to be absolutely sure. "You give me permission to tie you up?"

"I trust you."

Fuck. What did I do to deserve this woman? I don't deserve her trust. Not after the way I've acted over the past week, but here she is giving it to me without reservation.

"Do we need a safe word?"

We don't, but I want her to feel comfortable. "What do you suggest?"

"How about skunk?"

I shiver. I hate those rodents. She smirks and I realize she must know the story of how I got caught in a locker room with one. It took weeks for the smell to leave my skin.

"Skunk. I'll show you skunk." I tickle her ribs until she bats at my hands and begs for mercy.

I smile down at her before dipping my head to kiss her neck. I bite and suckle the area until she's squirming underneath me. Only then do I kneel and grasp the hem of her dress and pull it up and over her.

I grin at the green satin underwear revealed. I trace the edge of her bra with the tip of my finger. "Pretty. But it's got to go."

She arches for me, and I unhook her bra before dragging the straps down her arms. With my gaze focused on her breasts, I fling the garment behind me. I bend over to glide my tongue around her nipple, which tightens in response. I run my teeth over the tightened bud before rolling off of her.

I open my nightstand and remove the restraints and blindfold. I drop the blindfold on her stomach before crawling up the bed. I kiss the inside of her elbow before wrapping the restraint around her wrist and drawing her arm above her. I tie the end to my bedpost and check she's got enough room to maneuver before doing the same to her other arm.

Once her arms are secured, I pick up the blindfold. I dangle it in front of her face. "Still okay?"

She bites her lip. "More than."

I put the blindfold on her and her breathing increases until her chest is heaving. Hell, yeah someone is more than okay. Elizabeth is perfect for me. I don't know how I didn't see it before, but I'm aware now.

"I'll be back." I squeeze her hip before hurrying to my kitchen to gather a bucket of ice.

I set the bucket on the nightstand. I can practically feel Elizabeth's curiosity at the sound but she doesn't ask. Good girl. She should be rewarded.

I dig a feather out of my drawer and begin tracing it along her body. From her hands to her shoulders down her torso to her feet and back up again. She moans as I draw the plumage over her nipples. Back and forth. Back and forth. Until she's writhing and rubbing her thighs together.

I poke her hip with the pointy edge of the feather. "No! Open."

She doesn't whine or complain. She immediately opens her legs. Perfect for me.

I drop the feather and gather an ice cube in my hand. I rub it against her nipples, and she shouts, "Ow! Cold."

I lift the ice cube. "Too much."

She arches her back as if her body is chasing the ice. "No."

I trace the cube over her nipples until her breasts are covered in goosebumps and the ice has melted. I lean over to gather the wetness with my tongue, and she moans as she juts her chest into my face.

"More?" I ask.

"More."

I draw her panties down her legs before demanding for her to, "Open wide."

She follows my direction and I kiss her hip in reward.

"Tell me if this is too much," I order as I gather another ice cube in my hand. I wait for her nod before I place the ice cube in my mouth.

With my teeth clenching the ice, I trace her slit.

"Wow," she moans.

I use my tongue to push the ice cube into her opening and she nearly shoots off the bed as she comes.

"Yes! Oh god, River! Yes!"

I hold an arm over her hips to stop her bucking as I lick her through her climax. When she collapses against the bed, I stand and undress. I don a condom before crawling into bed with her again.

I situate my hips between her thighs and my cock bumps against her entrance. She wraps her legs around me and arches to pull me inside, but I'm the one running the show.

I pinch her nipple. "Behave."

"I've been a bad girl. Maybe you should discipline me again."

I chuckle. "Dirty girl."

I don't give her a chance to respond before I slam into her. I still when I'm fully seated in order to catch my breath. Holy crap. Nothing has ever felt better.

Why the hell have I been fighting this? I don't need to be in love with Elizabeth to have a relationship with her. My heart rejects those words, but I ignore what it could mean. I've got better things to be doing now.

I pull out while enjoying every second of her walls pulsing against me. When only the tip remains inside, I slam into her again. Her body jolts with the movement and her hands clench at the restraints. She's a goddess.

I hammer into her again and again until my lower back tingles and I know I won't last much longer. I bend forward to latch onto her breast as my hand sneaks in between us to strum her clit. I sweep my tongue across her nipple and her walls flutter around me.

"I'm coming. Can I come?"

Perfect for me.

I whip her blindfold off and she blinks up at me with hazy eyes. "Come when you're ready."

My words are barely out when her walls clamp down on me and she screams, "River!"

"Fuck. Yes. Elizabeth. Sweetheart."

I have no idea what I'm saying as my thrusts turn wild and my climax hits me. I continue to thrust into her until my energy is drained.

I collapse on her and reach to untie her hands. I roll to the side and rub her wrists.

"Sore?"

"Deliciously sore," she mumbles with her eyes closed.

"We need to talk." My words are met with a snore. I chuckle as I tuck her into my side and cover us with a blanket. There's plenty of time to talk because I'm not letting her go.

Chapter 27

Love – exists. That is all.

RIVER

Elizabeth lifts my arm and wiggles as she tries to roll out of bed. If she's trying to sneak out, wiggling her ass against my crotch is not the way to go. My cock wakes up and wonders if it's playtime. I ignore it since I have a woman creeping out of my bedroom to deal with.

She finds her panties and tugs them on before searching for her bra. It's hanging from a lamp on my dresser, but she doesn't notice it. She huffs as she gives up and puts on her dress. I've had enough when she grabs her boots and begins to tiptoe out of the room.

"Going somewhere?"

She shrieks and whirls around. She stares at me with eyes the size of saucers. "I didn't think you were awake."

"So, you thought you'd sneak out?"

She shrugs.

I jump out of bed and stalk toward her. Her gaze drops to my cock, and I smirk. Good thing I didn't bother getting dressed last night after she passed out.

"I thought we were done with sneaking out on each other."

I grasp her hand and haul her back to bed. I lean against the headboard and situate her between my legs with her back resting against my front. I don't think I can have this conversation while face to face.

"We never agreed to anything of the sort."

I kiss her neck. "We would have if you hadn't passed out."

"I didn't pass out. I fell asleep."

"What's the difference?"

"Passing out implies I lost consciousness due to the veracity of your lovemaking."

I bark out a laugh. "Veracity of my lovemaking?"

"I fell asleep because I was tired. I've been working my fingers to the bone to ensure *Glitter N Bliss* opens in the second week of the new year."

"We'll circle back to the spa in a minute. First, we need to talk."

She groans and drops her chin to her chest. "What now? Are you going to tell me it was only sex again? This is why I tried to sneak out. I don't need to hear this. I get it. We're friends. Friends with sometimes benefits."

I grasp her chin and turn her head until we're eye to eye. "Last night was more than sex. It was the best sex of my life." Her eyes widen in surprise. "You got off on every single thing I did to you. It was electrifying."

Her chest heaves. "I thought the same thing."

"Which is why I've decided to move this relationship along from friends to lovers."

Her eyes flare but she sasses at me, "You've decided, have you?"

"Yep." I bite her bottom lip to punish her disbelief.

"And am I allowed any say in this decision?"

I lick her bottom lip. "Your say was noted when you said you trust me."

She purses her lips. "But where can this relationship go? You don't believe in love, remember?"

"I don't have to love you for us to have a mutually satisfying relationship."

"Yeah. That's not going to work for me." She scoots away and begins putting on her boots.

"I thought this is what you wanted."

She pats my leg. "You thought wrong, honey. I don't want a dead-end relationship."

"You want flowers and chocolates and rainbows and unicorns," I growl. "Let me tell you, unicorns don't exist."

Finished with her boots, she stands. "I know. But love does. I don't understand why you don't believe in love. Your parents are in love. Your brothers are in love. Or do you think they're pretending?"

I scratch my beard. "No. I never said love doesn't exist."

"Really?" She scoffs. "I call your attention to exhibit number one. On the day of Aspen and Lyric's wedding, did you or did you not say, 'Love doesn't exist'?"

Fuck. I'm not having this conversation naked. I jump out of bed and dig a pair of sweats out of my drawer. I put them on before facing Elizabeth again.

"I meant love doesn't exist for me."

She crosses her arms over her chest and draws my attention to her breasts, which I happen to know are currently braless. My cock twitches and I fist my hands before I reach for her.

"Really? Did you not get the love gene when you were born? Is this some type of genetic deformity? Do you need to take medicine for the rest of your life? Should I start a fundraiser for this 'poor me'-gene deficiency?"

"Smartass," I grumble, but I'm smiling. "I don't have a genetic disease."

"What's wrong with you then? Why are you the one person on earth for whom love doesn't exist?"

"I'm not the only person."

"I'm not discussing sociopaths."

"You spend too much time with Lilac." I shackle her wrist and lead her to the kitchen. She scans the room with interest, and I remember she's never been inside my house before. Way to treat your best friend, asshole.

"You want coffee?"

I quickly make a pot. While I'm at it, I whip up some eggs and bacon.

She stares at the plate when I set it before her. "You can cook?"

"You've met my mom, haven't you? No way were her boys not learning how to cook and clean."

We sit next to each other at my kitchen island and while she digs into her food, I sip on my coffee and try to come up with a way to explain to her why love is a load of crap as far as

I'm concerned. I've never told anyone this before. I'm not sure where to begin.

"Begin at the beginning," she says.

"Can you read my mind?"

"You're hemming and hawing over there like one of the gossip gals trying to keep a secret inside."

"A gossip gal? You think I resemble a gossip gal?" I puff out my chest to show her I'm most definitely not a 'gal'.

She glides a hand up and down my naked skin. "This six-pack isn't going to excuse you from spilling your secrets."

I capture her hand. "Are you sure?" I press her hand down my body toward my waistline where my cock is eagerly awaiting her touch.

She yanks her hand away. "Start talking, Mr. Woe Is Me."

I gulp the rest of my coffee down before standing. I pace the kitchen in front of her.

"The beginning is Nancy."

She motions for me to continue. "Go on. Nancy."

"Nancy was my first college girlfriend." She drops her fork and gives me her full attention. Not helping. "After two weeks, she said she loved me. A week later she dumped me for the captain of the football team."

"Why is it always the captain of the football team?" she grumbles. "Okay. Nancy was a Class A bitch. You still haven't proved your point."

"After Nancy came Brianna. We dated for a week before she said she loved me. She also told my roommate she loved him.

When I called her on it, she said she could love more than one person at a time. I broke up with her."

"Kari was next. She told me she loved me after a whole month. When I didn't repeat the sentiment back to her after two months, she said she lied and never loved me at all."

Elizabeth raises her hand.

"What?"

"Did you get any studying done at college at all?" I glare at her. "Sorry. Continue. After Kari is …"

"Meg. She said she loved me after three weeks. The next week she cheated on me with my roommate."

"Is this the same roommate Brianna was in love with?"

"Yes."

"I hope you kicked him to the curb."

"We still exchange Christmas cards."

"What? Why would you exchange Christmas cards with the man who betrayed you?"

"He didn't betray me. Meg did."

She rolls her eyes. "It takes two to tango."

"I can list more names for you, but the story is always the same. Girls who told me they loved me, but their love would miraculously disappear if I didn't say the words back to them. Eventually, I gave up and decided to stick to having fun."

"You became a player," she clarifies.

"I don't disrespect women."

She waves away my objection. "I didn't say you did."

"And now you know why love is bullshit as far as I'm concerned."

She drums her fingers on the counter as she considers what I told her. "Huh."

"Huh? Huh, what?"

"I didn't realize you were this big of an idiot."

An idiot? She's not supposed to call me an idiot. She's supposed to commiserate with me.

"You want me to commiserate?" she asks proving the woman can read my mind. "I can commiserate. Shall I list all the boyfriends who lied and cheated on me?"

"No," I growl. I don't want to know about the men she's been with in the past.

"But I could."

"What's your point?"

"My point is almost every single person who's been out in the big wide dating world has been betrayed. You know what it means when someone betrays you?" She doesn't wait for me to formulate a response before answering. "It means they weren't your person."

"But all of those women said they loved me."

She shrugs. "Maybe they thought they did."

"Which just goes to show love is bullshit."

She shakes her head as she tsks at me. "River. River. River."

"What????" I bark out. I fucking hate how reasonable she sounds. Did I get the wrong end of the stick all these years? Did I throw away the possibility of love for all the wrong reasons?

"Love isn't bullshit. It's real. Just because some stupid college girls jumped the gun and declared their love way too soon doesn't mean love isn't real. I know you believe in love to some extent because you love your family."

Fuck. She's right. I do love my family and I do recognize the love my parents have for each other is genuine.

She walks around the kitchen counter to take my hands.

"I'm not saying you have to immediately change your mind and declare love is real. What I'm proposing is you open your mind to the possibility. Study what your brothers have found. I think you'll realize what they have with their partners is the real deal."

"Say I consider this. What do I get in return?"

She grins up at me. "Me."

"I'm in." I'm not going to lose this woman.

She lifts her eyebrows. "Just like that?"

"Yeah. I decided last night I was all in with you."

"Except you wanted to have a dead-end relationship," she clarifies.

"I said I'm willing to try." I run my nose along hers. "What do you say? Are you in?"

She leans back and studies me. "I need to think about it."

"Think about it?"

"Yep. I'm not sure I believe you're prepared to open your mind to the possibility of my awesomeness."

I lean close to whisper in her ear. "Oh, I'm open to exploring your awesomeness."

She shivers before shoving me away. "New rule. No using sex to get what you want."

"But sex is awesome."

She pushes up on her tiptoes and kisses my cheek. "It sure is. We'll talk later." She marches out of the kitchen to the front door. "Think about what I said."

I stare after her with my mind churning. Is she right? Am I being an idiot? No, it can't be. I'm not wrong about all the women who professed to love me without knowing me. How can I ever trust a woman to truly love me when they're all so eager to declare their love?

But is Elizabeth different? She obviously cares for me, but she hasn't uttered a word of love, and we've known each other for months. Is she the one? I did promise her I'd consider the possibility, and I don't break my promises.

Chapter 28

Perspective – changing it can rock your world

I DROP MY PURSE on the floor and shut the door to my apartment behind me.

"About time," Cassandra says, and I scream.

"What the devil are you doing here?" I ask as I clasp my chest to prevent my heart from galloping out of it. Shit. She scared me.

"I think you mean we." She points to Gabrielle.

Gabrielle waves. "Lilac sends her regrets."

"What's going on? Why are you both here? And how did you get into my apartment?" I groan. "Don't tell me Lilac taught you how to pick a lock."

"Lilac's no fun," Cassandra grumbles.

"What she means is, Lilac refuses to teach her how to pick a lock," Gabrielle clarifies.

"Then, how did you get in here? Did you keep an extra key when you moved out?"

She shakes her head no.

"I told her to keep an extra key, but she refused." Cassandra glares at Gabrielle.

"Tell me how you got in here and then get out."

I'm tired. I need a shower and then I'm going to crawl back into bed for a few hours before I have to check on the construction at *Glitter N Bliss*. The opening is imminent, and it will be perfect. I don't have time for whatever this is.

Cassandra chuckles. "You wish."

I cross my arms over my chest and stare at Gabrielle. Cassandra will never crumble but my baby sister might.

"It wasn't me!" she shouts after less than a minute. "Cassandra stole your keys out of your purse and had a replica key made."

"Way to keep a secret," Cassandra mumbles.

I hold out my hand. "Give me the key."

She digs it out of her pocket and drops it in my hand. "Fine."

I point my finger at her. "And don't think I don't know you plan to make another one. Wait. Did you already make extra copies?"

She nibbles on her thumbnail. "Nope."

"Liar." I guess I'm getting my locks changed. "Now, please vacate the premises. I've got things to do."

"Things such as shower to wash the sex off of you."

I narrow my eyes at my older sister. "Don't be jealous."

She springs to her feet. "Aha! The gossip gals were correct. You did spend the night with River."

I shrug. "He's my best friend. We talked. Watched a movie. And I fell asleep on the sofa."

She rolls her eyes. "How naïve do you think I am? I can spot sex hair a mile away."

"Really? And how does this skill help with your career op-portunities?"

"I have a career. I'm a mixologist."

"Mom and Dad would be very proud."

She flinches and I backpedal. "Sorry. Bitchy thing to say. I need sleep."

"Because you were up all night doing boom boom in the bedroom with River." She thrusts her hips and I wonder why I feel guilty for being a bitch to her. She certainly doesn't care when she's mean to me.

"Can we return to the subject at hand?" Gabrielle asks.

"Aha!" I shout. "You did come here with an agenda."

"Of course, we did. Teasing you is a bonus." Cassandra winks.

I tilt my head back and address the ceiling. "Why couldn't I have four brothers instead of three sisters and one brother?"

"You want four brothers going all protector whenever you date a new guy?" Gabrielle asks, and I cringe.

No, I don't want four brothers beating up the guy I had sex with who I think is the 'one' when he's actually using me for sex. But River isn't using me for sex anymore. Although, I don't know if he knows how to have an adult relationship. He's thirty-three years old and all his relationships were in college. College isn't exactly the time and place to learn how to have a relationship.

I collapse on the sofa as everything River said this morning hits me at once. Can he open his mind to the possibility love exists? Does he really believe he can give up his playboy ways with a snap of his fingers? Snap and all of a sudden, he's monogamous? And I'm the one to tame him? Not likely.

Gabrielle sits next to me and grasps my hand. "What is it? What happened?"

"Sex happened! I want all the details."

I sigh at Cassandra's demand. She knows I never kiss and tell, but it doesn't stop her from bugging me.

"Did River hurt you?"

"No." I blame my tiredness for what comes out of my mouth next. "He kind of declared we're together now and his playboy ways are done."

"Yeah! This is so exciting. You're going to marry my husband's brother and we're going to stay in Winter Falls together and live happily ever after."

Cassandra pretends to gag. "Gross."

My eyes widen when I realize the implication of what Gabrielle said. "What do you mean husband's brother? Did Phoenix propose?" She blushes and ducks her chin. "No way. He proposed on Christmas?"

"Yes?"

I reach for her left hand. My mouth gapes open when I spot the honking engagement ring there. "Congratulations!"

I wrap my arms around her as she giggles.

"What did Beckett say?" I ask after I release her.

Her nose wrinkles. "I haven't told him yet."

I chuckle. "Have fun with that."

"Welp. I guess you two are sorted. I'm off." Cassandra waves as she marches to the door.

I debate letting her leave. My older sister isn't exactly the best person in the world to ask advice from. Except, in this instance, I think I might need her. But you'll never hear me admit to needing her out loud. Forget it!

"I'm not sorted," I say.

She halts with her hand on the doorknob. "I'm confused. Did you or did you not explain less than five minutes ago how River wants a relationship with you?"

"I did."

"I don't understand the problem. You're in love with the dude and he wants to be with you. Sorted."

I don't bother arguing with her about whether or not I'm in love with River. I mean, it's true. There's no sense denying it. I do love the man, but I'm not discussing my feelings with anyone other than him.

I snort. "The man is the definition of playboy, but he's going to give up his playboy ways for me?"

"Why wouldn't he? Are you saying you don't think you're good enough for him? Nonsense. You may be a pain in my ass, but you're still better than any man."

"Thank you. I think. But why would the sexiest man alive give up on the smorgasbord of women available to him for me?"

I'm not begging for compliments. I genuinely don't understand why River would give it all up for me. He doesn't love me. In fact, until this morning, he didn't believe love existed for him. I'm not convinced I managed to change his mind.

"What are you talking about? You're gorgeous, smart, loyal, and funny when you forget to be nervous and awkward. You're a catch and any man who can't see how wonderful you are can shove it."

"She's right," Gabrielle agrees.

"Except all you have to do is strut in front of my boyfriends and they forget all about how great I am," I accuse Cassandra.

"Ugh." She groans. "Are you referring to Jared?"

I stand and stomp toward her. I poke her shoulder. "Of course, I'm referring to Jared. He was my high school boyfriend. Mine! And yet, you didn't give a flying fig about our relationship when you stole him away from me."

"I was doing you a favor."

"A favor? Stealing my boyfriend was doing me a favor? This is what I mean. I'm not the one to tame River. Not when Cassandra the boyfriend stealer will come along and tempt him away."

"Crap. We have to discuss this, don't we?"

"Discuss what? How I'm not woman enough?" I might be shrieking now if the banging on the ceiling by my neighbor is anything to go by.

Cassandra blows out a puff of air before straightening her back and grasping my hands. "Jared was cheating on you."

I roll my eyes. "I know. With you."

"No. With the entire cheerleading squad."

I rear back. "No, he wasn't. He hated those girls. He complained about their bleached hair and fake smiles all the time."

"And this is why I did what I did."

"I'm confused. Can you explain slowly for those of us in the back of the class?"

"I saw Jared making out with another girl at the mall. I tried to tell you, but you wouldn't listen to me."

My brow wrinkles. "I don't remember this."

"You wouldn't believe me."

"You should have tried harder."

"It wouldn't have mattered. You were enamored with Jared. No one was allowed to say a bad word about him."

What is she talking about? None of this sounds familiar.

She points to my face, which is probably looking mighty confused right now. "Exactly! You didn't believe a word I said. I needed to resort to drastic measures. You're welcome."

"Whoa. You want me to thank you for stealing my boyfriend away?"

"Yes. I did you a favor by getting that snake away from you."

Gabrielle clears her throat. "It's true. Jared was a jerk and a creep. He used to wait in the hallway outside of the bathroom whenever I took a shower and leer at me when I came out in my robe."

My head spins as my entire world tilts on its axis. "All this time I've been worried about my ability to keep a boyfriend because of Jared."

I'm such a hypocrite. Just this morning I told River he couldn't base life decisions on relationships he had in college, but I've been doing the exact same thing. Thinking I'm un-worthy because Cassandra stole my boyfriend away. All this time I thought she was the biggest bitch in the world while she was helping me out.

Does this mean I can be the woman to make River change his ways? Gulp. Who knew getting everything you ever wanted is scary as hell?

Chapter 29

Skinny dipping – an idiotic idea in December in Colorado

RIVER

I cross my arms over my chest and glare at my brothers and Beckett. "I'm not doing this." I sound like a five-year-old refusing to eat his vegetables, but I have no interest in skinny dipping today. The water in the falls is beyond freezing this time of year.

"The last time I refused to skinny dip in the falls you said I was a chicken," Phoenix points out.

"It was October. It's now the end of December. I have no desire to freeze my balls off."

Lyric slaps me on the back. The force of it causes me to fly forward. "But this is how we show you what an idiot you're being."

"I'm not being an idiot."

Beckett growls. "You're right. Treating my sister like a doormat is worse than being an idiot. Way worse."

I hold up my palms and back away. "I'm not going to fight you again."

He smirks. "Because you're afraid I'm going to beat the crap out of you."

"No. Because Elizabeth would be pissed at me for hurting you."

He snorts. "Because you give a shit what Elizabeth thinks."

I give a whole lot more than a shit. The woman has me tied up in knots. I told her I wanted a relationship with her, and she said she'd think about it. What's there to think about? We're best friends, we're fucking phenomenal together in bed, and we care for each other.

The woman has some magical woo-woo powers. Not only did she get me to confess my reasons for believing love doesn't exist, but she shot them down in less than five minutes flat. I can't stop thinking about how I might have been wrong. How I might have based my entire life philosophy on what a few college girls said.

"No one's beating anyone up," Lyric declares.

"Who invited the cop?" Beckett asks no one in particular.

Phoenix shoves his shoulder. "Lyric's our brother."

"And Elizabeth is my sister, and I won't stand for her being used. By anyone."

I rub a hand through my beard. "I'm not using Elizabeth."

He growls as he comes to stand in front of me. "What do you call it when you have sex with a woman but have no intention of asking her for more?"

"My past."

He crosses his arms and stares me down. Or, rather, he tries to. Beckett isn't a small guy at six-foot, but I'm two inches taller and I won't hesitate to use my height to intimidate him.

"Your past?"

"Are you deaf, old man? Need me to get you a hearing aid?"

"A leopard doesn't change his spots."

"Good thing I'm not a leopard."

"No, you're not a leopard. You're a manwhore who's going to break Elizabeth's heart."

Break her heart? I would never hurt Bessie. I rub a hand over my chest where a pain blossoms at the idea of hurting her.

"I'm not a manwhore."

Beckett cocks a brow. "No? What do you call your endless stream of one-night stands?"

"I told you. It's my past."

"And you expect me to believe you? You woke up one morning and decided 'Hey! I'm done being a player. I think I'll settle down with a plain girl.'"

I growl. "Don't you fucking dare say Elizabeth is plain. She's beyond gorgeous and fun to be around. Not to mention she's sweet and hard working."

"Hold up. Are you and Elizabeth a couple now?" Lyric asks.

I don't answer him since technically we're not. Elizabeth hasn't agreed yet.

"Damn," he swears. "I had Valentine's day. I underestimated Elizabeth."

Phoenix pats my shoulder. "Not as much fun when you're the center of attention, is it?"

I ignore my brothers to keep my focus on Beckett since his reaction is the one that matters. He studies me for a minute before nodding.

"Okay. I won't kick your ass. For now." He steps closer. "But if you hurt her again, your cop brother won't be able to stop me from beating the ever-loving crap out of you."

"I'm going to pretend I didn't hear that," Lyric announces.

"Are we done with this kumbaya shit?"

"I'm telling Mom you said discussing feelings is kumbaya shit," Phoenix taunts.

I cross my arms over my chest. "You want to go there? Should I tell Beckett how you proposed to his sister without asking permission?"

"Shows how much you know. I did ask for permission."

I know. I also know I don't want to talk about Elizabeth anymore. And switching the topic to Gabrielle is a surefire way to get the heat off of me.

"He knows. He also thinks he's off the hook." I glare at Lyric. "What? I've known you for thirty-three years. You can't fool me."

I'm done with this conversation. I toe off my boots before removing my coat and throwing it on the ground. I whip off my sweater and jeans and they join my pile of clothes. I leave my boxers on because I'm not a complete idiot.

I dash to the river and do a cannonball making sure to splash my brothers and Beckett.

Lyric and Phoenix strip and join me, but Beckett stands on the side of the river. "I'm not getting in the water."

I splash him and he curses. "It's fucking freezing out here."

"Who votes we phone Lilac and tell her what a sissy her fiancé is?" I ask and raise my hand.

"Not skinny dipping in freezing water in December doesn't make me a sissy."

"Bwak. Bwak," I taunt.

"Fine." Beckett begins to undress. I laugh when he removes layers of long underwear. He glares at me. "Not everyone is as cold-blooded as you are."

I wiggle my eyebrows. "I'm as hot-blooded as they come. Ask your sister if you don't believe me."

"Asshole." He jumps into the water but instead of chasing me, he turns right around and swims back to the riverbank. "Hell and damnation. This water is fucking freezing. What in the world is wrong with you people?"

"We get it," I taunt. "It takes a real man to handle the water of the falls."

He flips me off. "Make fun of me all you want. I don't give a shit. I'm not the idiot who's willing to flirt with hypothermia to make some stupid point. I'm going to the diner for breakfast."

I hurry after him. I'm literally freezing my balls off in here. "I could go for some pancakes and bacon."

I rush to put my clothes on. Not an easy feat when you're wet and you don't have a towel. My brothers follow my lead, and we trail after Beckett as he heads toward the diner.

Lyric slings his arm around my shoulders as we walk. "What's wrong, little brother?"

I growl at him. He knows I hate being called little brother. I'm barely a year younger than him, but he won't let me forget he's older.

I shove him away. "Why do you think there's something wrong?"

"Maybe because you jumped into the falls in December."

And it was as freaking cold as I predicted it would be. My balls tried to crawl back up in my body. I admit none of this to my brother, though.

"You followed me."

"I couldn't let my little brother outdo me now, could I?"

"I thought kumbaya hour was over."

"River. River. River." He tsks. "Kumbaya hour is never over in Winter Falls."

He's right. I have zero chance of escaping this conversation. I won't have it in front of Elizabeth's brother, though. I slow and wait until Beckett is too far away to hear us. "It's Elizabeth."

"Duh. What about her?"

"I told her I want a relationship and she said she'd think about it."

Lyric barks out a laugh. "This is precious. You finally found a woman you're willing to give up your slut ways for and she doesn't want you."

I scowl. "I'm not a slut. And she wants me."

"For more than sex," he clarifies.

"She'll come around," I claim, despite not being certain.

I thought all I had to do was tell Elizabeth I want a relationship and she'd jump for joy. Not hardly. First, she pressured me to tell her about my past. And then she said she'd think about it. What's there to think about? We're perfect for each other.

Phoenix claps my back. "Everything will work out in the end."

I narrow my eyes on him. "What do you know? What did Gabrielle tell you?"

"Nope." He shakes his head. "I'm not betraying her trust by telling you shit. Figure it out for yourself."

"I will." I hurry my pace. I need to get to Elizabeth.

Lyric catches my arm. "Not now. First, pancakes."

I yank my arm away from him, but he motions toward Beckett who's waiting for us around the bend before I can leave.

"Next time he tries to beat you up for hurting Elizabeth, I won't stop him."

"But you'll give me a running start."

He grins. "Hell yeah. It's a blast to watch you try and run from your mistakes."

Elizabeth is not a mistake. In fact, she might be the best thing to ever happen to me. Whoa. What? Am I falling in love with her? No, it can't be. Love doesn't exist, remember? Except Elizabeth blew holes in all my reasons for not believing in love. Maybe love does exist after all.

Damn. I'm in trouble.

Chapter 30

*Wish – a desire to do something that when expressed in front of
an entire town is likely to come true*

I ENTER *ELECTRIC VIBES* and scan the area. I expected the
bar to be decorated for New Year's Eve, but I was wrong.
There's probably some rule about decorations and balloons in
this town. Winter Falls is a great place to live, but there sure
are a lot of rules about things I've never thought about before.

Gabrielle squeezes my hand. "Everything will be fine."

Easy for her to say. She's engaged to the man of her dreams.
Although, who honestly thought a goat farmer would be
Gabrielle's dream man? Not me.

Stop being snarky, Elizabeth. She's being kind and supportive
because she knows I'm nervous. And why am I nervous? Because I decided to give River a chance.

To be honest, I don't have much choice in the matter. I love
the idiot who finds it hard to believe love exists. I have for a
while. And – if I don't take this chance – I'm going to regret
it. I only hope my heart survives.

"Where's Cassandra?" I ask because I don't want to discuss River anymore. It's all we've talked about for the past week. I'm done talking. It's time for action.

In response to my question, Gabrielle points to the bar. My eyes widen when I discover my older sister working there. When she said she'd meet us at *Electric Vibes,* I thought she wanted to start the party early. I didn't think she'd be working.

Gabrielle releases my hand. "Be brave."

"Why are—"

I swallow my question when I notice Phoenix and River saunter toward us. Phoenix wraps an arm around Gabrielle's waist and draws her near. When their lips meet, I look away.

My gaze falls upon River who's looking absolutely scrumptious this evening. He's wearing a button-down shirt with the top two buttons undone giving me a glimpse of his chest. A chest I love to scrape my nails down. He's already rolled the sleeves up past his elbows showing off his sexy forearms. Apparently, I now think forearms are sexy. It's all River's fault.

He leans over and kisses my cheek. "Hello, Elizabeth. You look beautiful."

At the feel of his lips and breath on my skin, I shiver. I wonder if it will always be this way. Will I be old and gray and still shivering every time the man touches me? I hope so.

He grasps my hand and tugs me further into the bar. "You ready for this?"

"What are we doing?"

He leads me to a table with a glass bowl filled with pieces of paper. Next to the bowl are pencils and empty cards. "Write down your wish for next year on the card and put it in the bowl."

"Is this a wish jar?"

"Not exactly," he hedges.

"What aren't you telling me?"

"Lennon reads the wishes out loud, and everyone guesses whose wish it is."

"What do I win if I get the most guesses correct?"

"The winner gets to drop the ball at midnight." He points to a shiny ball on top of the dance floor I hadn't noticed.

I rub my hands together. "You're on."

I know what I wish for next year. I quickly write it down and stuff the card in the bowl.

"What?" I ask River when I notice he hasn't moved. "Aren't you going to make a wish?"

He clears his throat. "Um, yeah."

"Get to it mister. I'll grab us drinks."

I push through the crowd until I make it to the bar where I wave Cassandra over. "Why are you working tonight?"

"One word. Tips."

Tips? It's not as if any of us Dempsey sisters 'need' money. What's she up to?

"What do you want?" Alrighty then. I won't be figuring out what she's up to today.

"Can I get a pitcher of margaritas and a pitcher of beer?"

"Margaritas?" She scoffs. "I've got something better for you."

"I'm fine with …" She leaves before I can finish my sentence. Good to know bartending doesn't affect her ability to ignore me.

When she returns, she's carrying a pitcher of neon blue liquid.

"What the hell is this?"

"Jack Frosties. You're welcome."

"What's in it?"

She waves as she walks away. I should know better than to think she'll answer me. I join Lyric and Aspen, Beckett and Lilac, Phoenix and Gabrielle, and River at a table near the dance floor.

Aspen glares at the pitcher of Jack Frosties on the table. "What the hell is that?"

"Jack Frosties?"

"Vodka, prosecco, Blue Curacao, and lemonade," Lilac reads from her phone.

Despite the strange color and list of alcohol contents, I'm certain it will be yummy. I give Cassandra shit about being a mixologist all the time, but she's actually quite good at it.

"Sounds yummy. Who wants one?"

Aspen makes a face. "Not me." She holds up her glass of bubbly. "I'll stick to the traditional stuff."

I pour glasses for Lilac, Gabrielle, and myself. I take a sip and cough as the alcohol burns its way down my esophagus. River slaps me on the back. "You okay?"

"I think Cassandra is trying to get me drunk."

"No getting drunk and streaking down Main Street," Lyric admonishes.

Who does he think I am? "I think you have me confused with someone else. I've never streaked in my life."

"Except for the time she was in college, and someone stole her clothes while she was showering in the communal bathroom and she ended up running down the hallway in a towel."

I glare at Gabrielle. "How do you know? You weren't there."

She giggles. "We went to the same college. The tale of Elizabeth Dempsey streaking down the hall while screaming *I'll get you my pretties* was legendary."

Beckett growls. "Who stole your clothes? Why haven't I heard this story before?"

Lilac pats his arm. "They're adults. Let them be."

"Easy for you to say. You don't know how it feels to be responsible for your sisters."

I tune out whatever Lilac's response is and focus on River. "How was skinny dipping?"

"No one in this town can keep their mouth shut," he mutters.

I wag a finger at him. "No complaining about gossip when you're the one who stripped off your clothes in public."

He snaps at my finger. "I didn't remove all of my clothes. I kept my boxers on."

I roll my eyes, but my response is cut off when Lennon taps the microphone. "It's time to get started."

Cheers erupt as he lifts the wish jar above his head. "Usual rules apply. I'll read the wish and call on the first person to raise their hand. If the person is correct about whose wish it is, we'll continue. If not, I'll call on the next person, and so forth and so on."

"We all know the rules," Feather shouts at him.

"Bets are closing," Sage hollers from her spot next to the stage.

"The first wish for next year is …." Lennon pulls a card out of the jar. "Never to have to wear pants again."

"Forest," everyone chimes in together.

"No points awarded," Lennon declares before removing the next card. "I wish the owners of *Naked Falls Brewing* would withdraw their plan to expand the brewery."

River raises his hand. "Eden."

"One point for River Alston."

"How did you know?" I ask him.

"Is it Miller or Elder?" Clove asks.

"I think Elder. He's dreamy," Petal answers.

"No. It has to be Miller," Cayenne claims.

"What are they talking about?" I ask River.

He doesn't get a chance to answer before Sage slams her hand on her table. "No bets about Eden will be taken as of this time. Project Lothario is still in play."

"What's Project Lothario?" I ask the table.

Lilac opens her mouth to answer but before she can, Aspen places a hand over her mouth. "Nothing," she says before yelping and pulling her hand away. "Ouch. You bit me."

"You don't silence me. You also know if you want me to lie, you need to explain in advance and give me a reason," she says.

"All requests for lying must be submitted to Lilac in advance in writing in triplicate," Aspen mimics.

I lean close to River. "What are they talking about?"

"You know Lilac hates to lie."

I narrow my eyes at him. "I wasn't talking about Lilac's distaste of lying and you know it."

"I'm not at liberty to say."

"You're full of shit."

"Next wish." Lennon reads the card, and his eyes widen as a smile spreads across his face. "I wish for River to be my boyfriend."

Ugh. My wish sounds dorky when read aloud in front of the town. I should have thought of something more witty or funny. Apparently, my awkwardness extends to writing. Awesome.

River cradles my face with his hands. His eyes are full of hope. "Yes? You made a decision."

"It wasn't hard."

He slams his lips on mine but all too soon he's releasing me and standing. He holds out his hand. "Let's go."

"We can't leave now. You're in the lead."

"You just announced to the entire town of Winter Falls you want me. We're not staying."

"But—"

He pulls me out of my chair and throws me over his shoulder.

"Project Lothario is a success!" Sage announces.

Ah. Now I understand what Project Lothario means. But why did the gossip gals set me up with Peace if they were intent on matching me with River? Unless they thought River would get jealous. Those ladies are sneaky.

"Who had New Year's Eve?" Cayenne asks.

"Gabrielle Dempsey."

What? My own sister bet on me. "Insider trading!" I shout. "She cheated." No one listens to me as Gabrielle jumps on stage to accept her winnings.

River steps outside and slides me down his body. I stomp toward the door to go back inside, but he maneuvers me until my back is against the wall and he has me caged in.

"Do you want to return to the bar to yell at your sister or do you want me to escort you home, strip you bare, and worship every inch of you?"

"I vote for worshipping!" Cassandra shouts through the window.

"What do you say?" River punches his hard cock against my stomach and tingles erupt throughout my body. For once, I agree with Cassandra. It's time for the ravishing to begin.

"Let's go home."

He kisses me quickly before grasping my hand and dragging me down Main Street toward my apartment. I giggle as I run to keep up with him. Considering his response, I'm pretty sure my decision to take a chance on us is the right one.

Chapter 31

Package – one size does not fit all

I wake with my arm draped over a naked body. *Elizabeth.* I nuzzle closer to her until my cock is snuggled against her ass.

"Sleep," she mutters. "I need sleep."

"I didn't wake you."

She wiggles her ass against my cock. It begins to harden and lengthen. "Something did."

I growl. "Keep wiggling your ass and there will be no more sleeping for you."

She wiggles her ass again and I spin her around until she's flat on her back and I'm looming over her. She stares up at me with bright, blue eyes. I tickle her ribs.

"You weren't sleeping."

She giggles and slaps away my hands. "Who could sleep with your thoughts going a hundred miles an hour?"

I freeze. "A hundred miles an hour?"

She bites her lip. "You weren't laying here thinking you made a mistake?"

"Elizabeth." I kiss her nose before laying my forehead against hers. "No. I wasn't. I promise."

I'm not lying. There's no urge to run away from her like I usually feel after I accidentally spend a night in a woman's bed. I'm not afraid of what the future will bring for us. In fact, I'm excited to discover our future. Together.

"We didn't get a chance to talk much last night."

I waggle my eyebrows at her. "We had much more fun things to do than talk."

She blushes and the color spreads from her cheeks down her neck to the top of her breasts. I glide the tip of my finger around her nipple. She shivers in my arms as goosebumps break out along her skin.

"You're distracting me," she complains, but she arches her back to thrust her breasts into my hands.

Who am I to reject such a wonderful gift? I knead the mounds until her nipples are hard and she's squirming beneath me.

"We're supposed to be talking," she gasps out as I pinch her nipple.

While I bend over to lick the petal soft skin around her areola, I glance up at her to ask, "What do you want to talk about?"

"What?" she wheezes.

"You wanted to talk." I drop my gaze, so she doesn't notice the humor in mine.

She wraps her legs around my waist and grinds against my cock. Fuck it. We'll talk later. I press my cock at her opening but before I can slide into heaven, her phone rings.

"Ignore it," I demand as I nibble on her neck.

"Can't. Family. May. Be. Emergency."

I growl in annoyance, but I reach for her phone on the bedside table and hand it to her.

"H-h-hello."

"Act normal," I whisper into her ear. I lick a line from her ear down to her shoulder. She tilts her neck to give me better access. "Phone," I remind her.

She clears her throat before answering. "Hello."

She listens for a second before responding. "What? You have a package for me?"

Satisfied the phone call isn't an emergency, I thrust my cock against her. "I've got a package for you."

She glares at me, but her legs tighten around my waist to keep my cock snuggled against her seam.

"It doesn't fit in my mailbox? How big is this package?"

I thrust my cock against her seam again. "It's big enough to do the job."

She slaps my shoulder. "Knock it off. I'm talking about a package delivery."

I waggle my eyebrows. "So am I."

She rolls her eyes. "Corny."

"I think you mean horny."

"I'm still here," she responds into the phone. Not for long if I have my way.

While she listens to whoever's on the phone, I decide to up my game. I sneak my hand down between our bodies until I find her clit. I rub it until her legs quiver before moving further down to plunge two fingers into her. Her walls clench around me, and I know she's close.

"I-I-I"

I grab the phone from her and end the call before throwing it across the room. It clatters to the floor.

"Come for me, sweetheart. Now."

I thrust my fingers in and out of her until her back bows and she shouts, "Yes! River!"

I wait until she collapses on the bed before removing my fingers and hitching my cock at her entrance. "Look at me, sweetheart," I growl.

Her chin dips until our eyes meet. Hers are full of wonder. Damn. I hope she spends the rest of her life looking at me this way.

With our gazes connected, I glide into her. She's hot and wet and freaking perfect. Heaven. I've found heaven and I want to spend the rest of my life here.

"You feel fantastic. Better than anything I've ever felt before."

I lift up onto my elbows and gaze down at our joining. My cock is covered in her juices. Shit. I'm not wearing a condom.

"Condom." I should pull out and put one on, but I don't want to move away from Elizabeth.

Her hands clench my shoulders. "No need. I'm clean and I get the shot."

"I've never had sex without a condom before."

She smiles. "I'm glad I can be your first."

"You're my first and last," I grit out before slamming into her. "There will never be another."

Her fingernails prick my skin as she holds on for the ride. There's no finesse. There's no teasing. I'm too far gone for either of those. My balls slap against her skin as I plunge into her again and again. It's not long before my lower back tingles as my climax draws near.

"I'm almost there. Join me."

Her hands move from my shoulders to play with her breasts. Fuck. Just when I thought this couldn't get any better. She plucks at her nipples and her walls quiver around my cock. Hell yeah.

The cliff is fast approaching. "Come. Come with me. Now."

Her head falls back as she moans. "Yeeeees."

Any rhythm I had fails me as I come. "Fuck. Fuck. Fuck."

I collapse on top of her. I know I'm squashing her, but I can't move yet.

"I'm getting tested today and then we're never using a condom again," I mutter against her skin.

Her body shakes beneath me. "Did you forget it's New Year's Day?"

I lift up and roll off of her. "It's not New Year's Day. It's Hogmanay."

"What's the difference?"

I stand and shackle her wrist before dragging her off of the bed. "You'll see. First, it's time to shower."

"My shower isn't big enough for the two of us."

I wink at her over my shoulder. "We'll make it work."

It doesn't work.

An hour later, Elizabeth emerges from the bedroom and stomps to the kitchen. I hand her a cup of coffee. "I said I'm sorry."

"Are you sorry for almost drowning me or for getting my hair wet?"

"Both?" I don't understand what the big deal is about getting her hair wet. Does she not wash it every day anyway?

She glares at me over the rim of her cup as she drinks her coffee.

"We'll have to use my shower next time."

She sets her coffee down on the counter. "We never did talk."

I circle her waist with my arm and draw her near. "What's there to talk about?"

She doesn't hesitate to answer. "Are you certain you're ready for a relationship?"

"If the relationship is with you, then yes, I'm certain."

She studies me for a minute before nodding. "Okay. Talk over."

"Just like that?" In my experience when a woman says we need to talk, she usually means she wants to rant and rage at me for at least an hour.

"Just like that."

I press my lips to hers for a quick kiss. "Perfect. You're perfect."

And she's all mine. I'm never letting her go.

Chapter 32

Faker – someone who pretends to be sick because he caught a case of the scaredy-cats

I skip as we walk toward the Alston family home. "What is Hogmanay? And how is it different from New Year's Day?"

"I can't tell you how it's different from New Year's Day since I've never experienced January 1st anywhere else than Winter Falls."

"Stop stalling and explain Hogmanay. Or is there a reason you won't tell me?" I stop and whirl around to face him when an idea hits me. "Or is this one of those lottery things?"

"Lottery things? What are you talking about?"

"You know the movie where they picked one person to sacrifice each year to guarantee good things for the rest of the residents of the town for the upcoming year."

"I thought you loved romantic comedies."

I shrug. "I also enjoy horror."

He tugs on one of my curls. "And yet you made me suffer through romantic comedies every time we had a movie night."

"You didn't seem to be suffering when you were stuffing your mouth full of popcorn and cookies."

He pats his stomach. "I had to spend hours and hours working out to make up for those evenings."

"Enough with the delays. Tell me. Do I need to be worried about being sacrificed?"

He wraps an arm around my waist and pulls me near before kissing my nose. "No, crazy girl with way too much imagination, you don't have to worry about being sacrificed. Although, I'm down to role-play tonight."

"If we're role-playing, I want to be someone strong. Maybe Wonder Woman."

"Will you wear the red bustier with a blue skirt and red boots while carrying a lasso?"

I narrow my eyes on him. His description was awfully specific. "Why do I have the feeling you already have the costume?"

He chuckles as he takes my hand. "We need to get going or we'll be late."

Notice he didn't answer my question. I need to drop it. I don't want to know about other women he's role-played with before. I knew he wasn't innocent the first time we were together. I can't exactly retroactively complain about it. And I refuse to compete with those women. None of them were worth making an effort for. I am, I remind myself.

I force a smile on my face. "Late for what?"

"For the first footing."

First footing? Is footing even a word? "What's the first footing?"

"Traditionally, it's when you visit family or friends immediately after midnight of January first in order to become the first person to visit them and enter their house in the new year."

I feign checking my watch. I don't actually wear one, but I know it's nowhere near midnight. "It's almost noon. We are definitely not going to be the first footers. Is that the right word?"

"No worries, sweetheart. Winter Falls changed the tradition to noon instead of midnight after a few kids walked in on their neighbors in compromising positions."

"Seriously? This is Winter Falls. You'd think Mrs. West would have used the opportunity to explain how sex is natural and a symbol of love, etcetera, etcetera."

"She tried, but she lost the vote to the parents who wanted to celebrate the new year without kids interrupting them."

I giggle. "Makes sense." I wouldn't have wanted anyone interrupting us last night. No way. No how.

"River," a man barks as we approach him on the sidewalk.

"Mercury. Happy Hogmanay. Have you met Elizabeth?"

I wave.

His eyes narrow on me. "Are you one of them Dempsey girls?"

"I am."

He harrumphs. "Don't cause any trouble," he orders before continuing on his way.

"Wow. Someone's the definition of grumpy old man," I say as I watch him walk away.

"That was him being sweet," River says.

"No way."

"Trust me. For some reason, the old man likes you Dempsey girls."

I beam up at him. "We are pretty awesome."

He tweaks my nose. "You ready for this?"

"Yep." He starts down the walkway to his parent's house, but I yank on his hand to stop him. "Wait. Should we have brought a gift?"

He lifts the bag he's carrying. "Dark rye bread and a lump of coal."

I frown at him. "I feel there's stuff about this Hogmanay you're not telling me."

"It's no big secret. Dark rye bread – aka black bun – is to ensure the people you visit don't go hungry in the year ahead and the lump of coal is to ensure the house remains warm in the coming months."

"But coal is bad for the environment." And Winter Falls does not compromise on the environment. I'd say they take it too far, but I'm dating a man who makes his living from providing environmental tours to tourists.

"Which is why the coal isn't real."

My nose wrinkles. "You're carrying a fake piece of coal and a loaf of bread in your bag? I thought your dirty underwear was in there."

"Nope. I left those on the floor of your bedroom."

I slap his chest. "You did not."

He leads me up the porch steps to the front door and barges inside without knocking. "Happy Hogmanay. The first footers have arrived."

"Too slow, brother. Too slow. We were here first," Phoenix claims.

"Liar. We were first," Lyric says. "Your streak of being the first footer has officially ended."

"Oh no. This is my fault. Well, it's not exactly my fault. There was a package delivery, but the package was bigger than I expected. It was too big for the mailbox and …" I trail off when I realize everyone is shaking with contained mirth.

"What? I'm not lying. There was a package delivery."

Lyric cocks an eyebrow. "Is that what we're calling it now?"

My face flames as I realize how my words sounded. "I wasn't referring to …" I wave a hand toward River. "I meant …"

Phoenix and Lyric burst into laughter. "Whatever. I'm going to find my sister."

River palms my neck to bring me near before kissing my forehead. "Be good, sweetheart."

Gabrielle's chatting with Aspen in the dining room. "How was your package delivery?" Aspen asks with a wink when I enter.

I groan. "You heard?"

She wiggles her eyebrows. "And how big was the package?"

Gabrielle holds up her hands. "I don't want to know."

I pull out a seat and fall into it. "Me and my awkward mouth."

Radiance sashays into the room. "Don't say awkward."

Aspen looks River's mom up and down. "And where have you been?"

She pats her hair. "Getting ready." She's lying. Her hair is a mess, and her lipstick is smeared.

Ever strolls in behind her wearing a shit eating grin. "I'll get the champagne." He slaps his wife's ass as he passes her, and she giggles like a teenager.

"Dad," River whines.

I sigh. I want to be like his parents when I'm older. Still having sex and embarrassing the hell out of my kids.

We gather in the living room and Radiance hands out champagne glasses. Aspen sniffs the bubbly and her head rears back before she shoves the glass in Lyric's hand and rushes out of the room. The sound of retching reaches us and Lyric grunts before following his wife.

"Someone celebrated a bit too much last night," Phoenix teases.

"I think an announcement is upon us," Radiance sings.

"It's about damn time," Ever grumbles.

I lean close to whisper to Gabrielle. "What are they talking about?"

"Do you think she's okay?" She bites her lip as she stares after the hallway where Aspen disappeared.

Phoenix pulls her near. "Lyric is with her."

I catch River drinking his champagne. "Knock it off. You have to wait for the toast."

"Aspen is a puker when she's been drinking. Trust me. I grew up with her. Ask me about the morning after she stole a bottle of peach schnapps sometime." He shivers. "This may take a while." He refills his glass, but I growl at him and he sets it down.

"This is the best Hogmanay in the history of Hogmanay," Radiance says.

"What are you talking about, Mom?" River asks.

"Aspen's obviously pregnant." The smile on her face stretches from ear to ear.

"It's true," Aspen says as she joins us. Her forehead is covered in sweat and her face is white, but she's glowing as she leans into Lyric for strength.

"But you were drinking champagne last night," River insists.

"Alcohol-free. I didn't want anyone to know about the baby until we had a chance to tell Radiance and Ever. And you know Lilac would have sussed it out if I wasn't drinking."

Radiance clutches her chest. "You didn't tell Ruby first?"

"Mom already has two grandchildren. This is your first."

Radiance squeals before rushing to Aspen and throwing her arms around her. I smile as I watch the woman I want to be my mother-in-law hug the woman who's already claimed me as her sister. I wind my arm around River. And this is the man I want to be by my side during it all.

I grin up at him, but he glances away. "I need to use the bathroom."

I frown as I watch him walk away, but I soon forget his grumpiness when Gabrielle joins me. "I don't fancy the idea of getting sick all the time."

I bump her hip. "Do you have something to tell me?"

She frowns. "Not yet."

For the first time since I discovered she's trying to get pregnant, I don't feel a ball of envy in my stomach clawing at me to lash out at her. Nope. I'm happy for my little sister. It helps I finally landed the man of my dreams.

"It'll happen. You haven't been trying long."

River returns to the room and announces, "I'm going home. I'm not feeling great."

Really? He was perfectly healthy this morning. "Let me get my things and I'll go with you."

"Nah. I'm no fun to be around when I'm ill."

Liar. The last time he got a cold he begged me to sit with him and watch movies because he didn't want to be alone.

"I'll phone you later," he calls as he waves and leaves.

Waves? What the hell? He couldn't bother to kiss me goodbye? What crawled up his ass? I don't know what's going on, but I will find out.

Chapter 33

Fault – cannot always be attributed to the 'bad' guy in the situation

I MARCH TOWARD RIVER'S front door like I'm on a mission. There's no 'like' about it. I am a woman on a mission. On a mission to figure out what crawled up his butt. This morning he was all 'you're fantastic' and 'I never felt better'. This afternoon he couldn't run away fast enough.

I know he hasn't been in a relationship for over a decade, but come on, you don't treat friends this way, let alone lovers.

I pause with my hand poised to knock on his door. Maybe I'm blowing this whole situation up because I'm feeling insecure. I never thought I – of the uncontrollable red hair and freckles – could tame a player. Why would River be any different? This is a bad idea. I should go home.

Home. Where I'll obsess about River all night and get exactly zero sleep. No. I straighten my shoulders. I need to know what's happening. I'm not putting this off.

I knock on the door and wait, but nothing happens. I can see lights flashing in the living room indicating River's watching television, but he doesn't answer the door. Maybe he's in the bathroom. Maybe he really is sick. And maybe I'm going to drive myself crazy with all these thoughts swirling around my mind.

I count to thirty and knock again. This time when he doesn't answer I begin banging on the door.

"Hold your horses, Lyric. I'm coming already."

He swings the door open, and his eyes widen. "Elizabeth. I thought you were Lyric."

I indicate my dress and three-inch heels. "Obviously not."

I wait but he doesn't greet me with a kiss on the cheek or even a smile. And he definitely doesn't invite me in. Damn. The minuscule drop of hope I was clinging to that I was blowing things out of proportion perishes. There's something wrong. Very wrong.

"Are you going to invite me in?"

I don't wait for his answer and push my way past him. He sighs as he shuts the door behind me.

"Feeling better?" I motion toward the remnants of a pizza and empty beer bottles on his coffee table.

"Um. Yeah?" He runs a hand over his beard.

I cross my arms over my chest and tap my toe. "You weren't sick."

"I wasn't sick," he admits.

"What's wrong?"

"You want a beer?"

He doesn't wait for my answer before going to the kitchen to grab two bottles. He hands one to me. When he makes certain our fingers don't touch, I realize the situation is worse than I thought.

Crap. I know what's going on here. The thrill of the chase is over and now he's regretting his decision. I should have known. I'm not the woman who can tame a wild man.

I slam my beer down on the table and the liquid explodes outward. I'm not going to apologize for the mess I made, though. Asses can clean up their own damn messes.

"What the hell is wrong with you?"

River glares at me. I don't know what he has to glare about. I'm the injured party here.

"What's wrong with me?"

I growl. I hate it when someone answers a question with a question. "Do you need me to repeat the question again? What. The. Hell. Is. Wrong. With. You?"

"I thought I could do this. I can't."

This? Us this? My heart stalls in my chest and I forget how to breathe.

"What are you saying?" I manage to choke out.

"You want children."

Can you get whiplash from a conversation? His answer makes no sense. "Where's this coming from?"

"I saw your face when Aspen announced she's pregnant. You want that. Babies. A family. A white picket fence."

"I don't understand what the big deal is."

"You didn't deny you want children."

"Because I do want children."

"I don't."

"Ever?"

"Ever."

I need a drink for this conversation. I pick up my beer and notice half of it spilled onto the table and floor. I down the remaining half while I contemplate the situation. At least he's not bored of me. Silver lining.

"Let me get this straight." I pace as I speak. "You were a complete jerk to your brother and sister-in-law after their big announcement because you don't want children."

"May—"

"I'm not done yet," I snarl. "Then, you took off without a proper goodbye to me – your supposed girlfriend of less than twenty-four hours – because I want children someday."

When he doesn't respond, I motion at him. "You may speak now."

"I'm not some villain in a crappy romcom movie."

"First of all, romcom movies are never crappy. Furthermore, I'm summing things up. If you sound like a villain…" I shrug. "If it looks like a duck and quacks like a duck, it's probably a duck."

He grunts. "I'm not evil because I don't want children."

"I didn't say you were." And I didn't. Did I imply he was a jerk? Why yes, yes, I did. "Aren't you excited to become an uncle?"

"Yeah." The corners of his lips tip up. "I'm happy for Lyric and Aspen. They hit a major bump in the road, but they managed to make it work."

"Maybe you should tell them how you feel," I suggest.

"Crap. I was an asshole, wasn't I?"

"I'm glad you're starting to see things my way."

"I'll call Lyric and soothe things over."

"Good."

"But this changes nothing."

"What do you mean?"

He motions between the two of us. "We want different things. You want your white picket fence."

I growl. "I swear if you say picket fence one more time …" I shake my fist at him.

He chuckles but quickly sobers. "You know what I mean. You want children, a family. I don't."

"Ever? You never ever want to have children?" I heard what he said the first time, but I need confirmation.

He shakes his head. "No. I'm sorry."

"How long have you felt this way?"

He glances away.

"Let me guess. The 'I never want children'-crap goes hand in hand with the whole 'love isn't for me'-crap."

"Maybe." He shrugs. "But I don't want to give you hope I'll change my mind."

"Give me hope? This is all about me, is it?" Snarky Elizabeth has arrived at the party.

He grasps my hands. "I don't want you to regret being with me."

Regret being with him? Is this the end of us? "Are you breaking up with me?"

Is there an award for shortest relationship ever? Because I think I just won. We didn't even make it a whole day. This is not an award I will cherish.

He squeezes my hands. "No. I mean maybe. I mean I don't know."

I yank my hands away and retreat a few steps. "Well, which is it? Yes? No? Maybe isn't an answer."

He stuffs his hands in his pockets and shrugs. "It's up to you."

My brow wrinkles. "It's up to me whether you break up with me?" I snort. "No. I am not shouldering the blame for this break-up, Casanova."

"I don't blame you. This is all my fault." His green eyes are full of sincerity as he holds my gaze. "I meant it's up to you. You have to choose if you can stay with me despite knowing I will never give you children."

Crap. This is not how I expected the first day of the new year to go after I decided to give River a chance. I knew the likelihood of ending up with a broken heart was high. Probably more than fifty percent given his history. But I had hope. Hope which is quickly fading away.

"You're firm on this? You won't consider the possibility of someday having children?"

Maybe I can change his mind. He changed his tune on the 'love is a crock'-thing after all.

"I don't want to give you false hope."

"But—"

He places a finger over my mouth to quiet me. "No, sweetheart. You can't change my mind."

My shoulders deflate and I take a step back forcing him to drop his hand. Can I stay with River knowing he will never want to have children with me? Never want to build a family with me?

Since Mom and Dad died when I was ten, all I've dreamed of is having my own children and building a family. I love River with all my heart. He's the man of my dreams. But can I stay with him when staying with him means I have to give up the biggest dream of my life?

"I need time to think."

"Of course. Take all the time you need."

"I …" I slam my mouth shut before I utter words of love. He has a hard enough time believing any woman could love him. I'm not going to say I love him now and bring up all his past issues. It's not the right time or place.

"I'll be in touch," I say instead. "I should go. I didn't get much sleep last night and I've got a busy day tomorrow. A busy week actually. It's T minus seven days until *Glitter N Bliss* opens its doors."

"Of course. How could I forget?"

He steps toward me, but I flee before he can touch me. If he touches me now, I'll throw away all my dreams without a second thought.

"See you," I shout as I rush out the door and down the steps.

I don't stop until I'm around the corner. I lean against a tree as I gulp in big breaths of air. I was this close to getting everything I wanted. This close! I should have known better. Good things don't happen to plain girls like me.

I sniff and suck up the tears welling in my eyes. I refuse to fall apart outside where anyone can see me. I wouldn't be surprised if the gossip gals have their binoculars trained on me now. I push off of the tree and march home where I can break down in private.

Chapter 34

Parent – someone who gives advice whether it's welcomed or not

I WANT MY MOM. I don't care how childish it makes me sound. I want my mommy.

There have been a million times I've wanted my mom since she passed away. When I had my first period, when I had my first crush, when I had questions about sex. But never have I needed to talk to her as much as I do now.

Especially as I don't have anyone else to discuss this messed up situation with. I refuse to burden Gabrielle with my problems when she's currently working on creating her own family. And Cassandra? Snort. No way will she be sympathetic. The woman's allergic to the l-word.

Do I stay with the man I love knowing he will never give me children? The question rolled around in my mind all night while I tossed and turned in bed. I finally gave up on sleep and now I'm pacing around *Glitter N Bliss.* I'm supposed to be reviewing the punch list, but I can't concentrate on the list of items to be completed before the spa can open.

"Hello!" someone hollers as she knocks on the front door.

I wasn't expecting anyone. Although, it's Winter Falls. I shouldn't be surprised. Dropping by unannounced is practically a national sport in this town.

I open the door to Ruby and Radiance. What are Lilac's mom and River's mom doing here? Together? And should I be scared?

Ruby hands me a mug of coffee. "Here. You need this."

I do, but how does she know?

Radiance lifts a basket. "And I brought strawberry muffins."

How does she know strawberry is my favorite? Silly question. There's probably a profile of my likes and dislikes floating around the town.

I sip on the coffee while they barge inside and make themselves comfortable on folding chairs since the furniture for the waiting room has yet to be delivered. Radiance taps the chair next to her.

"I always knew River was going to be the son to give me heartburn."

"Not Lyric?" Ruby asks.

Radiance rolls her eyes. "Lyric's been in love with your daughter since kindergarten. I never worried about him."

Ruby raises her eyebrows. "Not even when I suspended him for the skunk incident?"

"Teenagers," Radiance says as if the word is an answer.

"Come. Come." She motions me to the chair. "We have a lot to discuss."

I sit down next to her. "We do?"

"This place is coming along," Ruby says as she scans the area.

"Thank you?" I'm confused. Are they here to discuss the spa? Do they want jobs?

Radiance pats my hand. "There's no reason to be nervous, dear. We're here to help."

"You want to help me go through the punch list?"

"What's a punch list?" Ruby asks.

Okay, they're not here to help with the spa. Why are they here then? And can I ask them or is this some kind of Winter Falls business owner initiation ritual? I wouldn't be surprised if it is. Winter Falls put the K in kooky.

"No distractions," Radiance scolds Ruby before addressing me again. "We're here to help you with River."

"River? How do you know?"

She leans close. "Know what, my dear?"

"Know he doesn't want children," I blurt out.

Radiance frowns. "I was afraid of this."

Ruby chuckles. "Your boy does enjoy being contradictory."

"You remember the time he climbed to the roof of the school to prove he wasn't afraid of heights?"

"Of course. I was the one who called the fire department to help get him down when he froze with fear up there."

"But River is a volunteer firefighter now," I point out. Firefighters can't be afraid of heights, can they?

"Because he learned to conquer his fears."

I have a feeling there's an underlying conversation happening here. One I don't understand.

"I'm afraid you're going to have to spell things out for me. I haven't had a mother for twenty years. I don't understand the nuances."

Radiance clutches her chest. "Did you hear? She compared me to her mom."

"Naturally. You are her mother-in-law after all."

"Um. I hate to point this out – and no offense, Radiance, because you are lovely – but you aren't my mother-in-law." No matter how much I may wish it differently.

She grins. "Not yet."

"Actually, not ever if I can't accept River's announcement."

She digs a strawberry muffin out of her basket and hands it to me. "Here. I think you're going to need this."

My stomach growls as the scent of strawberry, vanilla, and almond hits me. Yum. I bite into the muffin and moan.

"This is good," I say as I chew.

"I make them from strawberry preserves I can in the summer."

I swallow. "Strawberry preserves?"

"I'll drop a batch off at your apartment."

I think I'm in love with River's mom. She would be a great mother-in-law to have.

Ruby consults her watch. "We need to hurry if we want to finish this discussion before the gossip gals arrive."

I gulp. "The gossip gals?"

I eye the back door to the alley. Maybe I can escape before they get here. Because those women scare me. Don't ask me how five elderly women can be terrifying. They just are.

"Okay. Let's hear it. What's wrong?" Radiance asks.

"What do you mean what's wrong? How does everyone know there's a problem?"

She smiles. "You're not used to Winter Falls yet, are you my dear?" I shrug and she explains, "You were seen leaving River's house last night with a devastated look on your face."

"I heard she was bawling her eyes out," Ruby adds.

"I wasn't crying. I waited until I got home to fall apart." Crap. I wasn't planning on confessing to anyone how much of a crybaby I am.

Radiance grasps my hands. "I'm sorry."

"Sorry for what?"

"For whatever idiotic thing my son did. I swear I did raise my boys right."

"She did," Ruby pipes in. "I was there. She taught them how to cook and clean and how to treat a woman properly."

Radiance's lips purse. "I went wrong with River somewhere. He hasn't exactly been exemplary in his treatment of women this past decade."

"It's not your fault."

Radiance ignores Ruby to tell me, "I've waited a long time for you."

"For me?" I croak.

"Yes. The woman to tame my River."

I shake my head. "I'm not the woman to tame any man."

I'm plain old Elizabeth with the crazy curly hair and more freckles than the law should allow. I can't compete with the plentitude of women throwing themselves at River.

She squeezes my hands. "Obviously, you're wrong since River is crazy about you."

My heart skips a beat. Is River really crazy about me? He did agree to try for a relationship with me and not any of the other gazillion women he's been with over the past decade. Maybe I am more than plain Elizabeth. Except he gave me an ultimatum last night.

"I'm sorry, Radiance, but I don't think I'm the woman for River."

"Which brings us to the point of this morning's gathering."

"Finally," Ruby mutters.

"What happened?"

This is what I get for wishing my mom was here. Now, I have two mothers to deal with. Two mothers who don't seem to understand the problem despite my telling them.

"I told you. River doesn't want children."

"Yes?" Radiance asks as if there's more to the explanation. There's not.

"There isn't anything more. He doesn't want children. I do. I've always dreamed of building a family and having children." I yank my hands from hers to motion to the area around us. "I built this entire business, so I could have flexible working hours when my children arrive. I even added a children's play area for when I bring my future children into work."

My eyes itch and my nose twitches, but I suck in big gulps of air to stop the tears from falling.

Radiance wraps her arms around me and pulls me near. She sways me from side to side. "There. There. Dear. There. There."

Ruby pats my back. "It's not the end of the world."

I push away from Radiance. "It's not? The man I love is asking me to give up my dream."

"No."

"No, what?" I ask Radiance.

"You are not giving up your dreams."

Ruby glares at her. "You can't make her decisions for her. She needs to make them for herself."

Radiance motions toward me. "Hasn't she already made it? She's only torturing herself with this."

I chew on my bottom lip as I listen to them. Is Radiance right? Have I already made my decision? My heart clenches and my stomach dips as I realize I have.

I'm going to let the man I love go. I can't give up my dream of having a family for anyone. Not even the man of my dreams. This is going to hurt worse than hell.

"You-hoo!" A knock on the door brings me out of my reverie. My eyes widen when I catch Sage and all her gossip gal gang waving at us through the glass.

Radiance pushes me toward the rear. "Go. We'll hold them off."

"How do you know they won't follow me?" I wouldn't put it past the gossip gals to chase me down the street.

She winks at me. "We got this."

I don't hesitate again. I sprint for the back door.

Chapter 35

Heartbreak – not metaphorical when you're experiencing it

"Hey," River greets when I open my door to him.

"Hey," I murmur with absolutely no enthusiasm at all.

His eyes flash with pain, but he blinks and his lopsided smile appears. "Can I come in?"

I motion him inside. As he passes, he kisses my cheek and I breathe in his outdoorsy scent of pine and grass. I need to memorize it for later because after this conversation I doubt we'll be alone in my living room again.

Damn. River was right. Having sex did ruin our friendship.

"You want a beer?" I don't wait for an answer before scrounging two beers from the refrigerator. It's official. I'm procrastinating.

Can you blame me? I don't want my relationship with River to end. I know it has to, but my heart doesn't want to let go.

I hand him his beer and settle on the sofa. He sits next to me. Close, but not touching. As much as I want to touch him, I'm thankful. I don't think I can have this conversation if we're touching. My mind turns to mush when we touch.

I sip on my beer as I gather my courage. I can do this. I'm a big girl. So what if it's the first time I've broken up with a man. It can't be difficult. Enough men have broken up with me. I know the drill. Although, I'm not going to call River plain or boring. There's nothing plain or boring about River.

I play with the label of my beer. "We need to talk."

"I kind of figured you wanted to talk when you sent me a message asking me to come over so we can talk."

I elbow him. "Wise guy."

He squeezes my thigh. "Go ahead, Bessie. I won't hurt you."

Won't hurt me? Does breaking my heart not count? Because my heart is currently bleeding and aching from being torn in two.

I swallow before setting my beer down and facing him. "I have to tell you something."

He smiles in encouragement.

"I love you," I blurt out.

His eyes widen in surprise. He's not the only one who's surprised. I didn't plan to say those three little words. I rehearsed this entire conversation in front of the mirror a gazillion times last night. In not one of those rehearsals did I say I love you.

Welp. I'm in this now. I might as well go with the flow.

He opens his mouth to respond, but I stop him with a finger on his lips. Mistake. I shouldn't touch him. I yank my hand away.

"I don't expect you to say the words back to me. I know you have a hard time believing in love." He nods and I continue, "I love you and I will always love you, but I can't be with you."

Pain flashes in his green eyes before he shuts them and his chin drops to his chest.

"I'm sorry," I croak out. I clear my throat and try again. "I'm sorry. I made a mess of things."

His eyes fly open. "No. You didn't make a mess of things, Bessie. You could never make a mess of things. You're perfect, sweetheart."

If I'm so perfect, why don't you want to have children with me? I know better than to ask the question out loud. Never ask a question you don't want to hear the answer to.

"I had a conversation with your mom yesterday," I say instead of bringing up the elephant in the room.

He cocks a brow. "Yeah?"

"She's awesome. I wish…" I shake my head as I cut myself off. I'm not going to make things worse by wishing for things that will never come to be. Radiance will never be my mother-in-law.

"She's pretty awesome until she figures out you stole the high school mascot's uniform and accidentally set the costume on fire ruining it."

"Accidentally?"

He shrugs.

"Aren't you supposed to be a firefighter?"

"Why do you think I became a firefighter?"

"To pick up girls?"

Damnit. Why did I bring up his player ways? Wait. He's no longer a player. His Casanova days are behind him. Shit. He's going to find another woman to love and it isn't going to be me. Meanwhile, we live in the same small town, and I'll have a front row seat to his falling in love.

"Never mind. I didn't ask you here to discuss your Casanova days."

"I'm here because you're breaking up with me."

I swipe at the moisture forming in my eyes. "Yeah."

"It's okay, Bessie. There's no need to cry."

He scoots closer and his hands cradle my face while his thumbs wipe at the tears falling down my cheeks.

"I'm not crying. You're crying."

He chuckles but the sound is empty of humor. "Please stop crying."

I hiccup. "I can't help it." Hiccup. "I finally found you and now I have to let you go."

"You'll find someone else. I know you will. You're sweet and supportive and funny when you're feeling all awkward. And totally cute when you're a klutz."

I shove his shoulders but he doesn't budge an inch. "I'm not a klutz."

"Of course not. And you don't accidentally spout sexual innuendos either."

"You're supposed to pretend not to notice."

He cocks an eyebrow. "When have I ever pretended with you?"

I squint my eyes and feign thinking about his question. "When you claimed to enjoy watching romantic comedies?"

He kisses my nose. "I do enjoy watching those cliché movies when I'm with you."

My mind flashes to all the evenings we spent sitting on this very couch laughing and watching movies while stuffing our faces with pizza and strawberry ice cream. I want more of those nights, but I can't have them. At least not yet.

"They're not cliché," I claim

"Really? Overused tropes aren't cliché?"

"I want to be mad at you, but I'm proud of you for knowing the word trope."

"I listened to you, Elizabeth. I heard every word you said."

The tears I'd managed to stop flow down my cheeks once again. "Stop being sweet. I can't break up with you if you're sweet."

He leans his forehead against mine. "How about I break up with you then?"

I hiccup. "Yeah?" Another hiccup. "Why are you breaking up with me? Am I not perfect?"

My attempt at humor falls flat when he winces.

"You are perfect. Too perfect for a fucked up mess like me."

"You're not fucked up," I whisper. "You're the man of my dreams."

He winces. "Except I don't want children."

"I'm sorry. I know I should compromise. Relationships are all about compromise."

"But you can't give up your dream," he finishes for me.

"I'm sorry."

"Stop saying you're sorry. This is my fault."

"Why don't we agree it's no one's fault?"

His hands caress my cheeks, and my eyes fall closed. I memorize the feel of the callouses on his thumbs touching me as he kisses my eyelids.

"I'll always care for you, Elizabeth Elaine."

"And I'll always love you, River Atlas."

He wraps his arms around me, and I fall into his embrace. I don't know how long we stay on my couch clinging to each other. It could be five minutes, it could be five hours.

I don't want to move. I want to take back every word I said, but I know it would be a mistake. I have to be true to me. No matter how much it hurts.

"I have no regrets."

And I don't. I may have ruined our friendship by pushing for more, but I wouldn't give up the moments I've spent with him for anything in the world. I'm going to cherish those memories for the rest of my life. And, hopefully, one day, I can remember without a shooting pain stabbing my heart.

His arms loosen until he can glance down at me. "Me either. I'd do it all over again."

He stands and I follow him to the door. He pulls on one of my curls and I bat his hand away. He smiles as he opens the door.

"See ya around, Bessie."

I nod because it's impossible to speak around the lump in my throat.

I watch him walk down the hallway and away from me. He doesn't glance back. When I can't see him any longer, I shut the door before collapsing on the floor. Why does doing the right thing hurt this much?

I want to run out the door and chase River and beg him to come back. I actually grab hold of the doorknob and start to stand, but I stop myself. I will not be the wishy washy woman who can't make up her mind. No, I will stick to my guns on this.

I curl up in a ball on the floor and let the pain wash over me.

Chapter 36

Sister from a different mister – a woman who has decided you're family and she's going to help you with your problems. Note – 'help' is subjective

I'M STILL LAYING ON the floor some time later when the door opens and bangs against me.

"It's stuck," Gabrielle says.

"Here. Let me."

Before Juniper can follow through, I stop her. "The door isn't stuck."

Gabrielle peeks her head around the door. Her eyes widen when she discovers me on the floor. "It's worse than we thought."

I ignore her comment to ask, "What are you doing here?"

Juniper appears behind Gabrielle. "We're your sisters. We're here to cheer you up."

"You're not my sister."

"I told you," Lilac says as she shoves to the front of the group, "the definition of sister is someone who has the same parents as you."

"What about sisters from a different mister?" Ashlyn asks.

This argument could go on forever. I get to my feet and open the door. "Come in before the entire apartment building knows my business."

Aspen laughs as she enters. "You still don't understand Winter Falls. Everyone already knows your business."

I groan as I shut the door behind them. I scan the group. All of the West sisters are here, but I'm missing a Dempsey sister. Well, two Dempsey sisters, but we don't discuss Olivia.

"Where's Cassandra?"

As if on cue, the door opens and she breezes in. "I'm here."

"Whoa. Someone's been playing with the one-eyed snake." Ashlyn points to Cassandra's shirt, which is buttoned incorrectly. "Who's the guy? And why don't we know about him?"

Cassandra quickly fixes her shirt. "Maybe because it's none of your business."

Ellery laughs. "Nice one. Try again."

"I thought we were here to cheer up my sister not to interrogate me."

Gabrielle studies our older sister. "She's deflecting. This isn't going to be good."

I shrug. I couldn't care less about Cassandra's love life at the moment. I've got my own troubles to drown in.

"Who brought the liquor?"

Cassandra flourishes the canvas bag she's holding. "Me."

"I hope it's not those Jack Frosties. My tongue was blue for days," Gabrielle complains.

"No worries. Today's cocktail of choice is corpse reviver."

"Corpse reviver?" Juniper shivers. "What the hell is in it? Does it raise the dead?"

"Gin, lemon juice, Cointreau, Lillet Blanc, and absinthe."

Aspen holds a hand over her stomach. "I never thought I'd say these words, but I'm glad I can't drink currently." Her eyes widen and she swears. "Shit. I'm sorry, Elizabeth. I didn't mean. I mean… Someone help me out here."

Lilac rolls her eyes. "She's embarrassed she reminded you of the reason you're heartbroken."

Aspen slaps Lilac. "What the hell? You made things worse."

"What?" Lilac appears genuinely confused. "Would you rather I pretend not to know? You should have—"

Aspen sticks her palm in Lilac's face. "Yeah, yeah, yeah. I should have filled out the form in triplicate."

Lilac's lips purse. "I do not make anyone fill out a form. I wish you'd stop saying I do."

I raise my hands and wait for them to stop bickering before asking, "Does everyone know?"

Ashlyn bats her eyelashes. "Know what?"

I stare at Lilac since I know she won't lie to me. "Yes, everyone knows you and River broke up because he doesn't want children."

Gabrielle grasps my hand. "What an idiot! Who wouldn't want children with Elizabeth?"

Cassandra stops her search of my kitchen cupboards to answer, "Me. I don't want children with my sister. Ew."

"She wasn't being literal," I point out.

Cassandra shrugs. "She should have said she wasn't being literal before posing the question."

"Can't you tell when a person is being metaphorical?"

Gabrielle sighs. "Too bad heartbreak doesn't influence your ability to bicker with Cassandra."

I snap my mouth closed. She's right. I shouldn't be fighting with my sister who came here to cheer me up. Except she's rummaging through my kitchen cupboards again.

"What are you looking for?"

"Cocktail glasses."

I stomp to the side table in the dining room and gather the cocktail glasses before walking to the kitchen and slamming them down on the counter.

"Stop going through my cupboards."

"Why? You don't keep your vibrator in here."

I'm not discussing vibrators with my sister. No way. No how. I return to the living room and collapse in my armchair.

"There's no use trying to cheer me up. All my cheer has left the building. Never to be seen again," I whine. Yes, whine. I'm allowed to whine after a break-up no matter how long the relationship lasted.

"You can't move away from Winter Falls." I'm not sure how Ashlyn's statement is supposed to cheer me up.

"Okay?"

"I'm serious. I've been looking forward to getting a massage at *Glitter N Bliss* since the town gave you permission to lease the building."

Aspen shoves Ashlyn. "We're not using her for her spa."

"Speak for yourself."

"We can swap apartments if you want," Cassandra offers as she hands me a cocktail glass filled with a cloudy liquid. "I wouldn't mind living in Winter Falls for a while."

"What about your job?"

She shrugs and walks away. What she doesn't do is answer the question.

"I'm not leaving town." I've worked too damn hard on my new spa to leave town now. I'll just avoid River until I don't feel as if my heart is breaking in two when I see him. It should only take a year or ten.

"Good. We'd miss you." Juniper smiles at me.

"White Bridge is a thirty-minute drive. She wouldn't be relocating to a foreign country," Lilac points out.

Juniper's nose wrinkles. "Who wants to live in White Bridge?"

"There's nothing wrong with White Bridge," Cassandra says as she hands out the rest of the cocktails to those who can drink alcohol. She raises her glass. "To getting over men who don't deserve us."

I have the distinct feeling she's not talking about River, but there's no sense asking her. She's all nosy as hell digging into your life, but when it comes to revealing information about her, she can't shut her mouth fast enough.

"Whoa," I say after a sip of my drink. "I hope someone brought food because one of these is going to have me drunk in no time."

Ashlyn rubs her hands together. "Awesome. Are you the type of drunk who would climb through a window into a person's house and steal their recipes?"

"Recipes?"

"Rowan won't give me the recipe for his red velvet with cream cheese glaze pancakes and mommy needs pancakes."

Ellery giggles. "Really? He gave the recipe to Cole."

"Which is why I'm asking Elizabeth to break into your house to get the recipe. You didn't seriously think I would ask her to break into my house, did you? Wait." Her attention returns to me. "Can you crack a safe?"

"Sorry. No."

"And Elizabeth isn't the type to do crazy shit when she drinks," Cassandra says.

"I leave all the crazy for my older sister."

"You got that right," Gabrielle mutters.

"Bummer." Ashlyn bats her eyelashes at Lilac.

"No."

"I didn't say a word."

Lilac raises an eyebrow. "You weren't going to ask me to crack the safe at your house?"

Ashlyn's nose wrinkles. "No?"

"Just because I don't lie doesn't mean I can't tell when someone's lying."

"But Rowan refuses to make me red velvet pancakes since I'm breastfeeding."

"Do you have a crowbar?" Aspen asks me.

"I don't think so."

"Too bad. We could use one to remove Ashlyn's foot from her mouth."

"What? I didn't …" Ashlyn's eyes widen when she realizes she was once again talking about her perfect family in front of the woman who will never have a family. Lucky for her, I find her amusing.

"We need to prank River." Cassandra slams her empty glass on the coffee table. "What do we know about him besides he's afraid of skunks?"

"Whoa! We're not pranking River," I insist.

"Why not?"

"Really? You don't remember the last time you pranked someone when you'd been drinking?"

"I only had one cocktail." Her hiccup at the end of the sentence makes her a liar. "Besides. It wasn't my fault the police showed up." She thumbs her finger at Aspen. "We've got police connections now. We won't end up in jail this time."

"I didn't end up in jail last time."

"Because you ran when you heard the sirens," Cassandra accuses.

"Of course, I ran! You dipped cotton balls in water and placed them all over the dean's car. And then you poured blue dye and dishwasher soap in the fountain in front of your dorm."

"It was a prank. I don't know why the police arrested me."

"The word you're looking for is vandalism," Aspen says.

"Who's in love with Cassandra right now?" Ashlyn's arm shoots into the air in response to her own question. "Why didn't I meet you before I had a baby?"

"What does being a mother have to do with anything? Did you lose the ability to prank when you pushed the munchkin out of you?"

Ashlyn sighs. "No, but I gained an overprotective husband who loses his mind whenever I even think of pulling a prank."

Her phone rings and she shows everyone the screen. *Molly-coddling man is calling.*

"This is interesting. You should answer the phone. I'd love to do a study on precognitive events."

Ashlyn snarls at Lilac. "Aren't you busy enough being CEO and presiding over a company?"

"I don't preside over the company. I'm the Chief Technology Officer."

"Whatever."

Ellery sits on the armrest of my chair. "I'm sorry. We did come here to cheer you up, but whenever all of us get together…" She shrugs.

"Actually, you did take my mind off my troubles. Too bad there aren't any snacks."

"Who was supposed to bring the snacks?" she shouts to be heard over her sisters who are now arguing about the difference between a board member and a manager. And I thought I knew how to squabble with Cassandra. I could follow a master class given by the West sisters.

"I brought movies," Juniper answers.

The doorbell rings and Aspen smirks. "And I brought the snacks."

"It doesn't count if you have your husband drive to White Bridge to pick up junk food," Ashlyn hollers after her.

"I guess you don't want any pizza then."

"I erase my comment from the record."

The first genuine smile I've felt in days crosses my face as I scan the room. I may not have love and children, but I've got a great family to support me when I'm down. It's not everything, but it's enough. For now.

Chapter 37

Dumbass – someone who doesn't realize he's making the worst mistake of his life

I nod to Lyric as I walk into the courthouse to meet my tour group. Thank god for the last-minute booking. I need something to do before I go out of my mind. I'm consumed with worry about Elizabeth.

Is she hurting? Does she hate me? Am I making a mistake? Should I have children with her? I'd do anything to make her happy. Maybe even have children. No, I shouldn't change for her. Should I?

"Hold up," Lyric hollers.

I tap my watch. "No time. I have a tour."

"Actually, you don't," Phoenix says as he joins us.

"What's going on?"

"We're here to stop you from making a dumbass mistake," Lyric answers.

"And I'm here to kick your ass," Beckett adds.

I rub a hand over my beard. I'm fucking tired of Elizabeth's brother threatening to kick my ass, although I probably deserve it after yesterday. Technically, Bessie broke up with me, but everyone in town knows it's my fault.

Sage rushes out of the police station. "Good. You haven't started yet."

Lyric points to the door she just exited from. "You need to return to work before I fire you."

She plants her hands on her hips. "You can't fire me. I changed your diapers."

"I need someone to be in charge while I'm away on business."

"I'll take over for you here with River and you can be in charge of the station."

A muscle ticks in Lyric's jaw. "This isn't a negotiation. Get back inside and do your job. I'm not going to ask you again."

"Fine," she huffs. "But if you screw this up and the gossip gals have to clean up your mess, I'm asking for double time."

"Get to work," he growls. A vein pulses in his forehead and he grits his teeth. He waits until the door shuts behind her before blowing out a breath. "Bane of my existence."

"Finally. It's time for some ass kicking."

"Who's tired of Beckett threatening to kick my ass?" I lift my hand and Lyric and Phoenix join me.

"You'd understand if you had sisters." He glares at me. "Sisters who you raised as your own after your parents died."

I lift my palms in surrender. "I know I fucked up."

I let the woman I love walk away from me. I more than fucked up. It took losing her for me to realize how I feel. But there's no denying it now. I love Elizabeth more than anything. She was right. Love is real and I'm a dumbass.

Lyric wraps an arm around my neck before rubbing his knuckles over my hair. "The first step to recovery is realizing your mistake."

I push him away. "Police brutality."

"Ah, did little River get his hair messed up by the big bad police chief?" he mocks.

I smooth my fingers through my hair. "You'd understand if you had good hair."

"Aspen thinks I have good hair. In fact, she enjoys threading her fingers through it while I—"

"Stop," Phoenix hollers. "You're talking about our sister-in-law."

Beckett and I nod in agreement. When he catches me agreeing with him, he scowls.

Lyric throws one arm around my shoulder and one arm around Beckett's shoulder. "Let's go."

Beckett plants his feet. "If you think I'm jumping into the falls again, you're out of your mind. It took two days for my balls to crawl out of my scrotum."

Lyric nudges him forward. "Okay, wimpy old man. We'll get a drink instead."

He's full of shit. Lyric had no intention of skinny dipping today. I follow him out of the courthouse building and down Main Street to *Electric Vibes*.

Lennon throws up his hands in surrender when we arrive at the bar. "Oh no. It's the fuzz."

Lyric rolls his eyes. "Can we get a pitcher of beer?"

Lennon leans close to whisper-shout. "I don't know. Can you? You're in uniform and strapped."

Lyric thumbs his finger at me. "It's for him."

Great. My brother is going to get me drunk and force me to talk about my feelings. I should have refused the tour group and stayed in bed. If I had known there was no tour group, I would have.

"Better add some chicken wings to our order. I'm not cleaning up River's puke," Phoenix adds.

I haven't thrown up after drinking since I was in college and some frat boy dared the 'country bumpkin' to play beer pong. Idiot didn't realize I was the beer pong champion of Winter Falls. Winning the dare was worth the two days I spent laying on the bathroom floor in my dorm room.

"I'm not puking."

He snorts. "You look ready to heave now."

"Whatever," I mumble since I am feeling nauseous at the idea of discussing my feelings with them.

We settle in a booth away from any other patrons. Although, considering it's not yet noon on a Tuesday, there aren't many people in the bar.

Lyric pours us beers and I down half my glass in one go. I wait for someone to speak, but everyone appears content to drink their beer in silence.

"Are you going to interrogate me or what?" I finally ask when the silence gets to me.

"I'll interrogate you," Lennon says as he drops a basket of chicken wings on the table. "What the hell were you thinking? I lost twenty bucks on you."

Phoenix chuckles. "You should have known better than to bet River would settle down. He's a player. He'll never settle."

"Yeah," Lyric agrees. "Our brother will spend the rest of his life having meaningless one-night stands. Eventually, he'll end up dying alone and his dog will eat his face off to keep from starving."

"I don't have a dog."

"Once he loses his hair, the women won't be interested anymore and he'll end up the pathetic old man who leers at women from his barstool," Beckett adds.

"What the hell? I'm not some pathetic loser."

Lyric cocks his brow. "You aren't?"

"Letting a good woman go because you're afraid of the future." Phoenix shakes his head.

"You're misrepresenting what happened."

Beckett sighs. "Too bad my sister fell in love with a coward."

"I am not a coward," I grit out.

"Really?" Lyric asks. "I'm pretty sure the definition of coward is a person afraid to do the hard stuff."

"I am not afraid to do the hard stuff."

Phoenix removes his hat and scratches his hair. "You're not afraid to have children?"

"Not wanting to have children doesn't make me a coward."

"Of course not. But you don't *not* want to have children."

"Wrong. I don't want children."

"Liar. You're afraid."

I growl. "Stop calling me a coward."

"If it looks like a duck, acts like a duck, it's probably a …"

"Duck!" Lyric and Beckett shout in unison.

"I'm not a duck and I'm not a coward and I'm not afraid. This is bullshit." I shove Phoenix to move out of my way. I'm done with this conversation.

My little brother doesn't budge. "I spent the night listening to my fiancée worry herself to death about her sister. I'm not done yet."

Fuck. I rub a hand over my chest where an ache blooms. "How's Elizabeth? Is she okay?"

"No," Beckett growls. "My sister is not okay. She's heartbroken over your dumbass."

"It was her decision," I argue.

"Lame," Lyric mutters.

"I'm not the same as you," I snarl at him. "I don't long for a wife and children."

"Does he think I'm stupid?" Lyric asks Phoenix.

"Sounds as if he does."

"I'm right here," I remind them.

"But are you ready to listen?" Lyric asks.

"Do I have a choice?"

"I saw you," is his bizarre response.

"I'm going to need more words."

"I saw you when you delivered Ashlyn's daughter. You looked at her baby with such longing in your eyes it hurt to look at you."

Fuck. He saw? "It wasn't… It's not…" I backpedal as fast as I can.

"And then," he continues before I have a chance to get my thoughts in order. "When Aspen announced we're pregnant, you had the same look of longing on your face. You." He points to me. "Want kids."

"But you're afraid," Phoenix adds.

Beckett's gaze travels over my brothers before landing on me. "This is almost better than kicking his ass. Almost."

I shrug and go for nonchalance. "Maybe I do, but how can I trust Elizabeth?"

"I lied. This isn't better than kicking his ass. You. Me. Outside. Right now." Beckett stands.

"I've got fifty bucks on Beckett," Lennon shouts.

"No one's going to bet against you," Lyric responds. "And there will be no fighting."

"There will be fighting." Beckett's nostrils flare as he stares down at me. "River claimed my sister isn't trustworthy."

"I didn't mean Bessie isn't trustworthy."

"You just claimed you can't trust her," he reminds me.

"I meant her love. How can I trust her love is real? What if it's all an illusion?"

"Can I beat him up now?" Beckett asks Lyric.

"Not yet."

"But he's a dumbass who's questioning my sister's trustwor-thiness."

Lyric shrugs. "He's been a dumbass since he returned from college."

Beckett points at me. "You're wrong about Elizabeth. I thought you were her best friend. Don't you know her by now? She's the most loyal person I know. Cassandra pushes her and pushes her, but Elizabeth won't give up on Cassandra because she's family and family is everything to Elizabeth."

He finally sits down but he's not done talking. "You're a complete dumbass if you don't want her to be the mother of your children. She'll be the biggest mama bear of the clan. No one – including you – will hurt her children."

Fuck. Maybe my brothers are right. Maybe I am a coward.

"Damnit. What do I do?"

Lyric slides the pitcher of beer across the table to me. "We need a plan."

"What we need is a grand gesture," Phoenix adds.

I gulp. A grand gesture? What have I gotten myself into?

Chapter 38

Grand Gesture – Not always grand, but always a gesture

MY HEART POUNDS IN my chest as I rush as fast as I can down Main Street. I can't believe this is happening. It's the day before the opening of *Glitter N Bliss* and Sirius phoned to tell me there's a water leak. It's a disaster.

I wave to Clove as I rush past *Clove's Coffee Corner*. She gives me two thumbs-up. Figures. The entire town knows about the problem already.

As I pass *Bertie's Recording Studio,* Ashlyn steps outside. "I've got twenty dollars on you."

I don't bother asking what she's betting on. The people of Winter Falls will bet on anything. I shake my head and continue on my way.

When I arrive at the spa, the door is locked and the lights are out. What the hell? Where's Sirius? Oh no, did we lose electricity, too? Can this situation get any worse? I've already taken bookings for the first month of business.

I unlock the door and enter. "Sirius!"

The lights switch on. "Surprise!"

I stumble and my legs give out on me. Before I can nose dive to the floor, River's there to catch me. He hauls me to his chest. "Careful, sweetheart."

I enjoy his arms around me for a moment before I remember. River isn't mine. We're not together. We're not even friends at this point. I think.

"Sweetheart?" I push him away, but he refuses to budge.

"Yes, sweetheart. You're mine."

"We broke up, remember?"

Personally, I don't need the reminder. My heart still feels as if it's been torn into two. It's bloody and tattered, and I don't know if I will ever be able to put the pieces back together again.

"I refuse to accept the breakup."

"You can't refuse to accept a breakup." Trust me. I've tried. My pleas always fell on deaf ears.

"I love you, Elizabeth Elaine. I'm not letting you go."

"But what about—" My mouth drops open when I realize what he said. "You love me?"

He kisses my nose. "More than I could have ever imagined."

I want to revel in his words, but love isn't enough. Not in our situation.

"But what about kids and that stupid white picket fence you're obsessed with?"

"Yes to kids. No to the picket fence."

"What about if we have a dog? We'll need a fence," I sass because I can't believe he's saying these things. I must be hallucinating. I must have fallen asleep in the library where I was working. Sirius didn't phone me. I'm probably drooling all over my business plan right now.

"If we get a dog, we'll get a fence for the backyard, but no picket fences."

I pinch myself. "Ow. Am I awake?"

He chuckles. "Yes, you're awake."

"But you said you never wanted children. Ever. You let me break up with you. You broke my heart," I whisper the last part.

He cradles my face. "I was an idiot. I was scared."

"A yellow bellied coward," Lyric shouts, and I startle.

"We're not alone?"

"You can't have a grand opening without a crowd."

My eyes widen. "Grand opening? But the grand opening is tomorrow. And there's a pipe leak." His lopsided smile makes an appearance, and I realize I'm an idiot. "There's no pipe leak is there?"

"Nope."

"You brought me here under false pretenses."

He smirks. "I did."

"Is the entire town standing behind me?"

"Yep."

"Did they hear our conversation?"

"We did. Can you explain the obsession with white picket fences?" Feather asks. "Is this some sexual thing I don't know about?"

My face warms, and I face plant into River's shoulder.

"There's no reason to be embarrassed," Petal adds. "Being adventurous in bed will keep the spice in your marriage."

"Who had today?" Sage asks the crowd.

"I did!" Aspen shouts. "I already ordered the new bookshelves for *Fall Into A Good Book*."

River grabs my hand. "We'll be right back," he calls as he drags me to my office. He shuts the door behind us before crowding me against it.

"Are you okay?"

"I don't know. Yesterday, I was convinced my dreams would never come true and today you're handing me everything I've ever wanted on a silver platter."

"Did she say silver?" Clove asks before she bangs on the door. "Speak up!"

River sighs before leading me to the chair. He sits on it before arranging me in his lap. "There. This is better."

"We aren't having sex when the entire town is standing outside the door eavesdropping," I hiss at him.

"We're not having sex," he agrees.

I wiggle on his lap. "Except I can feel how hard you are."

He growls and his hands go to my hips to hold me still. "Stop wiggling or you'll make it harder."

"It feels pretty hard already."

His fingers dig into my hips. "Sweetheart, I thought you wanted to talk everything out without an audience."

Right. I straighten my shoulders. "You want kids?"

"Yes."

"With me?"

"Yes."

"You love me?"

"To the moon and back."

"I'm good."

"Just like that?"

"Yep. I love you. You love me. You did some kind of grand gesture to prove your love. I'm good."

"I know it's not the biggest grand gesture."

"I don't need a grand gesture. All I need is you." I lean close. "Now, kiss me."

He smirks and hauls me near until my chest is plastered to his. He nibbles on my bottom lip until I grunt with frustration. Only then does he meld his lips to mine and plunge his tongue into my mouth. I groan as his outdoorsy taste hits my tongue.

He uses his hold on my hips to drag me back and forth against his hard cock. I dig my fingers into his shoulders as I rub myself against him.

"Aha!" Ashlyn shouts as the door bangs against the wall.

I jerk my lips from River's to glance over my shoulder. She's standing with her hands raised above her head in victory.

"Did you break into my office?"

"It's not breaking in if it's an office inside a building," she claims.

I don't bother arguing with her. Ashlyn has her own set of morals. There's only one way to deal with her.

"Rowan!" I yell for her husband.

"Sorry," he mutters as he claims his wife and drags her away. "Dream Girl, we discussed this."

I cuddle into River's arms. "Maybe we should escape out the back alley."

He lifts me from his lap and sets me on my feet. "No way. There's a party happening out there to celebrate your new business and we're not missing it."

"You made all this happen?"

He shrugs. "It wasn't difficult. The party was already planned for tomorrow. I just moved the catering up by a day."

"And finished the punch list. And put together the last of the furniture. And decorated for the opening."

"Phoenix and Lyric helped."

Gabrielle peeks into the office. "We all helped."

"I can't believe you kept this a secret."

She winks. "I can keep a secret."

"Apparently, I can't," Cassandra grumbles as she joins us, "since no one called me to help."

"Oh, there's cake," Ashlyn screams.

I blow out a breath of air. "We better get out there before she decides the cake is a pile of leaves she should jump into."

River holds tight to my hand as we wander back to the main room of the spa. It's slow going as every person we pass has to stop us to congratulate me. By the time we're in front of the cake, my heart is about to burst with pride for what I've built and happiness to have the man I love beside me.

"You happy?" River asks.

I look around the room crowded with the residents of Winter Falls, all of whom came out today to show their support for me and my new business.

"More than happy. Ecstatic."

"You ready to move to the next level?"

The next level. The spa hasn't had a single client yet. What would the next level be? Oh wait. He's not referring to the spa. "You don't mean the spa, do you?"

"Nope."

"What's the next level?"

"Phoenix, Lyric, and Beckett may have packed up your stuff and moved you to my house this morning."

"What? When? You couldn't ask me?" How long was I asleep in the library?

He tweaks my nose. "Don't pretend you're mad. You know you want to live with me. You can't live without me."

I roll my eyes. "Whatever. As long as they keep their hands off my vibrator."

He wiggles his eyebrows. "Don't worry. I packed up the toys before they arrived."

"I don't know how you managed to arrange this." I gesture toward the party. "And sneak into my apartment to move me."

"I am pretty amazing."

I push up on my toes. "Yeah, you are." I lean close but before I can kiss him, Cassandra screams.

"What the hell are you doing here?" she shouts as she glares at a man I don't recognize.

His brow wrinkles as he studies her. "What am I doing here? What are you doing here?"

She crosses her arms over her chest. "I asked first."

"Who is he?" I ask River.

"Cedar."

My brows scrunch. The name sounds familiar, but I can't place it.

"Rowan's brother."

"Holy cow. This is the man Cassandra has been fooling around with."

Cedar shackles Cassandra's wrist and drags her out of the spa and down the street. The gossip gals gather to follow them, but Lyric blocks them.

"Let them be."

"But how can we set up the bets if we don't have the proper information," Sage whines.

Lyric cocks his eyebrow. "As if you didn't know Cedar was back in town."

I smile up at River. "Things will never be dull in Winter Falls, will they?"

He kisses my hair. "Not with the woman I love in my arms."

He sounds completely corny, and I don't care. All that matters is that his words are sincere and heartfelt. Dreams do come true.

"What do you say we sneak out of your party and go back to our place?"

Our place? I love the sound of that.

"Let's go."

Chapter 39

Dare – a really bad idea when you're mad

CASSANDRA

I frown when I spot a man who reminds me of Archer in the crowd. But it can't be him. Archer doesn't know anyone in Winter Falls. He's camping on some land out of town to avoid the townspeople since he's a stranger.

Someone moves away from the man and his face becomes clear. What the hell? It is Archer. He lied to me. I hate liars.

I stomp in his direction. "What the hell are you doing here?"

His brow wrinkles. "Cassandra?"

"The one and only. Do I need to repeat my question? Should I speak slower?"

"What are you doing here?" he asks instead of answering my question. I grunt. I hate it when people answer a question with a question.

I cross my arms over my chest and throw daggers at him from my eyes. "I asked first."

The daggers must fail as he shackles my wrist and tugs me out of the spa and down the street. The gossip gals gather to follow us, but Lyric growls at them. "Let them be."

"But how can we set up the bets if we don't have any information," Sage whines.

Lyric's response is lost to me as we're now out of hearing range. Archer pulls me into the alley between *Naked Falls Brewing* and *Bertie's Recording Studio.* The same alley where I caught River laying a hot as hell kiss on Elizabeth a few months ago. I knew those two were destined to be together from the beginning. They should have listened to me and saved themselves a ton of trouble.

When we're halfway down the alley, I tear myself away from him and retreat a few steps. "What's going on? Why are you in town?"

He shoves his hands into his pockets and shrugs. He's not much of a talker. Normally, I'm fine with a man who doesn't speak much – more chance for me to talk – but not when he refuses to answer my questions.

I shrug and feign indifference. "Okay. Fine. I'll return to the party and ask them."

He grasps my shoulder before I manage two steps.

"You don't want to do that."

I rear back. "I don't, do I? You don't know what I want to do or don't do. You don't have the first clue about me."

He uses his hold on my arm to haul me near. "Wrong. I know lots of things about you. I know you melt in my arms when I nibble on your ear." I shiver at the memory of his teeth on my skin. "I know you taste of the sweetest honey."

When I realize I'm leaning into him, I shake myself and push him away. "Stop it. I'm not going to let you have your wicked way with me in an alley."

He smirks and my anger erupts. Enough with the avoidance already.

"How do you know everyone in town?"

"Rowan's my brother."

My jaw drops open. Is he serious? He's from Winter Falls? "Rowan as in Ashlyn's husband?"

"The one and only."

"But his brother's name is Cedar."

"Cedar Archer to be specific."

I poke his chest with my finger. "You lied to me."

He captures my hand and his thumb caresses my wrist. "I never said Rowan wasn't my brother."

I yank away. There will be no caressing when Archer is a big, fat liar whose pants are going to go up in flames any second now.

"You never said he was!"

"You didn't tell me you knew everyone in Winter Falls."

"Don't turn this on me," I snarl. "You know I've been working at *Electric Vibes*. Of course, I know the residents of this town. You're the one who lied and didn't tell me you grew up in Winter Falls." I lean close to hiss in his face. "In fact, you claimed you'd be gone by now."

I wouldn't have gotten involved with him had I known he'd stay in town for this long. There's a reason my college nickname was *One Time Cassie*.

He scratches his beard. "I planned to."

I snort. "Of course, you did. You're a wanderer. You can't stay in one place for very long or it will kill you."

He frowns. "It won't kill me."

I raise my eyebrows. "Oh yeah? I dare you."

"What are we? Kindergartners?"

"Never mind. You can't handle the dare. It's okay." I pat his chest.

He growls. "I can handle a dare. There's a difference between being able to handle something and not doing it because it's childish."

"I understand. You're scared to lose. It doesn't make you less of a man to back out before you have the chance to lose," I taunt.

He growls and I remember how much I love to hear the sound when we're naked. The man is a fucking liar, but he's fantastic in bed. The best I've had in a long time. Maybe ever.

"You can't trick me into accepting your dare."

I widen my eyes. "Me? Trick you? I could never." I totally could.

"I'm not going to accept this dare to prove you wrong."

I snort. "That would be silly, wouldn't it?"

"But what is the dare?" he asks and I know I've got him.

"I dare you to stay in Winter Falls for six months."

"Too easy."

"I'm not finished yet."

He motions for me to continue.

"You have to come into town and interact with the residents at least once a week."

"After today, they're not going to allow me to hide out anymore," he grumbles.

Hide out? What's he hiding from? The people of Winter Falls are super cool. Completely intrusive and overbearing sometimes but cool, nonetheless.

He crosses his arms over his chest. "And what are you going to do?"

"What do you mean? Dares aren't reciprocal."

"This one will be."

Well, shit. "What do you want me to do?"

He taps his chin as he considers the question. When a smile crosses his face, I know I'm in trouble.

"I dare you to keep a pet for six months."

"No problem," I immediately agree.

"And it can't be a cat or any type of rodent."

Damn. A cat would be a piece of cake. Cats are as relationship-averse as I am.

"What type of pets are left?" I ask as if I don't know where he's going with this.

"A dog. You need to have a dog as a pet for six months."

"What if I'm allergic to dogs?"

He shrugs. "I understand if you can't handle the dare," he mocks.

Crap. Why couldn't I be allergic to dogs?

"Fine. You're on." I hold out my hand. "What do I win when you flee town before the six months are up?"

"I'll pay for those business classes you've been eyeing."

I narrow my eyes on him. How the hell did he know I've been researching business classes?

He bops my nose. "I told you. I know you."

"Fine." We shake hands.

This is going to be fun. Plus, I don't have to worry about picking up extra shifts to pay for those business classes since there's no way I'll lose this bet. Archer will never survive six months in one place. This will be easier than stealing candy from a baby.

Chapter 40

Happy Ever After – when everything works out in the end

"WHAT DO YOU THINK?" I ask as I hold up the handheld mirror to the back of Gracious' head.

The diner owner's eyes widen. "Wow. I didn't think much of your idea of highlights, but this? I love it."

Phew. We argued for a good ten minutes on whether to add in the highlights or not. Afterwards, she argued about whether she should get bangs. I check the clock. I'm nearly thirty minutes late to meet River and I haven't had the chance to call him to let him know.

I whip the cape off of her. "Voila!"

She hurries off and I clean up my station as quickly as I can. "Are you good to lock up?" I ask Love Hill as I shrug into my jacket.

Yep. Love Hill. I initially didn't want to hire her. The woman is a total maneater and snarky to boot. But she's actually a good employee. As long as she keeps her hands off my man, we're good.

"I got it. Say hi to River for me."

Say hi from the maneater to my boyfriend? Not happening.

I rush down the street to *Electric Vibes.* I rear back when I open the door to discover the place covered in green. I should have known. It is St. Patrick's day after all. But Lennon doesn't usually decorate for the holidays. In his defense, it isn't easy to decorate when you can't use balloons and all decorations have to be made from recyclable materials.

I scan the crowd, but I don't see River anywhere. Shit. Did he leave when I didn't show up on time? His brothers are sitting at a booth with Aspen and Gabrielle. I wave to them and mouth *Where's River* to Gabrielle who shrugs in return.

I step toward them, but I'm stopped when an arm circles my waist. The woodsy scent of pine and grass hits me.

"Hey, babe. I'm looking forward to finding out if the carpet matches the drapes later."

I push River away. He's lucky I don't deck him for that lame line.

"You better go. My boyfriend's around here somewhere."

He whirls me around until we're facing each other. "What kind of man leaves a woman like you on her own?"

"The kind of man who trusts me."

"Yeah?" He steps closer until he's all up in my personal space. "He must be a pretty special guy to land a woman such as yourself."

I roll my eyes. "Corny."

He punches his hips and I feel his hard length against my stomach. "And horny."

Cassandra shoves her way in between us. "Nope. You're not leaving to go shake the sheets and rock the bed."

"Why not?"

My sister is usually the first person to leave a party if there's a chance of sex.

"Because it's St. Patrick's Day trivia."

My nose twitches. "Since when do you care about winning a trivia contest?"

She shrugs and avoids my gaze.

"Did you make another dare with Cedar?"

"Maybe?"

I groan. Cedar and Cassandra love to dare each other. The more outrageous the better. In my opinion, Cassandra is in over her head with Cedar, but I'm not saying a word. My bet is on them getting together before the fourth of July. Literally, I put money down with Sage.

"Hey, River," a woman shouts and my attention is pulled away from my sister to discover my boyfriend surrounded by a group of women.

I cross my arms over my chest to watch this play out. River never leads any of the women on, but he doesn't need to. With his appearance, women don't care if he's available or not. At least the locals know better than to try one on with him.

A woman grasps his hand and tugs. "You should come sit with us."

"Yeah," her friend agrees. "We have the best table in the house."

Another woman bites her bottom lip and bats her eyelashes at him. "There's five of us."

"And we don't mind sharing," the first woman says as she tries to drag him away.

River extricates himself from the woman and steps away from the group. "The best table in the house you say?"

They point to a table where their two other friends are sitting. The friends wave and send air kisses. Gag. Can they act more desperate?

River reaches behind him and holds out his hand. I know he wants me to take it, but I think it's good to make the man work for what he wants every once in a while. I mean I'm a sure thing, but I don't have to make it easy.

He glances over his shoulder and crooks his finger at me. I raise an eyebrow at him. He growls. This is fun. I should deny him what he wants more often.

He prowls to me and shackles my wrist before hauling me near. "Behave," he grumbles before kissing my hair.

"Did you come here with her?" one of the women asks.

"She can join us. Like I said. We don't mind sharing."

"I mind sharing," I tell River.

"Ugh. Is she selfish?"

I cock an eyebrow at River. If he doesn't handle these women soon, I'll be throwing out the trash myself. And if I throw out the trash, someone will be sleeping on the couch tonight. We have a perfectly good bed in the spare bedroom, but he won't be using it. Not when there's a couch in his office that's incredibly uncomfortable.

"She has every right to be selfish. She's my girlfriend," River declares without bothering to look at the women.

"Your girlfriend? But I was promised a weekend of sexy fun."

River chuckles. "I'm afraid I can't help you there. I'm taken. Happily taken."

Sage and Feather cheer. The rest of the gossip gals join them.

"Mission accomplished," Clove declares.

"This was our hardest assignment yet," Sage says.

River leans close to whisper in my ear. "I have something hard for you."

I shiver at the feel of his breath on my skin, but I feign indignation. "Stop being corny."

"You really should learn the definition of corny. It's not the same as horny."

"It's a good thing I love you, River Alston."

"Loving you is the best decision I made in my life."

I snort. "It's cute you think you had a choice."

About the Author

D.E. Haggerty is an American who has spent the majority of her adult life abroad. She has lived in Istanbul, various places throughout Germany, and currently finds herself in The Hague. She has been a military policewoman, a lawyer, a B&B owner/operator and now a writer.